Praise for *Stay Awake*

"[Chaon] is a master of psychological tension. . . . These stories demand and capture your attention, and they don't let go even after you've finished reading them." —*The Miami Herald*

"An understated master of the form whose occasionally devastating debut story collection *Among the Missing* was a National Book Award finalist in 2001. Chaon has returned to the format with more quietly haunting stories of isolation and disconnection that stick with you like faded images from a disturbing dream." —*Los Angeles Times*

"[Chaon's] command of language, and his empathy with his characters, leave you not shaking your head in disbelief, but simply, gratifyingly, shaken." —*The Wall Street Journal*

"If Chaon's 2001 [book] *Among the Missing*, which was nominated for a National Book Award, contained some of the best fiction written in the past twenty years, *Stay Awake* is its darker, more unsettling cousin." —*Esquire*

"The remarkable variety and depth within the limits Chaon has set makes *Stay Awake* an irresistible collection for those who don't mind risking a few nightmares of their own." —*The Columbus Dispatch*

"*Stay Awake* is a profound collection of contemporary ghost stories in the tradition of M. R. James and Peter Straub's *Houses Without Doors*. The prose unveils an atmospheric menace animated by a grief grounded in the real world." —*The Houston Chronicle*

"Moving . . . Dan Chaon deliver[s] some of the best of what contemporary short fiction has to offer." —*BookPage*

"Chaon has a knack for the dramatic . . . but there's more than a beguiling premise animating these stories. His real quarry is the pervasive nature of trauma's aftermath." —*Time Out New York*

"Grounded in realism but leading to some fantastic places, Chaon's stories keep the reader guessing as they blur the lines between dreams and waking nightmares." —*The Dallas Morning News*

"Chaon excels at inciting a gripping sense of foreboding; just as the reader realizes there's a monster in the closet, its shocking revelation only stirs the imagination further." —The Daily Beast

"With this arresting collection, Chaon again demonstrates his mastery of the short story." —*Publishers Weekly* (starred review)

STAY AWAKE

BY DAN CHAON

Stay Awake

Await Your Reply

You Remind Me of Me

Fitting Ends

Among the Missing

BALLANTINE BOOKS TRADE PAPERBACKS

NEW YORK

Stay Awake

Stories

Dan Chaon

2012 Ballantine Books Trade Paperback Edition

Published in the United States by Ballantine Books,
an imprint of The Random House Publishing Group,
a division of Random House, Inc., New York.

Originally published in hardcover in the United States by Ballantine Books,
an imprint of The Random House Publishing Group,
a division of Random House, Inc., in 2012.

The following stories have been previously published:
"The Bees" (*McSweeney's #10*, 2002), "Thinking of You in Your Time of Sorrow"
(*Mid American Review*, 2004), "Shepherdess" (*Virginia Quarterly Review*, Fall 2006),
"The Farm. The Gold. The Lily-White Hands." (*Avery Anthology*, 2007),
"Patrick Lane, Flabbergasted" (*Ninth Letter*, Fall/Winter 2007), "St. Dismas"
(*Santi: Lives of Modern Day Saints*, edited by Luca Dipierro and
N. Frank Daniels, Black Arrow Press, 2008), and
"To Psychic Underworld:" (*Tin House*, 2010)

ISBN 978-0-345-53038-7
eBook ISBN 978-0-345-53230-5

Printed in the United States of America

www.randomhousereaderscircle.com

2 4 6 8 9 7 5 3 1

Book design by Dana Leigh Blanchette
Title-page photograph: © iStockphoto

I had a dream I was awake and
I woke up to find myself asleep.

—STAN LAUREL

Contents

STAY AWAKE

The Bees

Gene's son Frankie wakes up screaming. It has become frequent, two or three times a week, at random times: midnight—three A.M.—five in the morning. Here is a high, empty wail that severs Gene from his unconsciousness like sharp teeth. It is the worst sound that Gene can imagine, the sound of a young child dying violently—falling from a building, or caught in some machinery that is tearing an arm off, or being mauled by a predatory animal. No matter how many times he hears it he jolts up with such images playing in his mind, and he always runs, thumping into the child's bedroom to find Frankie sitting up in bed, his eyes closed, his mouth open in an oval like a Christmas caroler. If someone took a picture of him, he would appear to be in a kind of peaceful trance, as if he were waiting to receive a spoonful of ice cream, rather than emitting that horrific sound.

"Frankie!" Gene will shout, and claps his hands hard in the child's face. The clapping works well. At this, the scream always stops abruptly, and Frankie opens his eyes, blinking at Gene with vague awareness before settling back down into his pillow, nuzzling a little before growing still. He is sound asleep, he is always sound asleep, though even after months Gene can't help leaning down and pressing his ear to the child's chest, to make sure he's still breathing, his heart is still going. It always is.

There is no explanation that they can find. In the morning, Frankie doesn't remember anything, and on the few occasions that they have managed to wake him in the midst of one of his screaming attacks, he is merely sleepy and irritable. Once, Gene's wife, Karen, shook him and shook him, until finally he opened his eyes groggily. "Honey?" she said. "Honey? Did you have a bad dream?" But Frankie only moaned a little. "No," he said, puzzled and unhappy at being awakened, but nothing more.

They can find no pattern to it. It can happen any day of the week, any time of the night. It doesn't seem to be associated with diet, or with his activities during the day, and it doesn't stem, as far as they can tell, from any sort of psychological unease. During the day, he seems perfectly normal and happy.

They have taken him several times to the pediatrician, but the doctor seems to have little of use to say. There is nothing wrong with the child physically, Dr. Banerjee says. She advises that such

things were not uncommon for children of Frankie's age group—
he is five—and that more often than not, the disturbance simply
passes away.

"He hasn't experienced any kind of emotional trauma, has
he?" the doctor says. "Nothing out of the ordinary at home?"

"No, no," they both murmur, together. They shake their
heads, and Dr. Banerjee shrugs. "Parents," she says. "It's probably nothing to worry about." She gives them a brief smile. "As
difficult as it is, I'd say that you may just have to weather this
out."

But the doctor has never heard those screams. In the mornings
after the "nightmares," as Karen calls them, Gene feels unnerved,
edgy. He works as a driver for the United Parcel Service, and as
he moves through the day after a screaming attack, there is a
barely perceptible hum at the edge of his hearing, an intent, deliberate static sliding along behind him as he wanders through
streets and streets in his van. He stops along the side of the road
and listens. The shadows of summer leaves tremble murmur-
ously against the windshield, and cars are accelerating on a
nearby road. In the treetops, a cicada makes its trembly, pressure-
cooker hiss.

Something bad has been looking for him for a long time, he
thinks, and now, at last, it is growing near.

When he comes home at night everything is normal. They live in
an old house in the suburbs of Cleveland, and sometimes after
dinner they work together in the small patch of garden out in back
of the house—tomatoes, zucchini, string beans, cucumbers—

while Frankie plays with Legos in the dirt. Or they take walks around the neighborhood, Frankie riding his bike in front of them, his training wheels squeaking. They gather on the couch and watch cartoons together, or play board games, or draw pictures with crayons. After Frankie is asleep, Karen will sit at the kitchen table and study—she is in nursing school—and Gene will sit outside on the porch, flipping through a newsmagazine or a novel, smoking the cigarettes that he has promised Karen he will give up when he turns thirty-five. He is thirty-four now, and Karen is twenty-seven, and he is aware, more and more frequently, that this is not the life that he deserves. He has been incredibly lucky, he thinks. Blessed, as Gene's favorite cashier at the supermarket always says. "Have a blessed day," she says, when Gene pays the money and she hands him his receipt, and he feels as if she has sprinkled him with her ordinary, gentle beatitude. It reminds him of long ago, when an old nurse had held his hand in the hospital and said that she was praying for him.

Sitting out in his lawn chair, drawing smoke out of his cigarette, he thinks about that nurse, even though he doesn't want to. He thinks of the way she'd leaned over him and brushed his hair as he stared at her, imprisoned in a full body cast, sweating his way through withdrawal and DTs.

He had been a different person, back then. A drunk, a monster. At eighteen, he married the girl he'd gotten pregnant, and then had set about slowly, steadily, ruining all their lives. When he'd abandoned them, his wife and son, back in Nebraska, he had been twenty-four, a danger to himself and others. He'd done them a favor by leaving, he thought, though he still feels guilty when he looks back on it. Years later, when he was sober, he even tried to contact them. He wanted to own up to his behavior, to pay the back child support, to apologize. But they were nowhere to be found. Mandy was no longer living in the small Nebraska town where they'd met and married, and there was no forwarding address. Her parents were dead. No one seemed to know where she'd gone.

Karen didn't know the full story. She had been, to his relief, uncurious about his previous life, though she knew he had some drinking days, some bad times. She knew that he'd been married before, too, though she didn't know the extent of it, didn't know that he had another son, for example, didn't know that he had left them one night, without even packing a bag, just driving off in the car, a flask tucked between his legs, driving east as far as he could go. She didn't know about the car crash, the wreck he should have died in. She didn't know what a bad person he'd been.

She was a nice lady, Karen. Maybe a little sheltered. And truth to tell, he was ashamed—and even scared—to imagine how she would react to the truth about his past. He didn't know if she would have ever really trusted him if she'd known the full story, and the longer they have known each other the less inclined he has been to reveal it. He'd escaped his old self, he thought, and when Karen got pregnant, shortly before they were married, he told himself that now he had a chance to do things over, to do it better. They had bought the house together, he and Karen, and now Frankie will be in kindergarten in the fall. He has come full circle, has come exactly to the point when his former life with Mandy and his son, DJ, completely fell apart. He looks up as Karen comes to the back door and speaks to him through the screen. "I think it's time for bed, sweetheart," she says, and he shudders off these thoughts, these memories. He smiles.

He's been in a strange frame of mind lately. The months of regular awakenings have been getting to him, and he has a hard time going back to sleep after an episode with Frankie. When Karen wakes him in the morning, he often feels muffled, sluggish—as if he's hungover. He doesn't hear the alarm clock. When he stumbles out of bed, he finds he has a hard time keeping his moodiness in check. He can feel his temper coiling up inside him.

He isn't that type of person anymore, and hasn't been for a long while. Still, he can't help but worry. They say that there is a second stretch of craving, which sets in after several years of smooth sailing; five or seven years will pass, and then it will come back without warning. He has been thinking of going to AA meetings again, though he hasn't in some time—not since he met Karen.

It's not as if he gets trembly every time he passes a liquor store, or even as if he has a problem when he goes out with buddies and spends the evening drinking soda and nonalcoholic beer. No. The trouble comes at night, when he's asleep.

He has begun to dream of his first son. DJ. Perhaps it is related to his worries about Frankie, but for several nights in a row the image of DJ—age about five—has appeared to him. In the dream, Gene is drunk, and playing hide-and-seek with DJ in the yard behind the Cleveland house where he is now living. There is the thick weeping willow out there, and Gene watches the child appear from behind it and run across the grass, happy, unafraid, the way Frankie would. DJ turns to look over his shoulder and laughs, and Gene stumbles after him, at least a six-pack's worth of good mood, a goofy, drunken dad. It's so real that when he wakes, he still feels intoxicated. It takes him a few minutes to shake it.

One morning after a particularly vivid version of this dream, Frankie wakes and complains of a funny feeling—"right here"— he says, and points to his forehead. It isn't a headache, he says. "It's like bees!" he says. "Buzzing bees!" He rubs his hand against his brow. "Inside my head." He considers for a moment. "You know how the bees bump against the window when they get in the house and want to get out?" This description pleases him, and he taps his forehead lightly with his fingers, humming, "*Zzzzzz,*" to demonstrate.

"Does it hurt?" Karen says.

"No," Frankie says. "It tickles."

Karen gives Gene a concerned look. She makes Frankie lie down on the couch, and tells him to close his eyes for a while. After a few minutes, he raises up, smiling, and says that the feeling has gone.

"Honey, are you sure?" Karen says. She pushes his hair back and slides her palm across his forehead. "He's not hot," she says, and Frankie sits up impatiently, suddenly more interested in something that is happening on the *Fuzzy Fieldmouse* show, which is playing on the TV in the living room.

Karen gets out one of her nursing books, and Gene watches her face tighten with concern as she flips slowly through the pages. She is looking at Chapter 3: Neurological System, and Gene observes as she pauses here and there, skimming down a list of symptoms. "We should probably take him back to Dr. Banerjee again," she says. Gene nods, recalling what the doctor said about "emotional trauma."

"Are you scared of bees?" he asks Frankie. "Is that something that's bothering you?"

"No," Frankie says. "Not really."

When Frankie was three, a bee stung him above his left eyebrow. They had been out hiking together, and they hadn't yet learned that Frankie was "moderately allergic" to bee stings. Within minutes of the sting, Frankie's face had begun to distort, to puff up, his eye welling shut. He looked deformed. Gene didn't know if he'd ever been more frightened in his entire life, running down the trail with Frankie's head pressed against his heart, trying to get to the car and drive him to the doctor, terrified that the child was dying. Frankie himself was calm.

Gene clears his throat. He knows the feeling that Frankie is talking about—he has felt it himself, that odd, feathery vibration inside his head. And in fact he feels it again, now. He presses the pads of his fingertips against his brow. *Emotional trauma,* his mind murmurs, but he is thinking of DJ, not Frankie.

"What are you scared of?" Gene asks Frankie, after a moment. "Anything?"

"You know what the scariest thing is?" Frankie says, and widens his eyes, miming a frightened look. "There's a lady with no head, and she went walking through the woods, looking for it. 'Give . . . me . . . back . . . my . . . head. . . .' "

"Where on earth did you hear a story like that!" Karen says.

"Daddy told me," Frankie says. "When we were camping."

Gene blushes, even before Karen gives him a sharp look. "Oh, great," she says. "Wonderful."

He doesn't meet her eyes. "We were just telling ghost stories," he says, softly. "I thought he would think the story was funny."

"My God, Gene," she says. "With him having nightmares like this? What were you thinking?"

It's a bad flashback, the kind of thing he's usually able to avoid. He thinks abruptly of Mandy, his former wife. He sees in Karen's face that look Mandy would give him when he screwed up. "What are you, some kind of idiot?" Mandy used to say. "Are you crazy?" Back then, Gene couldn't do anything right, it seemed, and when Mandy yelled at him it made his stomach clench with shame and inarticulate rage. *I was trying,* he would think, *I was trying,* damn it, and it was as if no matter what he did, it wouldn't turn out right. That feeling would sit heavily in his chest, and eventually, when things got worse, he hit her once. "Why do you want me to feel like shit," he said through clenched teeth. "I'm not an asshole," he said, and when she rolled her eyes at him he slapped her hard enough to knock her out of her chair.

That was the time he'd taken DJ to the carnival. It was a Saturday, and he'd been drinking a little, so Mandy didn't like it, but after all—he thought—DJ was his son, too, he had a right to spend some time with his own son, Mandy wasn't his boss even if she might think she was. She liked to make him hate himself.

What she was mad about was that he'd taken DJ on the Velocerator. It was a mistake, he'd realized afterward. But DJ himself had begged to go on. He was just recently four years old, and Gene had just turned twenty-three, which made him feel inexplicably old. He wanted to have a little fun.

Besides, nobody told him he *couldn't* take DJ on the thing. When he led DJ through the gate, the ticket taker even smiled, as if to say, "Here is a young guy showing his kid a good time." Gene winked at DJ and grinned, taking a nip from a flask of peppermint schnapps. He felt like a good dad. He wished his own father had taken him on rides at the carnival!

The door to the Velocerator opened like a hatch in a big silver flying saucer. Disco music was blaring from the entrance and became louder as they went inside. It was a circular room with soft, padded walls, and one of the workers had Gene and DJ stand with their backs to the wall, strapping them in side by side. Gene felt warm and expansive from the schnapps. He took DJ's hand, and he almost felt as if he were glowing with love. "Get ready, kiddo," Gene whispered. "This is going to be wild."

The hatch door of the Velocerator sealed closed with a pressurized sigh. And then, slowly, the walls they were strapped to began to turn. Gene tightened his grip on DJ's hand as they began to rotate, gathering speed. After a moment the wall pads they were strapped to slid up, and the force of velocity pushed them back, held to the surface of the spinning wall like iron to a magnet. Gene's cheeks and lips seemed to pull back, and the sensation of helplessness made him laugh.

At that moment, DJ began to scream. "No! No! Stop! Make it stop!" They were terrible shrieks, and Gene held the child's hand more tightly. "It's all right," he yelled jovially over the thump of the music. "It's okay! I'm right here!" But the child's wailing only got louder in response. The scream seemed to whip past Gene in a circle, tumbling around and around the circumference of the ride like a spirit, trailing echoes as it flew. When the machine finally stopped, DJ was heaving with sobs, and the man at the control panel glared. Gene could feel the other passengers staring grimly and judgmentally at him.

Gene felt horrible. He had been so happy—thinking that they were finally having themselves a memorable father-and-son moment—and he could feel his heart plunging into darkness. DJ kept on weeping, even as they left the ride and walked along the midway, even as Gene tried to distract him with promises of cotton candy and stuffed animals. "I want to go home," DJ cried, and, "I want my mom! I want my mom!" And it had wounded Gene to hear that. He gritted his teeth.

"Fine!" he hissed. "Let's go home to your mommy, you little crybaby. I swear to God, I'm never taking you with me anywhere again." And he gave DJ a little shake. "Jesus, what's *wrong* with you? Lookit, people are laughing at you. See? They're saying, 'Look at that big boy, bawling like a girl.' "

This memory comes to him out of the blue. He had forgotten all about it, but now it comes to him over and over. Those screams were not unlike the sounds Frankie makes in the middle of the night, and they pass repeatedly through the membrane of his thoughts, without warning. The next day, he finds himself recalling it again, the memory of the scream impressing on his mind with such force that he actually has to pull his UPS truck off to the side of the road and put his face in his hands: Awful! Awful! He must have seemed like a monster to the child.

Sitting there in his van, he wishes he could find a way to contact them—Mandy and DJ. He wishes that he could tell them how sorry he is, and send them money. He puts his fingertips against his forehead, as cars drive past on the street, as an old man parts the curtains and peers out of the house Gene is parked in front of, hopeful that Gene might have a package for him.

Where are they? Gene wonders. He tries to picture a town, a house, but there is only a blank. Surely, Mandy being Mandy, she would have hunted him down by now to demand child support. She would have relished treating him like a deadbeat dad, she would have hired some company who would garnish his wages.

Now, sitting at the roadside, it occurs to him suddenly that they are dead. He recalls the car wreck that he was in, just outside Des Moines, and if he had been killed they would have never known. He recalls waking up in the hospital, and the elderly nurse who had said, "You're very lucky, young man. You should be dead."

Maybe they are dead, he thinks. Mandy and DJ. The idea strikes him a glancing blow, because of course it would make sense. The reason they've never contacted him. Of course.

He doesn't know what to do with such anxieties. They are ridiculous, they are self-pitying, they are paranoid, but especially now, with the concerns about Frankie, he is at the mercy of his fears. He comes home from work and Karen stares at him heavily.

"What's the matter?" she says, and he shrugs. "You look terrible," she says.

"It's nothing," he says, but she continues to look at him skeptically. She shakes her head.

"I took Frankie to the doctor again today," she says after a moment, and Gene sits down at the table with her, where she is spread out with her textbooks and notepaper.

"I suppose you'll think I'm being a neurotic mom," she says. "I think I'm too immersed in disease—that's the problem."

Gene shakes his head. "No, no," he says. His throat feels dry. "You're right. Better safe than sorry."

"Mmm," she says thoughtfully. "I think Dr. Banerjee is starting to hate me."

"Naw," Gene says. "No one could hate you." With effort, he smiles gently. A good husband, he kisses her palm, her wrist. "Try not to worry," he says, though his own nerves are fluttering. He can hear Frankie in the backyard, shouting orders to someone.

"Who's he talking to?" Gene says, and Karen doesn't look up.

"Oh," she says. "It's probably just Bubba." Bubba is Frankie's imaginary playmate.

Gene nods. He goes to the window and looks out. Frankie is pretending to shoot at something, his thumb and forefinger cocked into a gun. "Get him! Get him!" Frankie shouts, and Gene stares out as Frankie dodges behind a tree. Frankie looks nothing like DJ, but when he pokes his head from behind the hanging foliage of the willow, Gene feels a little shudder—a flicker, something. He clenches his jaw.

"This class is really driving me crazy," Karen says. "Every

time I read about a worst-case scenario, I start to worry. It's strange. The more you know, the less sure you are of anything."

"What did the doctor say this time?" Gene says. He shifts uncomfortably, still staring out at Frankie, and it seems as if dark specks circle and bob at the corner of the yard. "He seems okay?"

Karen shrugs. "As far as they can tell." She looks down at her textbook, shaking her head. "He seems healthy." He puts his hand gently on the back of her neck and she lolls her head back and forth against his fingers. "I've never believed that anything really terrible could happen to me," she once told him, early in their marriage, and it had scared him. "Don't say that," he'd whispered, and she laughed.

"You're superstitious," she said. "That's cute."

He can't sleep. The strange presentiment that Mandy and DJ are dead has lodged heavily in his mind, and he rubs his feet together underneath the covers, trying to find a comfortable posture. He can hear the soft ticks of the old electric typewriter as Karen finishes her paper for school, words rattling out in bursts that remind him of some sort of insect language. He closes his eyes, pretending to be asleep when Karen finally comes to bed, but his mind is ticking with small, scuttling images: his former wife and son, flashes of the photographs he doesn't own, hasn't kept. *They're dead*, a firm voice in his mind says, very distinctly. *They were in a fire. And they burned up.* It is not quite his own voice that speaks to him, and abruptly he can picture the burning house. It's a trailer, somewhere on the outskirts of a small town, and the black smoke is pouring out the open door. The plastic window

frames have warped and begun to melt, and the smoke billows
from the trailer into the sky in a way that reminds him of an old
locomotive. He can't see inside, except for crackling bursts of
deep-orange flames, but he's aware that they're in there. For a
second he can see DJ's face, flickering, peering steadily from the
window of the burning trailer, his mouth open in a unnatural
circle, as if he's singing.

He opens his eyes. Karen's breathing has steadied, she's sound
asleep, and he carefully gets out of bed, padding restlessly
through the house in his pajamas. They're not dead, he tries to
tell himself, and stands in front of the refrigerator, pouring milk
from the carton into his mouth. It's an old comfort, from back in
the days when he was drying out, when the thick taste of milk
would slightly calm his craving for a drink. But it doesn't help
him now. The dream, the vision, has frightened him badly, and he
sits on the couch with an afghan over his shoulders, staring at
some science program on television. On the program, a lady scientist is examining a mummy. A child. The thing is bald—almost
a skull but not quite. A membrane of ancient skin is pulled taut
over the eye sockets. The lips are stretched back, and there are
small, chipped, rodentlike teeth. Looking at the thing, he can't
help but think of DJ again, and he looks over his shoulder,
quickly, the way he used to.

The last year that he was together with Mandy, there used to be
times when DJ would actually give him the creeps—spook him.
DJ had been an unusually skinny child, with a head like a baby
bird and long, bony feet, with toes that seemed strangely ex-

tended, as if they were meant for gripping. He can remember the way the child would slip barefoot through rooms, slinking, sneaking, watching, Gene had thought, always watching him.

It is a memory that he has almost succeeded in forgetting, a memory he hates and mistrusts. He was drinking heavily at the time, and he knows that alcohol grotesquely distorted his perceptions. But now that it has been dislodged, that old feeling moves through him like a breath of smoke. Back then, it had seemed to him that Mandy had turned DJ against him, that DJ had in some strange way almost physically transformed into something that wasn't Gene's *real* son. Gene can remember how, sometimes, he would be sitting on the couch, watching TV, and he'd get a funny feeling. He'd turn his head and DJ would be at the edge of the room, with his bony spine hunched and his long neck craned, staring with those strangely oversize eyes. Other times, Gene and Mandy would be arguing and DJ would suddenly slide into the room, creeping up to Mandy and resting his head on her chest, right in the middle of some important talk. "I'm thirsty," he would say, in imitation baby-talk. Though he was five years old, he would playact this little toddler voice. "Mama," he would say. "I is firsty." And DJ's eyes would rest on Gene for a moment, cold and full of calculating hatred.

Of course, Gene knows now that this was not the reality of it. He knows: He was a drunk, and DJ was just a sad, scared little kid, trying to deal with a rotten situation. Later, when he was in detox, these memories of his son made him actually shudder with shame, and it was not something he could bring himself to talk about even when he was deep into his twelve steps. How could he say how repulsed he'd been by the child, how actually frightened he was. Jesus Christ—DJ was a poor wretched five-year-old kid! But in Gene's memory there was something malevolent about him, resting his head pettishly on his mother's chest, talking in that singsong, lisping voice, staring hard and unblinking at Gene with a little smile. Gene remembers catching DJ by the back of the neck. "If you're going to talk, talk normal," Gene had whispered through his teeth, and tightened his fingers. "You're not a baby. You're not fooling anybody." And DJ had actually bared his teeth, making a thin, hissing whine.

He wakes and he can't breathe. There is a swimming, suffocating sensation of being stared at, being watched by something that hates him, and he gasps, choking for air. A lady is bending over him, and for a moment he expects her to say: "You're very lucky, young man. You should be dead."

But it's Karen. "What are you doing?" she says. It's morning, and he struggles to orient himself—he's on the living room floor, and the television is still going.

"Jesus," he says, and coughs. "Oh, Jesus." He is sweating, his face feels hot, but he tries to calm himself in the face of Karen's horrified stare. "A bad dream," he says, trying to control his panting breaths. "Jesus," he says, and shakes his head, trying to smile reassuringly for her. "I got up last night and I couldn't sleep. I must have passed out while I was watching TV."

But Karen just gazes at him, her expression frightened and uncertain, as if something about him is transforming. "Gene," she says. "Are you all right?"

"Sure," he says hoarsely, and a shudder passes over him involuntarily. "Of course." And then he realizes that he is naked. He sits up, covering his crotch self-consciously with his hands, and glances around. He doesn't see his underwear or his pajama bottoms anywhere nearby. He doesn't even see the afghan, which he'd had draped over him on the couch while he was watching the mummies on TV. He starts to stand up, awkwardly, and he notices that Frankie is standing there in the archway between the kitchen and the living room, watching him, his arms at his sides like a cowboy who is ready to draw his holstered guns.

"Mom?" Frankie says. "I'm thirsty."

He drives through his deliveries in a daze. The bees, he thinks. He remembers what Frankie said a few mornings before, about bees inside his head, buzzing and bumping against the inside of his forehead like a windowpane they were tapping against. That's the feeling he has now. All the things that he doesn't quite remember are circling and alighting, vibrating their cellophane wings insistently. He sees himself striking Mandy across the face with the flat of his hand, knocking her off her chair; he sees his grip tightening around the back of DJ's thin five-year-old neck, shaking him as he grimaced and wept; and he is aware that there are other things, perhaps even worse, if he thought about it hard enough. All the things he's prayed that Karen would never know about him.

He was very drunk on the day that he left them, so drunk that he can barely remember. It is hard to believe that he made it all the way to Des Moines on the interstate before he went off the road, tumbling end over end, into darkness. He was laughing, he thinks, as the car crumpled around him, and he has to pull his van over to the side of the road, out of fear, as the tickling in his head intensifies. There is an image of Mandy, sitting on the couch as he stormed out, with DJ cradled in her arms, one of DJ's eyes swollen shut and puffy. There is an image of him in the kitchen, throwing glasses and beer bottles onto the floor, listening to them shatter.

And whether they are dead or not, he knows that they don't wish him well. They would not want him to be happy—in love with his wife and child. His normal, undeserved life.

When he gets home that night, he feels exhausted. He doesn't want to think anymore, and for a moment, it seems that he will be allowed a small reprieve. Frankie is in the yard, playing contentedly. Karen is in the kitchen, making hamburgers and corn on the cob, and everything seems okay. But when he sits down to take off his boots, she gives him an angry look.

"Don't do that in the kitchen," she says icily. "Please. I've asked you before."

He looks down at his feet: one shoe unlaced, half off. "Oh," he says. "Sorry."

But when he retreats to the living room, to his recliner, she follows him. She leans against the door frame, her arms folded, watching as he releases his tired feet from the boots and rubs his hand over the bottoms of his socks. She frowns heavily.

"What?" he says, and tries on an uncertain smile.

She sighs. "We need to talk about last night," she says. "I need to know what's going on."

"Nothing," he says, but the stern way she examines him activates his anxieties all over again. "I couldn't sleep, so I went out to the living room to watch TV. That's all."

She stares at him. "Gene," she says after a moment. "People don't usually wake up naked on their living room floor, and not know how they got there. That's just weird, don't you think?" *Oh, please,* he thinks. He lifts his hands, shrugging—a posture of innocence and exasperation, though his insides are trembling. "I know," he says. "It was weird to me, too. I was having nightmares. I really don't know what happened."

She gazes at him for a long time, her eyes heavy. "I see," she says, and he can feel the emanation of her disappointment like waves of heat. "Gene," she says. "All I'm asking is for you to be honest with me. If you're having problems, if you're drinking again, or thinking about it. I want to help. We can work it out. But you have to be honest with me."

"I'm not drinking," Gene says firmly. He holds her eyes. "I'm not thinking about it. I told you when we met, I'm through with it. Really." But he is aware again of an observant, unfriendly presence, hidden, moving along the edge of the room. "I don't understand," he says. "What is it? Why would you think I'd lie to you?"

She shifts, still trying to read something in his face, still, he can tell, doubting him. "Listen," she says, at last, and he can tell she is trying not to cry. "Some guy called you today. A drunk guy. And he said to tell you that he had a good time hanging out with you last night, and that he was looking forward to seeing you again soon." She frowns hard, staring at him as if this last bit of damning information will show him for the liar he is. A tear slips out of the corner of her eye and along the bridge of her nose. Gene feels his chest tighten.

"That's crazy," he says. He tries to sound outraged, but he is in fact suddenly very frightened. "Who was it?"

She shakes her head sorrowfully. "I don't know," she says. "Something with a 'B.' He was slurring so bad I could hardly understand him. BB or BJ or . . ."

Gene can feel the small hairs on his back prickling. "Was it DJ?" he says.

And Karen shrugs, lifting a now-teary face to him. "I don't know!" she says hoarsely. "I don't know. Maybe." And Gene puts his palms across his face. He is aware of that strange buzzing, tickling feeling behind his forehead.

"Who is DJ?" Karen says. "Gene, you have to tell me what's going on."

But he can't. He can't tell her, even now. Especially now, he thinks, when to admit that he'd been lying to her ever since they met would confirm all the fears and suspicions she'd been nursing for—what?—days? weeks?

"He's someone I used to know a long time ago," Gene tells her. "Not a good person. He's the kind of guy who might . . . call up, and get a kick out of upsetting you."

They sit at the kitchen table, silently watching as Frankie eats his hamburger and corn on the cob. Gene can't quite get his mind around it. DJ, he thinks, as he presses his finger against his hamburger bun, but doesn't pick it up. DJ. He would be fifteen by now. Could he, perhaps, have found them? Maybe stalking them? Watching the house? Gene tries to fathom how DJ might have been causing Frankie's screaming episodes. How he might have caused what happened last night—snuck up on Gene while he was sitting there watching TV and drugged him or something. It seems farfetched.

"Maybe it was just some random drunk," he says at last to Karen. "Accidentally calling the house. He didn't ask for me by name, did he?"

"I don't remember," Karen says. "Gene . . ."

And he can't stand the doubtfulness, the lack of trust in her expression. He strikes his fist hard against the table, and his plate clatters in a circling echo. "I *did not* go out with anybody last night!" he says. "I *did not* get drunk! You can either believe me, or you can . . ."

They are both staring at him. Frankie's eyes are wide, and he puts down the corncob he was about to bite into, as if he doesn't like it anymore. Karen's mouth is pinched.

"Or I can what?" she says.

"Nothing," Gene breathes.

There isn't a fight, but a chill spreads through the house, a silence. She knows that he isn't telling her the truth. She knows that there's more to it. But what can he say? He stands at the sink, gently washing the dishes as Karen bathes Frankie and puts him to bed. He waits, listening to the small sounds of the house at night. Outside, in the yard, there is the swing set, and the willow tree—silver-gray and stark in the security light that hangs above the garage. He waits for a while longer, watching, half expecting to see DJ emerge from behind the tree as he'd done in Gene's dream, creeping along, his bony, hunched back, the skin pulled tight against the skull of his oversize head. There is that smothering, airless feeling of being watched, and Gene's hands are trembling as he rinses a plate under the tap.

When he goes upstairs at last, Karen is already in her nightgown, in bed, reading a book.

"Karen," he says, and she flips a page, deliberately.

"I don't want to talk to you until you're ready to tell me the truth," she says. She doesn't look at him. "You can sleep on the couch, if you don't mind."

"Just tell me," Gene says. "Did he leave a number? To call him back?"

"No," Karen says. She doesn't look at him. "He just said he'd see you soon."

He thinks that he will stay up all night. He doesn't even wash up, or brush his teeth, or get into his bedtime clothes. He just sits there on the couch, in his uniform and stocking feet, watching television with the sound turned low, listening. Midnight. One A.M.

He goes upstairs to check on Frankie, but everything is okay. Frankie is asleep with his mouth open, the covers thrown off. Gene stands in the doorway, alert for movement, but everything seems to be in place. Frankie's turtle sits motionless on its rock, the books are lined up in neat rows, the toys put away. Frankie's face tightens and untightens as he dreams.

Two A.M. Back on the couch, Gene startles, half-asleep as an ambulance passes in the distance, and then there is only the sound of crickets and cicadas. Awake for a moment, he blinks heavily at a rerun of *Bewitched,* and flips through channels. Here is some jewelry for sale. Here is someone performing an autopsy.

In the dream, DJ is older. He looks to be nineteen or twenty, and he walks into a bar where Gene is hunched on a stool, sipping a glass of beer. Gene recognizes him right away—his posture, those thin shoulders, those large eyes. But now, DJ's arms are long and muscular, tattooed. There is a hooded, unpleasant look on his face as he ambles up to the bar, pressing in next to Gene. DJ orders a shot of Jim Beam—Gene's old favorite.

"I've been thinking about you a lot, ever since I died," DJ murmurs. He doesn't look at Gene as he says this, but Gene knows who he is talking to, and his hands are shaky as he takes a sip of beer.

"I've been looking for you for a long time," DJ murmurs, and the air is hot and thick. Gene puts a trembly cigarette to his mouth and breathes on it, choking on the taste. He wants to say, *I'm sorry. Forgive me.* But he can't breathe. DJ shows his small, crooked teeth, staring at Gene as he gulps for air.

"I know how to hurt you," DJ whispers.

Gene opens his eyes, and the room is full of smoke. He sits up, disoriented: For a second he is still in the bar with DJ before he realizes that he's in his own house.

There is a fire somewhere: He can hear it. People say that fire "crackles," but in fact it seems like the amplified sound of tiny creatures eating, little wet mandibles, thousands and thousands of them, and then a heavy, whispered *whoof* as the fire finds another pocket of oxygen. He can hear this, even as he chokes blindly in the smoky air. The living room has a filmy haze over it, as if it is atomizing, fading away, and when he tries to stand up it disappears completely. There is a thick membrane of smoke above him, and he drops again to his hands and knees, gagging and coughing, a thin line of vomit trickling onto the rug in front of the still-chattering television.

He has the presence of mind to keep low, crawling on his knees and elbows underneath the thick, billowing fumes. "Karen!" he calls. "Frankie!" but his voice is swallowed into the white noise of diligently licking flame. "Ach," he chokes, meaning to utter their names.

When he reaches the edge of the stairs he sees only flames and darkness above him. He puts his hands and knees on the bottom steps, but the heat pushes him back. He feels one of Frankie's action figures underneath his palm, the melting plastic adhering to his skin, and he shakes it away as another bright burst of flame reaches out of Frankie's bedroom for a moment. At the top of the stairs, through the curling fog he can see the figure of a child watching him grimly, hunched there, its face lit and flickering. Gene cries out, lunging into the heat, crawling his way up the stairs, to where the bedrooms are. He tries to call to them again, but instead, he vomits.

There is another burst that covers the image that he thinks is a child. He can feel his hair and eyebrows shrinking and sizzling against his skin as the upstairs breathes out a concussion of sparks. He is aware that there are hot, floating bits of substance in the air, glowing orange and then winking out, turning to ash. For some reason he thinks of bees. The air thick with angry buzzing, and that is all he can hear as he slips, turning end over end down the stairs, the humming and his own voice, a long vowel wheeling and echoing as the house spins into a blur.

And then he is lying on the grass. Red lights tick across his opened eyes in a steady, circling rhythm, and a woman, a paramedic, lifts her lips up from his. He draws in a long, desperate breath.

"Shhh," she says softly, and passes her hand along his eyes. "Don't look," she says.

But he does. He sees, off to the side, the long black plastic sleeping bag, with a strand of Karen's blond hair hanging out from the top. He sees the blackened, shriveled body of a child, curled into a fetal position. They place the corpse into the spread, zippered plastic opening of the body bag, and he can see the mouth, frozen, calcified, into an oval. A scream.

Patrick Lane,
Flabbergasted

There had been several funerals of his old high school friends and Brandon hadn't gone to any of them. He was aware that this was a problem, a problematic decision, and sure enough, afterward one of the girlfriends of the dead called him up and told him how rude she thought he was. "It really shocked me," Rachel said. "Zachary was always a good friend to you and this just says something about you as a person that I wouldn't have expected. I lost a lot of respect for you today," she said.

He didn't know what to say. The truth was, he didn't have any excuse. He hadn't wanted to get dressed up, and he didn't like going into churches and being preached at. He had never really liked rituals, period. But he couldn't say this, and so instead he tried to tell her that he couldn't get out of work.

"Oh, come off it, Brandon," Rachel said. They had dated briefly in ninth grade and ever after she had had little use for him. "Everybody can get out of work for a funeral," she said. "Why don't you just admit that you have turned into a complete shitheel? That would be the decent thing to do right now."

"Okay," Brandon said. "I turned into a shitheel."

"Yes you did," Rachel said. "What happened?" And then she hung up.

Brandon probably could have argued with her, but he realized that it was not the kind of argument that you could win.

What could he say? He had known a lot of dead people recently. But was that a legitimate complaint? Was it enough of an excuse to say that he simply felt worn out?

To be honest, there were simply fewer and fewer things he felt like doing. That he could even *bring himself* to do. He'd stay up late playing video games on an aging PlayStation system he had hooked up to the television in the living room. He'd go to work at the grocery store. Sometimes he'd look at porn or read various message boards on the Internet. That was about the extent of it.

It seemed like he hardly ever talked to anyone anymore. At the grocery store he was working in the produce department stacking pumpkins when a beaming older woman came up to him holding some Seckel pears in her cupped palms as if they were delicate eggs.

"These are so adorable!" she exclaimed at him. "They are tiny little pears!"

"Yes," he said. "They are Seckel pears."

"Oh," she said enthusiastically. "And are they ripe? Could I eat one right now if I wanted to?"

"Well," Brandon said. He was a bit taken aback by her excitement. "Actually, these could probably stand to get a little riper. If you put them in a sealed plastic bag with a couple of bananas, and keep them at room temperature, they should ripen up pretty quickly. They will have a yellowish hue when they're ready to eat."

"Wonderful," the woman exclaimed. "You are really very knowledgeable and helpful."

"Thank you," Brandon said, and the woman clutched her tiny pears.

"No," she said. "Thank *you*!"

The depressing thing was, he realized later that this was one of the nicest conversations he'd had in quite a while.

He had been working at the grocery store for a number of years by that point. "What are you now?" his first grade teacher, Mrs. Love-Denman, had asked him. "Twenty-five? Twenty-six?" They had abruptly come face-to-face in an aisle where he was stocking cans of soup and he couldn't believe she recognized him. "You're Brandon Fowler, aren't you?" she said in that gentle, unnervingly sensual Southern accent. "Oh, my land! I can hardly believe it! Brandon Fowler—all grown up!" He guessed that he had known that she still existed, that she was still wandering around town, but nevertheless seeing her freaked him out a little. She must have been at least seventy years old but she was dressed like a much younger woman, wearing an ill-fitting, stiff blond wig—and he had no idea what to say to her. He supposed that he'd been rude for not talking to her. He did say "Hello," actually. And then he'd just smiled tightly at her and nodded in a kind of dazed way.

It was the sort of encounter that was really problematic and it took a long time to get over. At night, as they were closing, he paced slowly down the spice-and-cereal aisle pushing a wide dust mop, listening to music on his iPod, and trying not to think. In the parking lot he collected empty shopping carts, stacking them, inserting one into the next until he was propelling a kind of millipede of metal and wheels across the asphalt. Still not thinking. In the basement he lifted boxes of cabbages, crates of tangelos, rubber-banded bunches of beets and mustard greens and parsnips.

In the employee-only bathroom, he stood at the urinal stall and aimed toward the zinc cake that rested near the drain. Above the porcelain-and-silver piping of the toilet, people had written on the wall in pencil and ink and Magic Marker: various things.

His favorite piece of graffiti said: PATRICK LANE, FLABBERGASTED.

This had been scrawled above the urinal for as long as Brandon could remember, and he occasionally wondered about Patrick Lane as he peed.

Patrick Lane had apparently once been a grocery store employee, and Brandon liked to imagine that they might have become friends. He imagined that Patrick Lane was the sort of person who wrote odd, quirky, self-deprecating graffiti about himself, just for his own amusement. Perhaps Patrick Lane dreamed of becoming a cartoonist, or a singer-songwriter, or simply a perceptive and thoughtful wanderer in the mode of Sal Paradise in the Kerouac novel *On the Road*.

Did people ever hitch rides in the boxcars of trains anymore? Brandon wondered.

He liked to picture Patrick Lane, rambling across the country, leaving a record of his emotions—FLABBERGASTED—EXULTANT—INSULTED—DEVASTATED—and so forth, from bathroom to bathroom as he went.

This idea really appealed to him, but then someone said: *Oh, he's that poor kid that killed himself. I just couldn't bring myself to scrub his writing off the wall.*

Brandon was still living in the old house where he grew up, which he realized was probably a big part of the problem. His parents had been dead for two years, and his older sister, Jodee, was now living in Chicago with her boyfriend, Jake the Medical Resident.

After their parents' funeral, Brandon and Jodee had both agreed that the best thing to do was to sell the house and split the profits equally. The original plan was that Brandon would live in the house for a few months and fix things up a little to make it more presentable so they could sell it.

But the house didn't seem to want to be sold. Things that had never been wrong in the twenty years that the family had lived there together suddenly turned sour when the housing inspector came to check on the building.

One problem was called "deterioration of the structural roof deck" and cost an enormous amount of money to get fixed.

Other issues were smaller, and presumably should have been repairable by Brandon himself, with the help of a home fix-it book. These included improper wiring connections, bulges and crumbling spots in the drywall, some plumbing stuff, and so on—but much of this was more complicated than a person would think.

"But you're a smart guy," Jodee had told him. "You can figure it out. I think it's good for you to have a project to work on."

Brandon had spent some time at a couple of different colleges and then finally he had decided to take a while off and earn some money. He imagined that he would enjoy hanging around with some old high school friends, like Zachary Leven and Matty, and he was also kind of looking forward to having his mom do his laundry and so on.

And actually, Brandon's mom had thought it was a good idea. She thought that he still needed time to "find himself." This was right before she and his dad died.

Jodee was four years older, and she believed that their parents had been stricter when she was growing up.

"But honestly, I'm glad that Mom and Dad were harder on me," Jodee said once. "Because now I have a work ethic."

Then she hesitated. Brandon knew that she hadn't meant to be insulting, exactly. Nevertheless, he realized that she couldn't quite understand how it was possible that he was still living there, still fixing up the house, after almost five years.

Of course, Brandon was aware that things had probably deteriorated even more than Jodee realized.

Steadily, he had been relinquishing, withdrawing from portions of the house, and the actual living quarters had shrunk considerably.

There was, for example, his parents' bedroom upstairs, which he was naturally hesitant to enter, and Jodee's old bedroom, where he had decided to store all of the stuff that he'd eventually sell at an estate or garage sale, such as small pieces of furniture, vintage-esque clothing, his father's phonograph records and coin collection, his mother's jewelry and shelves of mystery novels, the boxes of photographs of the trips that they had taken as a family, Disney World, the Grand Canyon, New York City, and so forth.

There was the second-floor bathroom, which was now off-limits, following a weirdly disastrous attempt to replace the toilet's ballcock assembly and flush valve.

And then there were areas that he had started to clean or pack up but then had broken off for one reason or another.

For example, in the basement "rec room" area, on the upper shelf of a closet, he'd come across a bunch of games that the family used to play when Brandon and Jodee were kids: Monopoly. Yahtzee. Battleship. Which he'd planned to get rid of.

But then he opened the mildewy cardboard box of an ancient Scrabble game and an enormous number of cockroaches came scuttling out of it. Oh, my God! He chucked the game across the room and it broke open and all the little wooden tiles with letters printed on them scattered across the shag carpet.

His mom used to love to play Scrabble. He had this image of the four of them sitting at the kitchen table with the game board in the middle. He could picture his mother counting out her score and teasing their father, laughing and flourishing her little dictionary. She had seemed really happy at the time. It was weird to think that none of them had guessed how things would eventually turn out.

He knew it was childish, but after the incident with the cockroaches he had been unable to bring himself to pick up the scattered pieces of the game.

He had somehow gotten the idea that he would bend over and discover that the Scrabble tiles had spelled out some kind of eerie message.

When Brandon came home from work on the day that his parents died, he found a note that his mother had taped to the front door. It was a letter addressed to him, and he stood there on the stoop with his hand still on the side of the house, reading it.

Dear Brandon,

Your father and I have made a very difficult decision and I am writing to apologize for any pain that may be caused. Please, honey, don't feel guilty or as if this is all your fault because there is really nothing you could have done. Just always remember the happy times we shared as a family. You were a wonderful son!

> *All our love,*
> *Mom & Dad*

P.S. Please do not go up to our bedroom. Just call the police and tell them that you have found this note and they will come out to the house and help you take care of things.

P.P.S. I already sent a letter to Jodee so she should get it today.

This letter was one of the things that he tried not to think about too much, though sometimes little phrases from it would rise up for no reason to float on the surface of his consciousness.

You were a wonderful son! He thought. *You were a wonderful son!* There were a lot of ways to take that.

He often wondered about Jodee's letter, and whether they had told her something that they hadn't told him. Because she was older, or more responsible, or whatever. For example, had they explained to her in more detail about why they had killed themselves?

But he and Jodee had never actually talked about the letters.

Every once in a while, Jodee would call to check up on him and she would talk about how much she wanted to come back "home" for a visit, just to hang out and maybe even help with whatever finishing touches he was putting on the house. Give him that added "push" he seemed to need.

"I miss you, Li'l Bro," she said. "I can't believe how long it's been since we've seen each other."

"I know," he said.

"I hope you don't think I've abandoned you," she said.

"No, no," he said. He gave a kind of chuckle, and for a moment he thought again about the letter she had received from their parents. Did it say something like: *Jodee, please don't abandon Brandon!*

"*Abandon,*" he said. "Whatever."

"Well, you know what I mean," Jodee said. "We had a toxic childhood—I realize that—but there comes a time when we all have to move on."

"True," Brandon said. He hesitated. There often came a point in the conversation when Jodee would offer to put him in touch with a grief therapist who had been very helpful to her.

"When you grow up with people like Mom and Dad, they catch you up in a cycle," Jodee said. "You can't escape—that's the problem."

"Absolutely," he said. He considered. What did she mean by that?

There were times when he would have liked to tell her that something really weird had been happening to him—something to do with his sense of time . . . or?

But what could he say?

He was sitting on the fold-out couch in the living room, on the edge of the bare wafer of sofa mattress with the sheets and blankets crumpled at his feet, and the TV stand right at the foot of the bed with the PlayStation wires and the console and cartridges—Tekken 3, Q*bert, Crypt Killer, that kind of stuff—and the dresser from his bedroom and the computer and basically everything from his room upstairs that he wanted cluttered in a kind of fort around the sofa bed. He hadn't been upstairs to his bedroom in probably a long time.

"Well, anyway," Jodee said. "I know you're busy."

He took off his socks and rubbed the itchy soles of his feet, which were being very slowly consumed by a fungus. He had tried all sorts of ointments but the fungus appeared to be indestructible.

"Did I tell you about Zachary?" he said.

In the background, through the telephone line, he could hear the deep, jocky voice of Jake the Medical Resident asking Jodee a question, and she hesitated—maybe gesturing or miming or mouthing, "IT'S BRAN! DON!" exaggeratedly so that Jake the Medical Resident could read her lips.

"Zachary who?" she said. "Zachary Leven from high school?"

"Yeah," Brandon said. "Zachary Leven. He died, actually."

"Geez," Jodee said. "You sure have lost a lot of people from your class. What was it? A car accident? I hope it wasn't drugs."

"Um," Brandon said. He thought about it. "You know—I'm not completely sure what it was. It definitely wasn't a car wreck but . . . ? Some kind of, like, illness? I hadn't talked to him in a long time and I missed his funeral, so . . ."

He found himself sitting there in a state of pause. It was totally unnerving, because surely he had heard how Zachary Leven had died. Or read it somewhere . . . ? It reminded him of the day that his parents died, sitting there in the living room with the cop, a weight-lifter-looking guy named Mark Mitchell, who had a notepad he was writing in. *Had he noticed anything out of the ordinary about them recently?* Officer Mitchell asked. *Were they having marital problems? Had they made any statements concerning feelings of despair, had they verbally expressed any concepts of life not being worth living, that sort of thing? Were they having financial difficulties?* And Brandon had been unable to think of a single explanation. There was nothing unusual that he noticed, he said, and he sat there in the wingback chair, the cop on the sofa, the neat living room and the candy dish on the coffee table full of red and brown M&M's that he had never seen anyone eat.

He sat there remembering this, holding the phone against his face, and his eyes ran over the topography of the floor. It looked sort of like there was a kind of drain, a vortex around where the sofa bed was. A spiral of materials had begun to form an orbit: a spoon and empty yogurt container on the carpet, wasabi pea, Post-it note, throat lozenge, a sock in fetal position.

"Well—*anyways*," Jodee said at last, after the ellipses had trickled past for a while. She sighed in a gently emphatic way. "I don't want to keep you," she said. "I suppose I better let you get off the phone."

It had occurred to him that maybe something was going wrong with the world. Like global warming or an economic collapse or a coming plague. He could imagine that his parents had somehow intuited or found out about such an event, something so terrible that they couldn't bear to live through it. But what? He couldn't quite conceptualize such a catastrophe, though often he was aware of its presence, its *force*, something large and omnipotent hovering over not just himself and his house but also the neighborhood, the state, the country. Possibly the planet?

He noticed, for example, that many of the stores were closing and remaining empty—the old Beatrice Academy of Beauty across from the high school had shut down, and through the cracked windows you could see the hair dryers all piled together in a jumble, like dead spacemen. Parking meters along the block had been beheaded and were now just bare pipes sticking up out of the sidewalk. There were also more vacant lots than there used to be when he was growing up. These were lots where there once were houses, houses that he used to pass by on his way to school as a kid, and it seemed that they just came and took the houses away when he hadn't been paying attention. All that remained were patches of high grass and weeds, not even a foundation.

He had mentioned this to Patty and Marci, the two head

cashiers at work, but this didn't seem to make an impression on them. "Brandon," Patty said. "This city has been sliding downhill for so many years I barely notice it anymore."

"Hon, you have some writing on your arm," Marci observed.

In the bathroom in the basement of the grocery store, Brandon washed the pale underside of his forearm with a paper towel and some industrial liquid soap. But it seemed that he had written on himself with a permanent marker, so it wouldn't come off very well. *WTF . . . ?* he thought. He pulled his sleeve up and saw that the writing ran up the length of his arm from his wrist to his biceps; it was definitely his own handwriting.

On the lower part of his palm:

Intercerebral myiasis–
maggot infestation of the brain–
extremely rare but not unheard of.

And then crawling up his wrist, very shaky handwriting:

slab rat beg fed   garble fast bed   bad bag serflet

Then, more neatly, on his forearm:

Conclusion simply the place where you tired of thinking.

And finally, on his biceps, little teeny letters:

Flabbergasted. Flutterghosted. Flatterguessed. Flabergist. Fl

Back when he was in high school, he had the habit of writing notes to himself on his own skin when he didn't have a piece of paper handy. But he had no memory of writing any of this.

Maybe he'd done it in his sleep?

He tried not to let this concept freak him out. He rubbed at it until it had begun to fade a little and his skin felt kind of sore.

He was aware that he might be having sleep issues. He might be addicted to the Internet and video games and maybe that was part of it. That was why he couldn't seem to get the house cleaned up and that was why he kept missing important social-obligation-type things like funerals and that was why he was waking up in the middle of the night writing stuff on his hands and his arms and even his legs and so on which he couldn't remember writing in the morning though there would sometimes be a Sharpie pen clutched in his fist.

When he first started sleeping in the house alone he had found it comforting to have a little music playing when he tried to go to bed, or maybe the sound of the television, The Weather Channel, just the chatter of voices—but soon it was the video games and the computer as well, multiple programs stacked on top of one another, and before long there was a semicircle of electronic devices around the sofa bed where he slept. It was as if they were projecting a small force field around him. It wasn't a powerful force field, but it was at least enough to allow him to rest for a little while.

There were electrical outages in the city and then he couldn't sleep at all. He would sit there alone in the dark, clutching his flashlight. He was certain he could hear sounds in the house. In the ruined bathroom, his parents' bedroom, in the basement, where he imagined the scuttle of cockroaches or Scrabble tiles—

And he'd once actually fled out the back door in his underwear with his flashlight and sleeping bag in his arms and tried to sleep on the lawn under the old apple tree. But even that—the beloved apple tree of their childhood, "Jonathan the Apple Tree," their mother had called it—even that behaved strangely. Its leaves would get a white powdery substance on them and then they curled up and fell off, and the apples themselves were tiny and wrinkled and deformed in a way that made them look like little ugly heads, and as he sat in the backyard on the sleeping bag he heard one drop.

. . . tunk?

A sinister little questioning sound.

And then, after a long silence, another one—"tunk?"—and he imagined he saw the whispery movement as the shrunken apple rolled through the unmowed grass.

You could say that his problem had started with the death of his parents . . . or the death of his friends—you could say that it was just a stage of grief, maybe—but he worried that it was actually much bigger than that, it could be traced in concentric circles rippling back into the past who knew how long?

There was that time back in ninth grade, for example, when he and Zachary Leven ate some mushrooms, psilocybin mushrooms, and it had been a very unpleasant sort of psychedelic drug trip. At first there had been the mystical hilarity and talking trees and couches "breathing," etc.—but then it had become increasingly anxious, the world had begun to seem as if it wanted to commu-

nicate a dreadful, dire message, uncomfortable words and letters
began to emerge—for example, the long vine from his mom's
pothos plant in the kitchen was curling down in a way that appeared to be unreadable cursive writing, possibly Arabic, and the
shingles on the neighbor's roof seemed to be arranged so that
they formed *H*'s and *I*'s in a pattern: H I H I H I H I H I which
freaked him quite badly.

By that time Brandon's parents had found out and they drove
him and Zachary Leven to the hospital. Both he and Zachary
Leven had gotten paranoid and begun to imagine that their brains
were going to turn off. Like suddenly they would become vege-
tables. And both he and Zachary Leven were crying and his mom
said, *I am so ashamed of you, I hope you remember this when I'm
dead, after all I've done for you this is how you repay me, I hope you
think about this moment when I am gone,* and his father had looked
pained and said, *Oh, Cathy, that kind of talk isn't necessary,* and
the doctor gazed at them and said: "I am going to prescribe some
clonazepam—that should do the trick," and his mother said, with
enthusiastic disgust: "They are both of them throwing up and
they both have *diarrhea*!"

And though it had all been fine afterward, and his parents,
even his mother, had forgiven him, and he had gone on to college, etc.—even still there was occasionally a lingering memory
of that terrible message the world had been trying to telegraph.
Something had happened, he thought, something had happened,
something subtle but actually deadly had been implanted and was
possibly consuming his brain the way the fungus was consuming
his feet.

On the Internet he read about Hallucinogen Persisting Perception Disorder (HPPD). Could this condition have been caused by the mushrooms? And at the library he checked out the *Diagnostic and Statistical Manual of Mental Disorders* (*DSM*), published by the American Psychiatric Association (APA), and he tried to read up on HPPD, but afterward that didn't seem quite right, either.

"Halos around objects," he read. "Colors of objects changing while looking at them. Illusion that objects are moving."

He lifted his head and stared at the discarded white sock on the floor, which wasn't breathing, he was pretty sure.

"*Aeropsia,*" he read. "Floaters."

What if it was worse than just the lingering effects of a bad trip? What if something was really wrong? Maybe it was just Ohio, or just America, or just Homo sapiens as a species, but it might also be that the world, the entirety of Planet Earth was basically fucked.

There were long stretches when time seemed to have stopped working. The weather had stopped acting like it had when he was a child, with white Christmases and April showers and May flowers and so forth. Much of the time you would look outside and it would be gray and foggy, and you couldn't tell whether it was early morning or dusk. More and more frequently, the power would go out in his part of town and he would wake up and the clocks in the house would all say something different.

On The Weather Channel it said: "A large swath of dead clouds covered many areas of the Tennessee Valley to the Northeast yesterday."

His father used to enjoy watching The Weather Channel. His

father liked to sit in his recliner and doze in front of it, letting the gentle hysteria of distant blizzards and floods and tornadoes and hurricanes wash over him, and Brandon remembered how Zachary Leven used to joke about it. "Uh-oh, here comes the end of the world," Zachary used to say as they passed by Brandon's sleeping father on their way to the basement to play video games.

What would Zachary Leven say now? he wondered. He could imagine Zachary and Rachel stopping by for a visit, the two of them exchanging glances.

They might be like, "Um, how come you nailed your mom and dad's bedroom door shut?"

They might turn on the light in the second-floor bathroom and let out a cry of surprised disgust. "Holy shit! What is that greenish shit? Mold?"

They might say, "You need to get out of this house, man!" They might say: "You need to get out of this town! You need to get out of Ohio! You need to get out of this country! Hurry! Before it's too late!"

He was thinking of this again as he was on bag-boy duty that afternoon at the grocery store, standing at the end of Marci's checkout aisle—*Hurry! Before it's too late!* he thought, but he only stood there staring as various items came trembling down the conveyor, boxes of tea, a square of tofu, a can of organic chicken broth. They reached the end of the conveyor and began to cluster together, shoaling into a kind of tombolo at the end of the counter.

"Paper or plastic?" Brandon said, unfolding a bag, and he lifted up from his daze to see that it was the lady who loved Seckel pears—he recognized her at once, though it had been a while since he had seen her. She looked terrible. The skin around her mouth was raw and chapped, and glistened with some kind of ointment she had rubbed on it. Her eyes were large and sorrowful and appeared to be made up primarily of water.

"Can I have both plastic *and* paper?" she said.

"Of course," Brandon said.

"Thank you—you're very kind," she said, and she brushed her hand through her hair as she bent to write a check, and a few strands came out and remained attached to her fingernails like trailing moss. Beyond her, Brandon could see the customers moving along behind their shopping carts, and he thought about this old zombie movie that he and Zachary Leven had watched together—they had loved getting stoned and watching horror movies—and there was the one about the undead overrunning a shopping mall. "A trenchant critique of capitalism," Zachary had said, and of course that was one way to look at it. Another way was just that the undead were pissed off and bitter. "Youth is wasted on the young," his father used to say. "Life is wasted on the living." His dad thought this was hilarious.

More and more, he thought, his days at the grocery store were like being in a zombie movie except that here the undead appeared to be too depressed to be cannibals. You didn't even realize, most of the time, that they were dead, and he had the worrisome thought that he would look up and there would be his mom or Zachary Leven or there would be Patrick Lane, gray-skinned and surprised-looking, standing at the end of an empty checkout aisle, his hands moving slowly as if he were packing an unseen grocery bag with air.

It had occurred to him that if the undead don't realize that they are dead, he might easily be one of them himself.

But that wasn't it, either. Of course he was still alive! In the employee bathroom he pressed a ballpoint pen against the palm of his hand and naturally he could feel the pen poking against his skin, of course he still had feeling. *Hello?* he wrote. *Anyone home?*

That was what his mom used to ask him. He would space out, he wouldn't hear what she said to him as they sat there at dinner eating and he'd be gazing down at his plate and she'd touch her finger to his shoulder.

"Hello, Brandon? Is anyone home? Do you hear me talking to you?" And she'd look over at his father in her very ironic, conspiratorial way. "I think there's something missing there," she said. Referring to Brandon.

The memory made him shift uncomfortably. He took off his apron and hung it up in his locker and ran his time card through the ancient punch clock and smiled at Marci who was looking at him curiously and then he was walking home, walking home from work, taking the same route he had taken for years now so that he hardly saw the houses and trees and the unscrolling sidewalk beneath his feet.

"You know," his mother had once said to his father, "it worries me—he never really seems to grasp cause and effect very well," she said. Brandon was sitting right there watching TV but she spoke as if he weren't, and his father gave him a mournful expression.

"Now, Cathy," his father said, "some people just don't think in that way."

And it occurred to Brandon as he stood once again in the doorway of his house that perhaps he *didn't* understand cause and effect—maybe that was the problem. He kept trying to put together a sense of what had happened to him, and it refused to cohere.

"A conclusion is simply the place where you got tired of thinking." That was one of his father's sayings, and this, too, was a kind of joke, a kind of sad joke between his father and his mother; they had both laughed in that way that he had since realized was more than just laughing, though even now, Brandon didn't understand it.

Is anybody home? he thought, and he could remember the day that his parents had died, he walked back from the grocery store like he always did and there was that note taped to the door and he had come into the house and stood in the foyer.

"Hello?" he said uncertainly, the note held loosely in his hand. Obviously it seemed like a suicide note but he felt almost certain that it wasn't. Of course not.

"Mom?" he said. "Dad?" and he was shaking a little as he picked up the phone in the front hallway and called the police like the note told him to do and he knew that he should go up there because there was a sound up there, a thud, as if someone had jumped down on the floor and he was aware that someone else probably would have gone up, gone running up, but he just stood there, his feet gesturing agitatedly as if they were going to start walking.

There was something that he should have understood that he hadn't understood. That he still didn't understand. *Hello? Is anyone home?*

...

He was sitting there in the living room of the house with the video-game controller, and the geometric shapes of Tetris were slowly floating past on the TV screen like protozoa under a microscope.

"People get through things," Jodee told him once. "People who have suffered a lot worse than we have. Like the Holocaust, for example. Or slavery. Or the Depression. I mean, you think about what a lot of people have endured, and you could almost be sort of thankful. You've just got to try harder.

"Like me, for example. You know? That semester that Mom and Dad died, I could've taken the rest of the term off, or whatever, but I didn't. And I was taking really hard classes! Chemistry. Calculus. But I just *focused*, and I ended up getting three A's and a B plus. Do you understand what I'm getting at?"

"Mm-hm," Brandon had said—and now, thinking of his sister's report card, he cupped his palms over his forehead.

As if to prove something to himself, he actually got some tools out—a pipe wrench and a hammer—and he had his home-repair book open and he read: "Remove the valve plunger and you'll see one or two washers or O-rings . . ." and he hesitated, feeling vaguely shaky, standing there at the bottom of the stairs, looking up to where the closed doors lined the hallways.

He just had to get himself together, he told himself. That was what Jodee always said. He was just a little lazy, that's what Jodee said, lazy, unmotivated, and if only he applied himself a bit more—

He could imagine that there was a way in which all the pieces came together and interlocked, some kind of lines that could be drawn from the funerals of his classmates to the plumbing problems in the house, which also connected the clutter of hair dryers in the abandoned beauty academy with his old grade-school teacher, which was associated with the time he and Zachary Leven had watched that zombie movie, which was linked to the scattered tiles of the Scrabble game and the graffiti in the grocery-store bathroom and the note that his parents had left him—it was a map, he thought, a net that cast itself outward, and if he only applied himself he would see how the weather would lift and he would get the house finished and the economy would shift again and he would go back to college and meet some new friends and the wars would come and go and he would move to a new place and maybe get married and he would tease his own children about how they never seemed to grasp cause and effect very well.

He sat there, huddled underneath the hum of electrical equipment that made a halo around the sofa bed, but the house crept gently closer. He could sense the house, the way you sense someone leaning over you and watching while you're sleeping. He could hear the rattle of the apple tree in the wind, the shifting sound of the floorboards upstairs, the red flutter of an emergency vehicle on a distant street. Outside the window, some streetlights winked off and on, hesitating.

Then, with a sigh, the power shut down again. All across the city the light folded into itself, and the darkness spread out its arms.

Stay Awake

Zach and Amber's baby was born with a rare condition that the doctors told them was called craniopagus parasiticus. This meant that their baby had two heads. Or—more properly—it meant that there had once been two babies, conjoined twins, but the second one had failed to develop completely. They were connected by the fused crowns of their skulls, and shared a small portion of the parietal lobes of their brains.

The second twin, which was called the "parasitic" twin, had a head and a neck but didn't really have a body. The neck stump below the head contained fragments of bone and vestiges of a heart and lungs, and there were tiny buds attached to the neck that were the beginnings of limbs.

Nevertheless, the head of the second twin was perfectly formed, with a beautiful little face.

Naturally, there was interest in the media, though they had tried to keep their situation as private as possible. Everything that was written felt upsetting, invasive, even cruel. It was reported that a number of world-class surgical specialists were being consulted, but that "there was little hope for survival."

The whole baby—the "host" baby, as it was termed—was named Rosalie, the newspapers informed their readers, and then they explained that "the parasitic head that is to be removed from Rosalie is capable of blinking and even smiling, but not of independent life."

One reporter called them to ask whether they had given the parasitic head a name, and Zach sat there at the kitchen table, hesitating. Across from him, Amber appeared to be watching her folded hands, her face blank.

"No," Zach said. "No, we have not."

Not long after this, he was driving home from the hospital.

Should they have given the other head a name? he was wondering.

This was a little after ten o'clock at night. It was snowing slowly, and the headlights of the cars shimmered in a way that struck him as particularly vivid. Even the white trail of steam from the steel plant seemed deliberate and painterly, but perhaps that was because he was so tired, perhaps the world was already half in dream.

Amber was asleep back at the house. When he got home, they would lie together in the same bed for a few hours, and then he would get up and go to work. In the few months since the birth they had honed their routines, their daily schedules, their lives separate and divided into hours and half-hours and posted side by side on the refrigerator.

In his dream, Zach pulled into the snow-boughed, pine-darkened driveway and pressed the button so that the automated garage door lifted gently open. Things seemed almost normal, almost like they were before Rosalie. His keys jingled as he unlocked the back door and stepped into the darkened kitchen, where the yellow tabby cat was sitting on the counter, blinking solemnly at him in the moonlight. He slipped off his shoes at the foot of the staircase and began to undress as he ascended, slipping off his shirt and unbuckling his belt and feeling his way down the hallway toward their room, where the bed was waiting with his wife curled up and warm on the right-hand side, and she would sit up and smile, squinting sleepily, tenderly, pulling a strand of her hair away from her lips.

He was just about to bend down to kiss her when his car went off the road.

He was only dreaming that he was home, he realized. He had fallen asleep while driving and he awakened with a start as the steering wheel lurched beneath his hands.

His head jerked up just in time to see a sign fly up over the hood and past the windshield, and he watched in surprise as the red octagon with the word STOP printed on it lifted up and whisked away over his head like a balloon.

Then the windshield smashed, and the car hit a tree, and the safety air bag punched him in the face as it expanded, blocking out his vision.

In her bassinet, baby Rosalie was asleep, though the other head, the parasitic head, was apparently alert. Was it conscious? The other head seemed to sleep less than Rosalie did, and even late at night the nurses would find it blinking slowly and gazing serenely into the darkness, peacefully awake. The other head didn't seem to be in pain, the way Rosalie often was. While Rosalie balled her fists and scrunched her face and screamed, the other head let its eyes drift along the ceiling, its mouth puckered and moving, as if nursing.

Zach had often wondered what was going on inside their brains. Could they dream each other's dreams, think each other's thoughts? Could they see what the other one saw, the two pairs of eyes looking at the world both right side up and upside down?

Or perhaps they weren't aware of each other whatsoever. After all, they couldn't see each other. They'd never looked in a mirror. To Zach, this was a terrible thought—that they had no idea that anything was wrong. It was awful to think that the babies both assumed that this was the way the world was supposed to be.

Of course, he realized that this probably wasn't an accurate way to think about things. He knew that it was not appropriate to attempt to interpret the various expressions and glances that passed across the faces.

"It's a bad idea," one young, friendly doctor told him.

"You don't want to get into a relationship with . . . Well. You don't want to anthropomorphize—is that the right word?—anthropomorphize the deformity. If you see what I mean."

According to the doctors, the other head was probably blind and almost undoubtedly had very low levels of brain function. It had no thoughts or feelings.

Zach woke up in a bed in the hospital. Despite the air bag, he had sustained multiple injuries to his neck, spine, arms, legs, and pelvis, and he was held in spinal traction, in a halo crown and vest. He could feel the titanium pins that held the halo ring to his head, fixed tight to his skull, a pressure just behind his ears. His legs, too, were in traction, but he was not as aware of the splints that held them immobilized. When he opened his eyes, the ceiling swam hazily above him.

"You're very fortunate," a nurse whispered to him. He lay there, motionless, and he had an image of himself drifting upon a wide sea. The nurse was checking his blood pressure and intravenous tube. "Very lucky," she murmured.

He assumed that she meant that his injuries weren't permanent, that he would walk again, that he wasn't a quadriplegic. He had vague memories of conversations being held in the air above him, the voices of doctors undulating. *Some function remained below the level of spinal injury,* they'd told him. *Early immobilization and treatment are the most important factors in achieving recovery,* they said.

"Am I . . . ?" he said, and he thought he felt his fingers flex.

"They tell me that you're Baby Rosalie's father," the nurse said after a moment. Her face hovered briefly over him, her severe eyes and the pointed white nurse's cap, and then she withdrew. Zach couldn't turn his head far enough to maintain eye contact, so he wasn't certain what her expression was like. No doubt there was a lot of gossip among the hospital staff about Rosalie. And there had been that short segment on a television news program that had focused—rather unsympathetically, he thought—on the fertility treatments that they'd undergone.

"Yes," he said, his voice parched. "Yes. That's right. I'm Rosalie's father."

"I've seen her," the nurse said. "Them." There was a pause and Zach flexed his fingers again. Something about her tone of voice disquieted him.

"You . . . saw her?" he said. But the nurse was silent, busy with some task, and maybe she didn't hear him. He could sense her presence, her movement at the periphery of his vision, the winged tip of her nurse's hat. He didn't know they still wore those.

"You know," the nurse said, after he had almost decided that she wasn't going to answer him, "I've always believed that God puts every one of us on earth for a reason."

He cringed inwardly, but tried to smile. "Yes," he said. Ever since Rosalie's birth, people had been quoting such homilies to him, and he had gotten used to accepting them—gracefully, he hoped. He was not a particular fan of religion.

"I think you've been blessed," the nurse continued, in her oddly singsong voice. "That's just my opinion. Some people might tell you otherwise."

Zach felt the woman's hand brush lightly across the lower part of his abdomen. "Thank you for your kind thoughts," he said. He wasn't sure what else to say.

He rolled his eyes downward and he could vaguely see the white shape of her uniform. There was a tube that had been inserted into him, a catheter. Tape had been applied to his skin below his navel and he felt her fingers smoothing it down.

"Poor baby," the nurse said softly, almost musically. "Poor baby."

Of course no one was to blame for Rosalie's condition.

Though he often felt guilty about it—it seemed as if, with some people, there was a kind of unspoken condemnation hovering in the air, his sister, Monica, for example, Monica and her two healthy children. He would be describing their struggles with conception, all the biological and scientific complexity, all the tests and methods—gamete intrafallopian transfer. Superovulation. Intracytoplasmic sperm injection. Gonadotropins. And then he would sense a very light film of judgment in her voice. *What about adoption?* Monica said. *What about adopting a baby from China? They have such beautiful babies.*

"We want to have a baby of our own," he said.

Was that wrong? he wondered, after Rosalie was born. *Were they being punished?*

When Zach woke again, Amber was sitting at his bedside. It was dark outside, and he could see the entire hospital room mirrored against the surface of the window. Here was Amber in the foreground, reading through a sheaf of papers. Here he was, in the bed nearby, posed like a statue in his various braces. Snow was falling through their translucent reflections.

It had been, he guessed, several days since he and Amber had actually spoken. In the months since the baby's birth, their paths seemed to cross less and less. He would sometimes come into a room and it would surprise him to find her there and she, in turn, would seem to stiffen, alert and wary as he entered. It was like finding a deer or some other sort of woodland creature grazing in the backyard.

The two of them had been married for five years, and increasingly much of that time had been occupied by the issues of fertility. The process of conception, in all its arcane biological complexity. Long stretches of their married life together had been given over to such concerns—packets of materials arriving in the mail; hushed, endless waiting rooms and the subsequent conversations with condescending specialists and gently manipulative quacks; silent drives home afterward.

He could often sense Amber brooding as he drove. She was a lawyer by training, and she was bothered by the unfairness of it—by the simple fact that so many women had babies without even trying. They hadn't had to struggle, as she was; they hadn't even had to ask. Sometimes, in a supermarket or on the street they would encounter a mother who was not taking proper care of her baby. The mother would be swearing at it, or carrying it in the bright sunlight without a bonnet, or holding it carelessly against her hip, ignoring it, letting its nose run as she gossiped with another mother. At such times, Zach would watch Amber's eyes settle on the woman. It would seem that the very molecules of the air vibrated with Amber's disapproval, with her intense dislike.

Once they had heard on the radio a program about a woman who had drowned her two toddlers during some kind of postpartum depression and Amber's hands had tightened against each other in her lap.

"I'd like to see that woman tortured," Amber had said quietly. "I'd like to see her burned alive."

Zach hadn't said anything then, though the light in her eyes had disturbed him. They didn't really argue about things, the way he imagined other couples did—though the ghosts of their disagreements would waft underneath their conversations, curling like the fingerlets of incense smoke that Amber would sometimes burn. RELAXATION, the incense said. GOOD FORTUNE, HAPPINESS.

He looked up at her face from his hospital bed and he was reminded of the grim look she would get as she lit her little incense sticks and candles. She had never expected to have so much hardship in her life.

Amber had looked up from her reading at last, and she'd noticed that his eyes were open. They regarded each other, and he could see her expression tighten. It felt as if her thoughts were withdrawing backward into the shadows so that he couldn't see them.

"You're awake," she said softly.

For a moment, he expected that Amber was going to tell him that their baby had died. That was, of course, what would happen eventually. Sooner or later, some member of the hospital staff would emerge from a closed room to speak to them in a hushed voice: *Mr. and Mrs. Dixon.* They both knew this was coming. *I'm so sorry to tell you—there was nothing to be done.* The doctors had more or less assured them of this, even as they prepared for the surgeries. There had never been a successful separation.

On the Internet, Zach had found one example of a craniopagus parasiticus baby who had survived into childhood. This was the so-called Two-Headed Boy of Bengal, who was born in 1783 in the village of Mundul Gait. He had apparently lived for four years without any special medical treatment, and had purportedly died of a cobra bite, rather than anything relating to his condition.

The skull of the Two-Headed Boy was still on display at the Hunterian Museum of the Royal College of Surgeons in London.

Zach would sit in front of the computer late at night after Rosalie was born, searching the Internet. He downloaded a photo of the Two-Headed Boy's fused skull. He read various accounts.

He read that the parents of the Two-Headed Boy were poor farmers who soon realized that they could earn money by exhibiting their child. In Calcutta, they would cover him with sheets to prevent people who hadn't paid from glimpsing him.

After the Two-Headed Boy died, he was buried near the Boopnorain River, outside of the city of Tumloch. The grave was later plundered by an agent of the British East India Company, who dissected the child's decaying body and carried the fused skull away with him to England.

Sometimes Zach would fall asleep in front of the computer and wake up with his forehead pressed against the keyboard.

One morning after he'd been up nearly all night, he awoke and Amber was standing above him. "Zach," she was saying, her hand against his shoulder, and when he lifted his head he could feel the tooth marks of the keyboard impressed into the skin above his eyes. "Zach," Amber said, and she stared at the screen of his computer, at the photo of the Two-Headed Boy of Bengal's skull in its glass museum case—

"It's seven-thirty," she said, and glanced at her cellphone. He didn't know what she had been doing with her own night, while he had been following various branching trails of information, one Internet search leading to another and then another. Sometimes he would find her sitting in the television room, watching a sitcom; sometimes he would find her sleeping, curled up on the bed, on top of the covers with her shoes off, and he would lean over her, wishing that he had found a useful bit of information to give her, some kernel from his long foraging.

"I'll see you at the hospital at six," she said. She touched the screen of her phone, used her thumb to scroll, furrowed her eyebrows, and he ran a hand through his hair.

"Even when a child's death is imminent, the parent must forever carry the image of the child moving forward, alive, into the future." After Amber left, he had found this written in his own handwriting on a Post-it note on his desk. Was it a quote from something? Had he thought of it himself?

He was thinking about all of these things as Amber spoke to him. "You're awake," she said and he opened his eyes and Amber's face floated above him.

He was aware of specific thoughts, images, connections: the fused skull in the museum, the movement of Amber's fingers against her phone, the little Post-it note. All of these things had been in the process of sliding into place, connections were being made, and then the links seemed to unfasten as his mind rose out of sleep. He lifted his hand and some kind of monitor was clipped to his index finger.

"I'm sorry," he said, and there were so many things that he didn't even know what he meant. Was he sorry for the two-headed boy, exhibited by his parents; for all the time he'd spent reading such stories, staring at his computer while Amber moved through another part of the house; for falling asleep at the wheel and leaving her alone to deal with the terrible details of their child's last days; for being yet another burden to worry about; for the life they had been thrust into, which was unexpectedly difficult and unexpectedly unexpected; for his hoarse voice, which was a crackling of paper. *I'm sorry, I'm sorry, I'm sorry.*

"Zach," Amber said firmly, as if she hadn't heard him. "Are you able to focus? Can you hear me talking to you?"

There was still a little paperwork to be done concerning Rosalie's upcoming operation. Release forms and so on. These documents needed to be signed immediately.

"Yes," he said. "I'm listening."

Meanwhile, upstairs, the babies had opened their eyes again as well.

Above them, a mobile was turning in a slow circle: blue giraffe, yellow duck, red doggy, bobbing on wires, turning slowly around an axle, and the babies followed the motion of the shapes as they wheeled by.

Rosalie moved her tongue inside her mouth and the other one's brow furrowed. Rosalie's hands waved gently in the air and the other shifted her eyes back and forth, searching. After a time, they could see the pointed cap of the nurse above them, a blurry white peak on the horizon. A hand emerged and lowered itself toward them and they felt the cold of the air as their diaper was undone. The legs gave bright, athletic kicks, a burst of energy or excitement, and the parasitic head smiled dreamily.

"There, there," the nurse murmured. "It's all right, it's all right." She began to hum, and the babies liked the music, the sound of a lullaby and the touch of the warm cloth as their body was cleansed.

The surgery would need to be performed immediately if there was to be any possibility of saving Rosalie's life.

The parasitic head had begun to grow faster than Rosalie's own, and the doctors feared that the pressure from the growth would start to hinder Rosalie's brain development. Because the two brains shared common arteries that were dependent on Rosalie's organs, Rosalie was now in constant danger of heart failure. The other head was getting nutrition from Rosalie's body, blood from Rosalie's heart, oxygen from Rosalie's lungs. Keeping both heads alive was becoming a daily struggle for the body.

Zach listened as Amber repeated these things to him. She was reporting the information in a careful, formal voice, the way one might recite a lesson in a foreign-language class. "Sagittal sinus," she said. "Venous drainage."

"Well," he said. He considered for a moment. He was a college graduate, but he had no idea what to say. No one had ever prepared him for such an occasion. *After the head was removed, would they bury it?* he wondered vaguely. *Would it require a headstone?*

"You don't have to say anything," she said. Her expression flinched, and she looked at the hand he had lifted to hold out to her. She patted her palm against his knuckles, pressing his hand back down to the bed. "Just rest," she said.

When this is over, he thought. When it was over, there would have to be a way to repair their marriage. They would have to find their way back to the life they once had. Maybe a trip, he thought. They had once liked to travel. They had gone bird-watching in the cloud forests of Ecuador; they had walked through Roman ruins in the Dordogne of France, holding hands as they passed through the archway of an ancient gladiatorial arena; they had driven recklessly on one-lane roads in the Scottish Highlands, singing. They were a happy childless couple once. They could be that again.

"Everything will be all right," he said.

"Yes," she said.

He lay there, waiting, awake. The operation would take many hours. He didn't know how much time had passed. It was now the middle of the night and he could see the snow was falling again onto the parking lot outside his window.

From time to time he would hear the *clip-clop* of someone's hard-soled shoes against the floor of the hallway outside his room. The footsteps would gradually grow louder and then they would grow softer.

The doctors would need to separate Rosalie's brain from the conjoined organ in small stages. Blood vessels and arteries were shared between the two heads. The doctors planned to slowly cut off the blood supply to the extra head. The doctors would clip the veins and arteries and finally close Rosalie's skull, using a bone-and-skin graft from the second head.

If Rosalie died, he imagined that someone would come to tell him. Or—if the operation was successful, they would come and tell him that, too. He had called once and a nurse's aide had come to assure him that he would be the first to know. Whatever happened, she said.

The television had been turned off for a while now, its gray face blank and neutral. *If there was consciousness,* he thought; if there was consciousness, even if there was some rudimentary consciousness, the head would be asleep, under anesthesia. It would not be aware of the moment in which the blood supply stopped, the oxygen cut off, the brain cells began to shut down.

The room was dark but he could see something trembling on the ceiling. A piece of light, a reflection, quivering like a leaf on the surface of a pond. He moved his fingers, then his toes. He could feel the screws that held the halo crown to his skull, and he knew that once his condition had stabilized he would have to begin rehabilitation; that would have to be discussed at some point, once the situation with Rosalie was resolved.

His life had started out pleasantly enough. He and his sister growing up uneventfully in a suburb of Chicago, moving dutifully through elementary school and middle school and high school and college and finding jobs not far from their parents, who had then died abruptly when Zach and Monica were in their early twenties. Their father, a heart attack in his car, in the parking lot outside of the little strip-mall office where he'd had a dentistry practice. Their mother, about six months later, in the same car, sitting in the garage of their old childhood house with the engine running.

It was not something he liked to think about. "You should get a little therapy," Monica had said. "I've found it very helpful, just to talk about my feelings, and sort of put everything in perspective," and he agreed that it sounded like it would be a good idea and he'd visited a mental-health professional who had given him some medication, temporary medication, which had basically been enough. Shortly thereafter he had met Amber and they had fallen in love and gotten married and his life had moved back onto the track; they had their honeymoon in Scotland and they'd bought a house and two cars, and they'd worked fastidiously to pay off their student loans and mortgage and tried to save a little for the future.

Even when our death is imminent, we carry the image of ourselves moving forward, alive, into the future. He had read that somewhere, but it came to him like a voice speaking from the back of his mind, and he shuddered. The titanium pins that held his halo traction in place, the pins that had been drilled into the skull above his ears, felt like they'd loosened a little. It was as if he could sense them twisting and untwisting.

He fingered a buzzer that would call a nurse to help him, but didn't press it. What did he need help for? He could feel the nipple of the button beneath his thumb.

He was remembering an article he had read on the Internet about the transplantation of heads. In 1970, Dr. Robert White first successfully transplanted the head of a rhesus monkey onto another monkey's body. It lived for several days, paralyzed from the neck down but aware. Eating. Following people with its eyes. Sometimes trying to bite.

He came alert abruptly and the nurse was leaning over him. She looked surprised, drew back abruptly.

"Mr. Dixon," she said, and adjusted her nurse's hat, which looked a little like a paper boat. "Mr. Dixon," she breathed, and he felt the pinch of an injection. "You shouldn't be up at this hour," she murmured, and then she began to hum to him. An old lullaby he thought he remembered, the whispered words barely audible, coming as if from a great distance.

. . . while the moon . . . drifts in the skies . . . stay awake . . . don't close . . . your . . . eyes. . . .

And then suddenly morning sun was streaming into the room. The morning, and Amber appeared, backlit against the window with a rind of light around her.

"Is—?" Zach heard himself whisper. "Dead?"

It was the first thing that he thought of, the first word that his lips formed. He couldn't see her expression, but he felt fairly certain. "Dead?" he whispered, and she came forward and bent down and the features of her face came into focus.

"No," Amber said. Her face was pinched and her eyes were lit and fierce, in the way of a marathon runner, or an all-night gambler. Her lips drew back and she showed her teeth but it was too exhausted and intense to be a smile. "She's alive," Amber said. "She made it through. She—"

He watched as her eyes scoped along the edges of his traction, the halo crown and the metal bars that ran past his ears and attached to the vest at his shoulders; the web of rope and pulleys that held his legs suspended—as if she had noticed for the first time.

"It's not—as they expected," she said at last.

Rosalie's condition was described as *serious but stable*.

After the surgery, she had been given barbiturates, which put her into a beneficial pharmacologically induced coma. Over the course of several days, she would be slowly weaned from the drugs, and this, it was hoped, would help to reestablish normal blood flow. Her heart was accustomed to beating faster to pump out more blood for the second head, and now it had to learn to pump more slowly. Otherwise, she was likely to have heart failure. In her bassinet in intensive care, you could see the scar that ran along the top of her head, the seam over which skin had been folded over and closed. Zach had not actually seen Rosalie since the operation, but Amber had brought photos for him to look at. One of the pictures had been taken by a photographer for the Associated Press, and had gone out over the wire service to news outlets across the world. It was probably the most flattering of the photographs. In it, Rosalie appeared to be sleeping blissfully, her eyelashes like little feathers.

The doctors were said to be *cautiously optimistic*. At the same time, they reported to the media, "Rosalie's survival of the operation was a big achievement in itself."

"I'll just have to take everything one step at a time," Amber told him as she sat there by his bedside. "Get through one thing and then worry about the next thing. Right? Isn't that the way life goes?"

"Yes," he said. He was elevated into a sitting position, and Amber was spooning small cubes of gelatin into his mouth. Occasionally she would wipe his lip with a napkin. "That's right," he said, though he didn't like it that she said "I" instead of "we."

"We'll get through it," he said. His voice croaky, tiny. "We'll . . ."

Behind Amber, the nurse poked her head into the room from the doorway and peered in. Checking, he guessed, to see if Amber was still there. He watched as the nurse paused and observed them for a moment, then withdrew.

"I know that it's going to be touch-and-go for the next few months," Amber was saying. "For the next few years, probably. It might be premature to say anything, but I just feel like . . ."

"I know," Zach said. "I know what you mean. I haven't even had time to think much about my own situation. I imagine I'll have to start rehab soon, and then I'll eventually be able to help more, instead of just—"

"Mmm," Amber said. Her eyes rested distractedly upon his hand, and he made an effort to flex his fingers. "Mmm," she said. "Yes, well . . ."

"—instead of just lying here."

"Everything will be fine," she said, and gave him a firm, noncommittal stare. "Why can't it all be fine? I mean, it's a miracle she lived through the surgery and we should just be grateful for that, and then whatever else happens . . . we don't have any control over that. . . ."

"Right," Zach said. "Of course." He watched as she put the spoon down on the tray, next to the empty gelatin container.

They were silent. They were both looking forward—

momentarily, looking forward very cautiously—thinking about the possibility of life together with a living child. Zach was aware that they were probably considering some of the same images in their minds.

For example, Rosalie walking for the first time. Rosalie's uncertain feet, her arms held out, Rosalie wearing one of those bell-shaped dresses that little girls wear. Or, for example, Rosalie starting kindergarten. Her hair would be long enough to cover the scar on her scalp—it wouldn't even be noticeable—and she would carry a lunch box and backpack and there would be certain cartoon characters that she liked, certain favorite books and songs. She would have her own personality at that point.

They were still silent. Of course it was bad luck to say any of these things, probably bad luck even to think about them.

Amber tapped her knuckle against the fiberglass vest across his chest. It was a weary but gently playful gesture, Zach thought. Partly, it was meant to bring good luck, like knocking on wood. Partly it meant: I can't really think of anything else to say at the moment. "Well," she said. "I guess—"

"Sure," he said. "You better get going."

They both tried out a smile, experimentally. But it felt a little dangerous to be smiling, and they stopped almost at once. As if their greedy sense of hope might be spotted—and punished?!—by some stern Higher Power.

After Amber left, Zach lay there for a long time, staring up at the ceiling. *It will be okay,* he thought. It was all going to be fine. He tried again to picture them—himself, Amber, baby Rosalie—in the future. Standing in the backyard, beside the tree with the old swing. All three of them smiling. He could see it as if someone had taken a photograph.

He would undergo rehabilitation, and eventually, after a struggle, he would walk again. Perhaps there would always be a limp, he thought.

And even if his body didn't ever start to work again, at least his brain continued on. Right? He still had his mind, and really wasn't the flesh just a container, a shell that you inhabited?

Back when he was spending his nights on the Internet, he had come across a long article about astral projection. According to some philosophies, the self existed outside of the physical body. There were many religions that believed the soul could lift away, a noncorporeal version of your mind could rise up from the tether of muscle and skin and bone and blood and float off on its own.

Its own journey.

People who experienced astral travel reported that it seemed to happen from a vantage point such as high in the sky looking down. Astral travel was frequently reported by people who had near-death experiences, in which they could view themselves from above, watching themselves as hospital staff worked on their bodies. Frederik van Eeden presented one of the first studies of out-of-body dreams to the Society of Psychical Research in 1913, and he described a "silver thread" that connected his projected self to his sleeping physical form.

"In these lucid dreams," van Eeden wrote, "the reintegration of the psychic functions is so complete that the sleeper remembers day-life and his own condition, reaches a state of perfect awareness, and is able to direct his attention, and to attempt different acts of free volition."

Zach didn't know whether he believed in this or not, but he thought that there must be—well, *something*—

There was a snail track of sweat moving down the back of his neck, leaving an insistent itch in its wake.

Outside the window, in the parking lot, there was a female clown holding a bouquet of blue and pink helium balloons, each with a cartoon face printed on it. He watched as the woman stood there, flipping through a small notebook. The balloons were revolving upon the axis of their strings, the smiling faces slowly rotating, facing his window and then turning away in a slow circle.

Zach was aware of the sound of a small voice calling to him, a sound in the back of his mind, and then another trickle down the back of his neck, an odd feeling in his hair, like the ticklish legs of an insect. Movement.

Why do people, he thought. He was thinking of something that Amber had asked him once, right after the baby was born.

Why do people want to have babies? she had said, her eyes upon him heavily. *What does a baby have that we want from it?*

Well, he had said. It's . . . it's part of life. It's . . .

She had been going through a kind of depression, postpartum depression, he thought, she wasn't herself—and they were driving along the interstate; he was behind the wheel and there was that feeling you have when the car is just an extension of your body, when you are at least partially a machine and your movements are also the automobile's movements and he was both listening and not listening; part of him was talking to her and part of him was watching the road, steering.

All the babies in the world, she was saying. *All the babies that need homes and we had to create another one. It's greedy, isn't it? Avaricious and acquisitive. We had to have a baby of our own, right? No one else's—it's got to be ours, only ours. Isn't that what it is?*

No, he said. No, of course not. There's nothing . . . avaricious . . . about it. It's about being in love . . . and you want to . . . create something that no one else can create, right? And . . . it's biological. It's normal to want to have a baby.

Is it? she said, and she looked at him for a long moment and he could feel it but he was also watching the traffic. He didn't want to look her in the eyes, in any case.

Then she seemed to lose herself in thought—perhaps to forget what she had been talking about, or dismiss it, or else it vanished along with the majority of her depression after she got some prescriptions. In any case, they never spoke of it again.

But he had thought of it, later, considered it from time to time over the ensuing months as the drama of their deformed baby had played itself out, and now he found himself remembering it once again.

Why do people want babies? he thought, and of course there were the usual things. Urges.

You want a child because it is a piece of yourself that will live on after you are dead. That is one answer.

You want a child because it is a specific kind of love, a specific kind of experience of love that you feel certain can't be replicated in any other way. The way your parents loved or failed to love you, for example.

You want a child because it is a link in the bridge that you are building between the past and the future, a cantilever that holds you, so that you are not alone.

He opened his eyes and the nurse hovered over him, drawing blood from his arm, and he watched a thread of his own blood weaving its way upward through a thin tube.

There was that odd feeling in the back of his head, that little ticklish feeling that didn't seem to want to go away. He tried to give his head a shake, but of course it was held in place by the halo, held in traction.

For a moment he had the impression that something moved at the back of his skull. There was a subtle quiver of the skin like an expression shifting, and he thought of the blinking of eyelids, a mouth opening and drawing breath.

Even when we are dead, we carry the possibility of ourselves moving forward, alive, into the future.

"I didn't realize that I was sleeping," he said to the nurse, and she looked down at him silently. Her face was thoughtful and private, as if she were gazing down into a reflecting pool. She tilted the tube that was filling up with Zach's blood, but she didn't respond. It was the same way that Amber had seemed to stop hearing his questions. As if he were not even there.

Upstairs in the intensive-care ward, Rosalie was comatose. Her coma was an expanse of gray ice water, a sensation of bottomless sinking; perhaps it was nothing at all. It may essentially have been the same as the nothing that was now being experienced by the other head, which no longer existed except as pieces of skin and bone grafted to Rosalie's scalp and skull, as ashes that sifted in a fine layer at the bottom of the incinerator.

Nearly asleep, Zach could feel the shadowy stirrings of presences and absences. The perception of that other brain must surely have been a tangible thing. Rosalie must have felt it. She must have felt it rising, he thought, connected by a thin silver thread, drifting up and up as it was removed.

In the same way, Zach was himself hovering over his own body. The corporeal Zach was a sad, stick figure of a person, arms and legs spread like a child's drawing, and he gazed down toward it tenderly, even as it grew smaller and more distant.

He understood, now, vividly, what it would be like, and as he drifted up he wished he could tell someone. Amber, perhaps? Or Rosalie herself?

At some point, perhaps, at five or thirteen or twenty-seven, his daughter, Rosalie, would wake up and remember the way someone else's thoughts felt as they grazed lightly against the surface of her own. A flicker of consciousness would wink on and off.

Hello, a voice would say. *I'm still here. I'm still with you.*

Rosalie, someone would whisper. *I'm still awake.*

Long Delayed,
Always Expected

When January turned forty-four she began to have gloomy thoughts about the future, about mortality, and so forth. Her daughter had left home to go away to college, and had been gone for one month, which was part of it. It occurred to her that a whole segment of her life had come to an end.

Wow, she thought. *So that was what it was like to raise a child.*

Then she thought: *I guess I won't be doing that again!*

Which was kind of disturbing, after she considered for a moment. She didn't like to think of the things that—more than likely—she might have already done for the last time.

She sat there at the open window and stubbed out a cigarette into the dirt of a potted plant.

It wouldn't have been so weird if it hadn't been for the fact that it seemed like many other women her age were just beginning—they all seemed to have babies and grade-school children—and they had spent their youth getting their careers under way, making lots of money and having fun and probably getting laid frequently as well. Now their skin had a rosy, post-maternal glow, and they spoke in gently therapeutic voices as they walked around carrying their babies in expensive papooses. She, meanwhile, had the haggard eyes and quick temper of a woman who had just lived for five years with a teenager.

Personally, she didn't like the looks of this stretch between forty-five and fifty. She felt very uncomfortable about it.

She drank a glass of wine and then called her ex-husband, Jeffrey, and invited him to come over to the house for dinner.

Jeffrey had been severely injured—brain-damaged, actually—in a car accident after they had divorced and now he lived in a group home with a number of other mentally challenged men. He was generally in better shape than the rest of them—he was the only one of them who held a Ph.D. in mathematics, for example—but he seemed basically content with the situation. She imagined that it was a little like his old fraternity house.

"Jeffrey," she said. "I'm sorry to bother you. But I'm wondering if you would mind keeping me company if I made you dinner. Do you want to rent a movie and come over?"

"Are you drinking?" he said.

"Yes," she said. "But I'll stop if you come over."

"You're smoking, too," he said. "I can hear you breathing smoke."

"Well," she said. "I've got the window open."

Lately, he'd been quoting various horrifying cigarette-smoke statistics to her, and she didn't mind it, really. She hoped that maybe he would be able to scare her into stopping.

They had been divorced for almost five years when Jeffrey had his accident. Their daughter, Robin, was fifteen, and she'd grown used to shuffling between the two of them, their houses about twenty minutes apart on either side of the city, and she'd been very good about accepting the fact that her parents were going to have separate lives, though they both loved her still, they were both connected *through* her, and they continued to be very cordial to each other, despite some lingering bitterness. They were basically on friendly terms.

But when it became clear that Jeffrey's injuries were more extensive than they had expected, Robin began to give her long, impatient looks. She grew judgmental, then outraged.

"Aren't you going to help him?" Robin said. "Aren't you going to do something?" This was during the period when it was becoming clear that he couldn't return to independent living. When the doctors were suggesting a nursing-home facility.

"Honey," January said. She found herself shifting under Robin's scrutiny. "Listen," January said. "*I'm* not going to take care of him. I hope you realize that he can't live here."

Robin had gazed at her bleakly.

"Robin," she said. "I'm not going to dedicate my life to caring for a man I divorced five years ago. I'm sorry for him. But it's just tough luck. Seriously."

Tough luck. Had she really said that?

Now, thinking back, she was aware that it was one of those things that Robin would later repeat when people asked what kind of person her mother was. She remembered how Robin's eyes had lingered on her face. A defining moment, Robin probably thought.

Jeffrey took the bus from the group home and arrived about a half an hour early. She saw him from the window, pacing back and forth along the sidewalk in front of her house and pausing to read his watch. He could tell time but it took some processing on his part, and she never understood why he couldn't just get a digital watch.

She came out onto the porch and folded her arms. "Jeffrey," she called out as he was walking past, and he stopped and looked startled. Agape. "What are you doing?" she said.

"I'm early," he said.

"You can still come into the house," she said. "It's okay."

He hesitated.

Over the last few years, since his accident, he had changed a lot. He had lost quite a bit of weight, for example, and his face had taken on a certain kind of sloe-eyed, sleepy quality that might be associated with marijuana smoking or post-coital tristesse. His hair, once carefully and severely close-cropped, had gotten thick and wavy in a way that made him seem younger. The old Jeffrey would have probably been pleased about all of this—he had once been quite vain about his looks, his body. But the current Jeffrey couldn't have cared less, which was part of his charm. He had magically returned to the mind of the sweet, nerdy eleven-year-old he had probably once been.

"Are you hungry?" she said. "Come in, come in."

She thought that she was almost used to this new Jeffrey. It was actually as if he were a nephew of Jeffrey, rather than Jeffrey himself. Occasionally there would be little resemblances between the Jeffrey of the past and the current version. There was, for example, a certain boyish way of rolling his eyes up toward the ceiling when he was remembering something—a cute and endearing expression on both of the Jeffreys. It was problematic to regard a brain-damaged person as "sexy," but he was, somehow.

It had been about seven or eight years since she had last slept with him—the old Jeffrey. They had still been married when it stopped and she actually couldn't remember when the very "last time" had been. It was probably one of those dutiful married-person fucks that happened right before they went to sleep or right after they woke in the morning, and no doubt it had been fine; sex had never been a big issue in their marriage—

—but of course there was a part of her that placed importance on the notion of "firsts" and "lasts," of "mosts" and "leasts"; she had been, after all, a little girl who had memorized parts of the *Guinness World Records* book and so it was troubling that she wasn't able to recall such an important milestone: the Last Time I Slept with My Ex-Husband.

She had considered asking him. She was a little curious about whether Jeffrey—this new, childlike Jeffrey—had any memory of their sexual relations, but of course it was probably better not to know. He appeared to have the emotional life of an intelligent preadolescent, and there had never been any hint of, well.

"Jeffrey," she said. "Would you like a Coke?"

"Yes, thank you," he said, watching sternly as she put her empty wineglass on the counter, next to the sink.

He had been injured by a drunk driver, and now he disapproved of alcohol on general principle.

The last time January went on a date, she had been trying out an Internet matchmaking service that brought people together based on a complex personality survey. "Our total compatibility system takes into account the 'whole' you—personality, life and lovestyle, values and preferences—matching you on what counts in a lasting relationship!" the website said, alongside a series of testimonials from happy customers who had gotten married, found love, happiness, and so forth.

And the man that she eventually met was, honestly, a very nice person. Steve Schiller: fifty-four years old, a curator at the natural-history museum, a trim, sweet, dapper little man, a widower with two adult children. They had gone to the same midwestern liberal arts college, albeit ten years apart, and they liked a lot of the same music and books, and he had a dry, pleasantly low-key way of speaking, and they had gone to a funny little Ethiopian restaurant that she had actually been interested in going to—they were so compatible, she thought, it was almost irritating.

Why do I hate him so much? she kept wondering. *What's wrong with me?*

There was a certain kind of earnestness, that was part of it. Something eager and hopeful and slightly embarrassing. "You know what they say," he told her. "Fifty is the new thirty." He said it wryly, with a little ironic shrug, but she could see how much he'd like to believe it.

"Really?" she said. She put her hand to her chin thoughtfully. "Does that mean that thirty is the new ten?"

Which was bitchy, of course. She saw what he meant, she really did. The desire to remake that shrinking expanse of life they were still allotted, to make use of it, to fill it up with possibility. Oh, please: one more transformation.

He looked at her, and she could see the pinch and fuss of museum curating beneath the charming exterior.

"Ha," he said awkwardly. "It's stupid, I know."

"I've also heard that one hundred is the new eighty," she continued. "And thirteen is actually the new negative seven."

"Okay," he said. "Cut it out. I get it."

She had made hamburgers for Jeffrey. Hamburgers and French fries and macaroni and cheese—everything starchy and salty and blandly meaty, which is where his brain-damaged taste buds seemed to have settled.

Back when they were married, he'd been a finicky eater, the kind of person who wouldn't eat chicken breast because he didn't like the "texture" of it, who had to have his apples and pears cut into slices, who didn't like bread crust, the kind of person you never wanted to cook for because he made every meal seem like an examination he was grading.

It was like that with a lot of things in their marriage. He had been her teacher when they first met—a handsome young assistant professor, only a few years older than she was, teaching a course called Math for Mystics, which she'd hoped would satisfy the general education requirement and not be too difficult—though, actually, most of what they talked about in class was over her head—Pythagoras and the golden ratio and Venus's pentacle . . . and later she wondered if he'd let her pass only because he was attracted to her.

In any case, the "lenient teacher" and "underachieving student" template had lingered on in their relationship. He'd had a set of unspoken, unspecific rules in his mind, tests she always felt as if she were failing, though he'd never admit it. "What's wrong?" she would ask, as he sat at the table looking skeptically at the food she had prepared, or when he made a little grunt while she was driving, or when she came downstairs in the morning and he let his eyes run over the clothes she was wearing.

"What?" she'd say. "You don't like this shirt?"

And he'd shrug and turn back to his crossword and coffee: No comment.

How weird it was that he'd once had such power over her, that he could once shame her with only a glance.

Of course, she was not that person any longer. In the years since their divorce, she had developed a thicker skin, a resilience. She was the type of person who didn't take anyone's crap—that's what her friend Joni told her. "That's what I like about you, Jan," Joni said. "You tell it like it is. You speak your mind. You call it like you see it."

"Thank you," January said, though actually she thought of

herself as fairly restrained. If she *actually* spoke her mind, she probably wouldn't have any friends at all.

They worked together at the library, and mostly they shelved books together and gossiped unkindly about their coworkers. She had been an employee for years, but had never advanced very far in the ranks. In the beginning, the flush of independence, the sense of making her own way alone in the world, had been enough. Now, it wasn't quite so enthralling. One quiet late afternoon, as she was rolling her cart through a narrow, desolate row of bookshelves, a line abruptly came into her mind: *She is the type of person who has rejected love at every turn.*

What was this from? A movie? A novel? It sounded to January like some bullshit chick-lit claptrap, and she dismissed the thought with annoyance. But it returned to her as she sat watching TV with Robin later that night, and for a moment she considered speaking it aloud.

Then she reconsidered. She was afraid it might be an assessment that Robin would agree with.

And perhaps Jeffrey would as well. As he sat eating his hamburger, he gave her one of those inscrutable looks that reminded her of the days when they were married. He considered her in a way that seemed, she thought, vaguely judgmental, and then he bent to sip his Coke with a kind of dedicated, trancelike seriousness.

"What?" she said. "The hamburger isn't well done enough?"

"It's good," Jeffrey said, and he took a moderate bite, and chewed, and swallowed. "I like it," he said.

"I know my lips look weird," January said. "They've been very chapped—it's gross."

"Oh," Jeffrey said. He peered at her lips thoughtfully, scratching along the bite-shaped line of scar along his forehead, where he'd had some surgery or another. "Hmm," he said.

"So have you talked to Robin recently?" she asked.

"I talk to Robin every day at eleven o'clock," he said. "She calls me on my cellphone before lunch."

"Oh," January said. And—well, yes, it did bother her, a little. A small twinge of hurt, or jealousy, a momentary recurrence of *she is the type of person who.*

As it happened, Robin hadn't called *her* since being dropped off at the dorm room on the first day of New Student Week. Robin had declined January's offer to help her unpack, and hadn't wanted to be taken out to a bon-voyage dinner at a nice restaurant, either—instead, trotting off with her new roommate, leaving January to walk alone to her car and sit there for a moment in the parking lot (not crying) and drive silently through the rude Chicago traffic toward the miles of interstate that would take her back to her empty home.

She gave Jeffrey a smile.

"So," January said. "How is Robin doing? She's settled in all right, I presume? She's meeting new people and enjoying her classes? Lots of excitement keeping her busy, I would imagine."

"Yes," Jeffrey said. "She's doing okay, I think."

"Well, good, then," January said. "Good for Robin." She put a French fry to her mouth, and the shape of it made her wish for a cigarette. She sighed, and Jeffrey raised an eyebrow, cocking his head with puzzlement.

"Are you sad?" he asked at last, and he peered at her face as if it were one of the crosswords he used to do. Since his accident, he had some difficulty interpreting facial expressions and emotions. He had been working on this in his weekly rehabilitation therapy sessions. He had shown her the flash cards he was studying—close-up pictures of people miming various exaggerated feelings.

"No, no, no," she said reassuringly. "I'm not sad. It's been a frustrating week, that's all."

"Hmm," Jeffrey said. "It's hard to concentrate when you're frustrated."

"It really is," she said. Without thinking, she licked her napkin and leaned over to dab a spot of ketchup from the edge of Jeffrey's mouth, and he didn't appear to mind—though it was weird because she hadn't done the napkin-licking thing since Robin was about three.

"I'll admit," she said, "it hasn't been an easy time. I've been in a mood. You know what my moods are like."

"Yes," Jeffrey said.

She shook her head. "There's a lot of stuff to deal with, you know? I mean: the empty nest. And middle age, or whatever you want to call it. And coming to terms with your own mortality in general, you know. I'm kind of afraid of dying, Jeffrey. Does that seem childish to you?"

"Why?"

"Why what? Why am I afraid of dying? Aren't you afraid?"

Jeffrey shrugged. "It's just like going to sleep."

"Yes, but you never wake up. That's the problem."

"How do you know?"

"How do I know what?"

"You don't know that you never wake up," Jeffrey said. "Because you're dead. You don't know anything anymore."

"Good point," she said. She looked at him thoughtfully. Though he was almost four years older, he looked younger than she did. Abruptly, he reached out and patted her hand.

"Don't be scared, Jan." he said. "It's okay."

And that was how it happened: He patted the back of her hand.

He patted the back of her hand and she turned her hand over so their palms were touching and their fingers moved vaguely into one another in a melancholy, exploratory way, and then the fingers interlocked and she hadn't seen the familiar lines of his palm in so long, the palm she had once tried to read using a chart, a silly game of fortune-telling, and there was something sad and naked about the creases that marked the segments between his finger joints—thumb, index, middle, ring, pinkie—and she bent down and kissed the fleshy pad where his fingerprints were whorled; it was completely impulsive, she'd had only a couple of glasses of wine, and then, well, shit, despite the brain damage, his instincts were still intact and they were kissing, he pressed her up against the stove and caught her wrists in a grip and his body was leaner and more solid than she remembered, and she could feel his erection through his jeans, and she was really, really lonely and sad, damn it, unzipping him and reaching beneath her skirt to push her panties down and etc., etc.

Don't judge me, you fuckers, she thought, as her eyes turned upward and squeezed shut.

...

For the next couple of months, things went like this. October, November. The leaves turned color and there were a few minor snowfalls, and she went to work at the library and when she came home Jeffrey was there waiting for her, sitting in the wicker chair on her porch with his hands folded in his lap.

Usually, she made dinner for him, and she discovered that he would dutifully eat whatever she cooked for him, even the spicy curries that he used to hate, even the much-loathed chicken breast, though he widened his eyes sadly when she said, "You're going to eat your chicken, aren't you, Jeffrey?" Which was, she guessed, a little cruel. Sometimes, he would stand with her on the porch, shoulders bunched and hands thrust in his coat pockets, watching as she took her time and smoked her cigarette, shivering as his own breath fogged in the cold air. Then she would feel guilty and they would sit on the couch together and watch a movie—his preference now being lowbrow comedies or animated children's films like *Shrek*, which they watched probably fifteen times, and which, after a couple of glasses of wine, she had come to enjoy even in its repetition, the charming indie-rock soundtrack and the way, at the end, the princess decides that she wants to be an ogre, too, just like her rescuer. She imagined that this must be significant to him.

Usually, though, there was no prelude or small talk. They would move toward the bedroom almost as soon as they'd eaten their dinner, wordlessly undressing and falling onto the bed, grappling and kissing and moving against each other, not even making eye contact.

He was a better lover, as a brain-damaged person, than he used

to be—less self-conscious, less likely to come up with pronounce-
ments like "I understand the importance of the clitoris," which he
said to her once when they first began to sleep together and then
he went down on her politely for about eight minutes—
whereas now, it was kind of like having sex with a monkey, and
sometimes, okay, she found herself getting a little rough with
him, digging her fingernails into his back or biting his nipple or
gripping his etc. hard until he emitted a small yelp that, okay,
really turned her on—and she thought, *Oh my God I'm a monster—
no one must ever know about this* . . .

And then afterward they stood outside her house and waited
for the bus that would take him back to the group home, and he'd
sigh, and shift his backpack from shoulder to shoulder: not much
to say.

When he was gone, she sometimes felt as if she'd landed back in
the first years of their marriage. That late-night feeling, that insomnia, that floating sense of having lost herself. She would remember what it had been like after Robin was born and she
realized how permanent a choice she had made.

Back then, she found herself waking in the middle of the
night. Even though the baby had been sleeping until morning for
quite some time, she still found herself wide awake, listening for
something she couldn't identify. The baby was not crying, though
for a minute she could almost hear it, vague, distant, melting
away into other sounds—a plane's metallic yawning overhead,
the soft breath of her pulse in her ears, the assorted implacable
clicks and hums of the house settling.

Once she was up, she felt better. She turned on The Weather

Channel soft and studied the temperatures of distant places; she looked through her old books from college, the earnest notes made in the margins by the teenage girl she had once been; she stood at the window in her nightgown and brushed her long hair.

Always, always, a few minutes after she woke, a bus would stop in front of their house. Often, she'd be standing at the window looking out. Presently, the empty bus slid down the street.

Who rode it? she wondered. She imagined people on their way to factories or hospitals, or on their way home from bars. She saw, or imagined herself—just a solitary silhouette alongside the street sign: a woman working a double shift? Or on her way to a tryst? A drunk, the lit end of her cigarette the same size and color as taillights passing in the distance? Another life? Another life?

After the bus passed, everything was still. She even walked down to the sidewalk sometimes, and there were only the shadows of trees and bushes crisscrossed on the asphalt, rows of streetlights stretching down to where the streetlight blinked yellow. There weren't even any cars on the road.

It had actually been her idea to have a baby. Some of her friends had them by that time, and she'd been stunned by a longing the moment she'd touched them, their soft skin and beautiful, half-blind gaze, downy hair along their ears and neck. One night after she and Jeffrey had talked about it, he went out to a movie—a Kurosawa double feature—and when he came back, he said he had come to a decision. "Yes. I've thought it through. I think we can manage it," he said, and her heart quickened. They lay down together, no birth control, and he began his strategic kissing of her body, his hands fluid and considerate along the graph of her.

She stared at the ceiling uncertainly as he passed a gentle tongue along her belly. Wait, she wanted to say. *Do I really want to do this?* she thought. *Am I making a mistake?* But it seemed like it was too late.

This occurred to her often after the bus had passed. She could pinpoint the moment when she almost said, "No! Stop!" And her baby, and her life as it was, would have ceased to exist.

And then, without warning, the baby, Robin, was all grown up, and the young woman who had stood at the window brushing her hair was like a ghost in an attic. January read an article in a newspaper about "bucket lists," which was a list of things you wanted to do before you died, and she found herself looking at the various suggestions with growing dread. Skydiving? Absolutely not. Visiting Florence? Extremely doubtful, given her salary and fear of flying. Learning to play a musical instrument? Too complicated and boring. All the things that people longed for seemed a little stupid, she thought.

Meanwhile, in the living room, Jeffrey had inserted *Shrek* into the DVD player, and there was that jolly music yet again, *maybe I'm in love, maybe I'm in love,* etc.

And then Robin was coming home from college for the Christmas holidays, and January and Jeffrey stood in the baggage claim area of the airport, awaiting her.

He had promised that he wouldn't tell Robin. She had extracted this vow after that first night, and he had agreed, and she basically trusted him, although she worried a little.

"So," she said to him now, as they sat watching a cluster of people withdrawing luggage from a conveyor belt. "So, anyways . . . I think it's really not a good idea for us to talk to Robin about what's going on with us."

"About . . . ?" said Jeffrey. He had been hypnotized by the slow trundling of baggage along the carousel, and now looked up at her, perplexed.

"About us having *sex*," January said. "Don't tell Robin about that."

"Why would I tell Robin about that?"

"I don't know, Jeffrey," she said. "You have brain damage. I have no idea what your thought processes are like. I'm just reminding you, okay?"

"Okay," he said.

"I'm not trying to be mean," she said. "Do you think I'm mean?"

"No," he said, and folded his hands in his lap. She looked at her cellphone to check the time.

"She should be here by now," January said.

Outside, it was sleeting a bit. The news had spoken hysterically about a "monster storm" spreading across the Midwest, but she hadn't paid much attention until now. She stood below the monitors and found Robin's flight. DELAYED, it said.

This was the kind of thing that used to make Jeffrey crazy. He hated disruptions to his schedule, he hated being made to wait, he would descend into tantrums of outrage when he encountered a long queue or was put on hold on the telephone or, God forbid, had to sit in an actual waiting room—she could remember how he had once behaved at the obstetrician, sitting there with his legs crossed and his foot jiggling, flipping irritably through the pages of *Parents* magazine and *Good Housekeeping* with wrist flicks that seemed almost like slaps, and she'd said, "Please, Jeffrey, will you just go for a walk or something," which sent him spiraling into a decline, and he spent the entire rest of the afternoon radiating gloomy, silent resentment. (Note: *He* had not in fact been the one who was eight months pregnant at the time.)

Now, on the other hand, as they lingered and lingered in the airport, Jeffrey seemed perfectly content. He was still as a potted plant, and had a little transcendent smile as they sat there in the uncomfortable plastic chairs. A few rows away, a young mother was struggling to keep her toddler from running amok; she had him strapped into his stroller and he was flailing and arching his back like a torture victim, letting out low, guttural, straining cries as the mother attempted to calm him with that gently therapeutic voice they all used these days.

"She's *reasoning* with him," January remarked to Jeffrey as they observed the unfolding drama. "It's so stupid. It's like trying to explain something to a cat."

"Hmm," Jeffrey said. "Cats don't really understand human language."

"Do you remember that time when Robin was about four and she would have those terrible fits of rage? Pulling her own hair and throwing herself around like something out of *The Exorcist*? God, that was awful."

"I don't remember that," Jeffrey said.

"You were very good with her, actually," January said. "Very matter-of-fact. I thought you were a good father."

"I don't really remember anything about what Robin was like as a little girl," Jeffrey said. He was still observing the mother and toddler a few rows over, who were in the midst of a great contest of wills. "I remember when I look at pictures," Jeffrey said. "I remember taking the pictures."

"Hm," she said. The photographs had begun to taper off precipitously not long after Robin turned five. Whatever urge there had been in the beginning to document every "first" they experienced had faded, and soon the photo albums were only bare outlines of their years together: a few posed portraits on birthdays, or in front of some vacation landmark, or a Christmas tree. She wasn't sure how much she herself could recall of those last years of their family life, so distracted had she been by unhappiness. It was kind of chilling, in a way.

"Well," she said at last. "Memory's not all it's cracked up to be, anyway."

"Probably not," Jeffrey said, and after a moment he leaned into her, tilting his head so that it rested lightly on her shoulder. He was capable of such gestures every once in a while, and sometimes she thought that, even without his memories intact, some residue must still remain. It was weird to think that she had known him for longer than she had known anyone else in the world.

Across the way, she saw that the toddler had calmed. Freed from his stroller, he now rested comfortably and quietly in his mother's lap, his head leaned against her shoulder, his blanket clutched to his mouth.

She looked back at Jeffrey.

Oh, she thought, and absently reached up and put her fingers through Jeffrey's thick, shaggy, beautiful hair, and he nuzzled a little, comfortably. Jeffrey had his fist pressed to his mouth, as if he were holding an imaginary blanket.

Oh.

But she tried not to think any further. She arranged a calm look on her face. She would not step even a tiny bit more into the future that seemed to be settling over her.

The buzzer for another baggage conveyor began to bleat, and luggage began to emerge from another mysterious cave, but neither the toddler nor Jeffrey lifted his head. Above, on the screen that listed arrivals and departures, she saw that Robin's flight had been changed from DELAYED to CANCELLED.

She would just sit there a while longer, she thought. He was resting so peacefully.

Outside, the sleet had gotten thicker. You could hear it pebbling against the large glass windows, you could see it swirling wildly through the spotlights of street lamps. It was the kind of night when you might expect to see a skeleton flying through the air, its ragged black shroud flapping in the wind.

I Wake Up

Twenty years passed. Then one summer my sister Cassie began to call me on the phone. She'd call me up every week or so, just to chat, and it was a kind of weird situation. I hadn't known anything about her whereabouts since I was very small, and at first I didn't really know what to say to her.

But Cassie acted as if it was the most natural thing in the world. "Hey, babe!" she said. "What's up?" She had the kind of voice that made her sound as if she was smiling affectionately as she talked, and I found that I enjoyed hearing from her. "What's been going on, sweetie?" she'd ask me, and we'd end up talking for hours, talking until her voice began to blank out and get static as her cellphone ran out of power. She would go on about some movie she'd seen, or tell a story about some eccentric person she used to know; she would ask me to describe my friends and my job and my daily life, and when I said something she thought was funny she would laugh in this great way that made me actually feel a kind of glow.

Sometimes she would call very late or extremely early in the morning, and she would be in a strange mood. She would want to talk about our other brothers and sisters, who she was also in contact with; or she would go into very inappropriate subjects, like her sex life; or a few times she even wanted to talk about our mother, who she referred to as "Karen."

"What do you think Karen's doing right now?" she asked me once, and for a minute I didn't even know who she was talking about. It was about five in the morning, and I was in my apartment above Mrs. Dowty's garage, sitting in my narrow twin bed with the covers wrapped around my middle.

"Who's Karen?" I said groggily, and Cassie was silent for a moment.

"Our *mother*," she said. Outside the window, some branches were moving in the darkness when I looked out. I noticed how the spaces between boughs cut the sky into shapes.

"Don't you ever feel sorry for Karen?" she asked me. "I mean just a little?"

"I don't know," I said. "I never really thought about it."

To be honest, until Cassie started calling, there were a lot of things that I hadn't thought much about. I knew the basic facts,

of course. I knew, for example, that my mother was thirty-two
years old when she was sent to prison. She had given birth by that
time to eight children. They were:

Cassie
Cecilia Joy
Ashlee
Piper
Jordan
Me
LaChandra
and Nicholas

We all had different dads. All of us were living with her when
LaChandra and Nicholas were killed. Then our mother's paren-
tal rights were terminated, of course, and we all went to different
foster homes, and she was sentenced to life without parole.

So we had been sent on various separate paths away from her,
and from one another. I guess I had always assumed that this was
for the best, but Cassie didn't see things that way. She told me
that she had been gathering information for years, tracking each
of us down, one by one. She was the oldest—she was almost fifteen when our mother got sent away—and she said she'd always
felt like it was her responsibility to keep an eye on all of us. "They
can tear us apart, but they can't make us stop loving one another,"
she had told me the first time she called, and I soon came to recognize this phrase as one of her mottoes. "Only connect, Robbie," she said to me from time to time. "That's what I firmly
believe. *Only connect.*"

"Uh-huh," I said, though to be honest I wasn't totally sure what she was talking about. I guess what she meant was that we were all still connected, even though we were scattered, even though so much time had passed. I guess it was a legitimate way to feel about things.

According to Cassie, most of us had done very well for ourselves, despite our rough beginnings. Cecilia Joy, for example, lived with her husband and two beautiful children on a sheep ranch in Montana and she'd had some of her poems published. Ashlee was taking acting classes while working as a receptionist for a movie studio in Los Angeles, and Piper had taken her first job as a mechanical engineer for a company in Houston. Jordan had come out of her coma, recovered completely, and now was attending medical school at Princeton University.

Sometimes, I have to admit, I wasn't completely sure I believed everything Cassie told me. It seemed like she might be exaggerating certain things, maybe stretching the truth a bit. She claimed, for example, that her ex-husband was a rich construction contractor with mob connections, which was why she was always changing her cellphone number. She said that she had spent some time in law school, and that she was a certified public accountant, though now she worked as a home caregiver for the elderly in St. Augustine, Florida. Sometimes she would call and I'd think I could hear the background noise of what sounded like a bar or a party.

Once, I thought I could hear the boxy voice of some kind of official announcement being made in the distance—maybe the last call at an airport terminal: *All ticketed passengers must be on board.*

"Cassie," I said, "Where are you right now? What are you doing?" And she made a shrugging sound in her throat.

"I'm at home," she said innocently, though I could've sworn that I very clearly heard the murmur of people in the background, and a baby crying.

"I'm just sitting here at the kitchen table, having a cup of tea," she said thoughtfully. "Just sitting here looking out at the moon shining over the ocean."

My own life wasn't as interesting as the stories that Cassie told about herself and our siblings. Perhaps that was the problem; perhaps that was why I didn't always quite believe her. My foster parents, the Dowtys, were simple, kindly, middle-of-the-road people: a math teacher and his wife. I grew up with them in Cleveland, Ohio, and then I remained there afterward, mostly of my own free will, with one year of college to my credit and four years working as a housepainter for my foster cousin Rob Higgins. I lived in a little converted apartment above my foster mom's garage, and I paid her a hundred dollars a month for rent. I was twenty-five years old, and I'd visited only three other states, and zero foreign countries. These were the bare numbers of my life, which I kept in my head. I had 7,891 dollars saved up in the bank. I had ten toes and nine fingers. I got up at six in the morning six days a week. Sometimes I worried, wondering what Cassie was telling the other siblings about me, because there was so little interesting to say.

It was funny, I suppose, that Cassie and the others had so quickly come to occupy such a large part of my daily thoughts. The truth was, I'd hardly considered them at all in those long years since I'd last set eyes on them. They had almost completely faded out of my mind before that one day when Cassie called me for the first time.

"Happy birthday, Robert!" Cassie had said. Those were the first words out of her mouth when I answered the phone. "You'll never guess who this is!" she said.

It was actually the day after my birthday, and I was still a little hungover. I was sitting in my recliner, watching TV, and I put the sound on mute with my remote. I sat there blankly for a bit.

"This is your sister Cassie," she said at last. "You probably don't even remember me, do you?"

I hesitated. What does a person say to a question like that? I thought I could feel a kind of glimmer of recognition, though I wasn't sure if it would officially be considered "remembering." For some reason, I pictured her with red hair and freckles, and I thought hard about it until I pulled up a momentary flash of recollection. Here was the kindly policeman who carried me on his shoulders; here were the tops of the heads of my siblings below me; here was the weeping voice of my mother, who was locked in the bathroom with the water running. *My babies!* my mother was crying. *Come help Mommy! Come save Mommy!* And from my perch on the kindly policeman's shoulders I could see more policemen coming with crowbars, and a shiny puddle of water was emerging from under the crack of the door.

I sat there silently for a moment, considering this memory. Then I slid it slowly to the back of my mind again, and shifted the phone from one side of my face to the other.

"Cassie," I said. "Sure I remember you."

...

I opened my eyes.

The electricity had been off the night before, another power outage, but now it was back on. The bedside lamp bent brightly over me. The digital clock was blinking, the television over in the corner had come on and was sending a mist of static into the room. I noticed that there were some hard objects in the bed, and when I felt underneath me I discovered my flashlight and the cordless phone, and I sat up. It was morning, basically. Late August.

The night before, I'd fallen asleep while still talking to Cassie, and little scraps of our conversation floated back into my head. *Tell me,* she'd said. *What's the first thing—*

"—the first thing you remember," she said.

"I'm thinking," I said, and she let out a breath.

"Don't blow a gasket," she said. "Geez. It's not such a difficult question."

"Well," I said. I considered again: nothing.

"Okay," she said. "So just tell me about Cleveland—how about that? Tell me about the first time you came to your new—"

Your new family, she said, and I shifted.

"Um," I said. I considered. I tried to think of interesting anecdotes.

I was so boring, I thought.

I had become aware of it, more and more, as the summer wore on, as the first rush of enthusiasm and excitement began to grow cooler. I thought of Cassie a lot while I was at work. What kinds of things could I tell her next time we talked? What would I say?

I tried to save up little jokes I'd heard, articles from the newspaper. I moved through the days watchfully, waiting for a quirky little moment I could package up for Cassie.

I arrived in Cleveland the summer I turned twelve. A social worker put me on the train in St. Louis. I guess things had been explained to me in some fashion or another and I was aware that my new foster parents were going to meet me when I got to my destination. I was given some papers to carry with me and someone had packed me a lunch in a paper bag, a juice box and some baby carrots and a peanut butter sandwich.

It must have been around 2 A.M. when we got in. I remember, at least, that it was the wee hours of the morning, though I don't know why I would have come in at such a time. I remember only that the conductor came to the seat where I was sleeping and ran the beam of his flashlight gently across my face. "This is your stop coming up, young man," he whispered. The social worker had spoken with him when I was being put on the train, so he must have known some part of my story. He looked down as if he knew some terrible secret about me, stern and sorrowful the way old workingmen get in the years before they retire, and he stood there waiting to be sure I was awake before he moved on down the aisle. There was the faintly dusty smell of the old air-conditioning and the hiss of the pneumatic door opening between the train cars. Beyond the window was dark but you could hear it raining.

Mr. and Mrs. Dowty were there on the platform when the train stopped. Water was trickling down from the awning that led toward the station building and passengers were opening up their umbrellas as they got off the train. I stepped down the metal stairs with my old alligator-skin suitcase and that was when I saw Mrs. Dowty looking right at me. She was a skinny little woman in a blue navy pea coat, and I saw that her eyes had rested on me—hopefully, though also a little concerned, I thought. She had a little sign that she had made on which she had printed my name. ROBERT POTTER, it said. WELCOME HOME.

Mr. Dowty had been standing there holding her hand, and when he saw me coming forward he untwined his fingers from hers and came forward, smiling. He was a short man, only a little taller than Mrs. Dowty was, with a bald head and square black glasses.

"Robert?" he said to me. "Robert?" And I was surprised to see that his hands and fingers had a lot of dark hair growing on them, despite his baldness.

"How do you do?" he said, and we shook hands.

"Let me take that for you!" he said, and he slipped the handle of my suitcase out of my grasp.

"Did you have a good trip?" he said. "It's awfully early in the morning for a boy to have to get up and around!"

I nodded and followed along beside him. All during this time Mrs. Dowty had continued to stand there holding her sign, the two of us watching each other as I approached, and I wasn't sure what to make of it at first. I thought maybe she had been expecting something else, a different type of boy altogether, and there were butterflies in my stomach.

She had her hand up holding the throat of her coat closed and there was a gust of wind off the lake.

"Anna," Mr. Dowty said, "I believe this is our boy," and she stood there for a minute longer.

"Yes," she said.

We drove home through the silent, faded city and I sat in the backseat with my head pressed against the window. Did we talk? I don't remember that we said anything—Mr. Dowty driving, Mrs. Dowty next to him in the passenger seat, planes of light tilting and passing across our faces. I saw some men sleeping on steaming grates on a sidewalk, and blank brick fronts of empty warehouses. The halogen streetlights bent their heads over us, the traffic lights hanging like lanterns from braided black wires. No one else seemed to be awake, and we passed under a cement train bridge and curved up a hill lined with dark trees, houses and apartment buildings hidden between the branches. I closed my eyes and opened them, and then we were pulling into a driveway and here was the house where I would be living from now on.

I don't remember what I was feeling at the time. I could never very clearly recall the foster home where I was living before I came to the Dowtys', and perhaps even then I had almost forgotten it. I thought of myself as an object, a box, and my mind was clenched in the center of it and muffled under layers of packing, in hibernation, and I imagine that I must have moved mechanically when Mr. Dowty opened the door of the car, holding my suitcase in his hand, speaking in a voice so soft that it seemed to be only inside my head. *Come on, now, Robert, let's go to sleep in a nice soft bed, come on now,* and I followed him through the back-

yard gate and through the doorway and up the stairs to where a
room had been prepared for me.

It was a small, neat room on the corner of the second floor,
and even at that hour, sleepy and dazed as I was, I was aware of
the room as a kind of empty space, a place that hadn't been lived
in for some time. The carpet had been freshly vacuumed—you
could see the lines where the vacuum had brought the shag of the
blue carpet up into tufts, like artificial grass. The bed was tightly
made, the pillow folded under the bedspread and tucked like a
package, a quilt folded over the foot. There was a little desk with
a lamp on it and a blotter with a single pencil in the center, and
above the desk was a bookshelf with the books arranged, it
seemed, from shortest to tallest, the spines all even with one another in a single, smooth wall, as if they were bricks. Mrs. Dowty
went in ahead of me with the polite, careful steps of a nurse,
which she was, and I stood in the doorway as she went to the
dresser along the wall and opened the top drawer, displaying its
dustless vacancy as if she were showing me a cabinet of knickknacks that mustn't be touched.

"You can put your clothes in here," she said. "But you don't
need to do that tonight. I imagine you're very tired and want to
go right to sleep."

"Yes," I said. I looked down at my shoes, a pair of ragged,
cracked high-tops with laces the gray color of dishwater, and I
felt lonely and ashamed.

Later I would learn that this had been the room of the Dowtys'
son, Douglas, who had been dead three years by the time I came.

Douglas had been sixteen, had died in a diving accident, Mrs. Dowty said; he broke his neck on the cement bottom of the town swimming pool, and by the time he was pulled out of the water his brain had been deprived of oxygen for too long.

"We were able to donate some of his tissue. His bones," she said. "Corneas . . ." She considered, and I assumed that there was a long list of things that she had memorized, items that recited on in her mind, though she was silent. "So," she said, after a pause. "So. I like to think that not only does his spirit live on in our hearts, but his physical body lives on to some extent as well."

I had been there for months when she told me this; we were sitting at the kitchen table and Mr. Dowty had already gone off to work at the high school, but I was staying home with the flu. It was winter and outside it was all snowy white and shoveled pathways along the sidewalks.

I was glad that I didn't know, that first night, that I was going to be sleeping in the room of a dead boy. Still, I suppose that in some ways I *did* know, as I unbuttoned my shirt and unlaced my shoes and took off my jeans. There was a kind of steady, weighted stillness in the room as I folded my clothes as best I could and put them into a pile. I got into the bed, in between the cool, dry sheets, and put my head against the thick pillow and folded my hands over my chest as if I were in a coffin. After a moment my eyes closed without my noticing.

When I woke up the next morning, it had been daylight for a while. It was a day in April and for a moment I expected to still be on the train. I could not remember where I was, I didn't recognize the room, and I felt that blank, open space in my mind, which is what it must be like to have amnesia or Alzheimer's disease, that sense of grasping, a foot coming down and not finding the ground. I sat up, and I could just barely hear them talking in some other part of the house and my brain pulled out a little flash: the Dowtys standing on the train platform in the rain, in the night, two silhouettes under umbrellas, but it might as well have been an old black-and-white movie I had seen a long time ago on a television in the recreation room of the group home, a memory light as a piece of ash.

I was aware again of the room I was in, that silent feeling of disapproval, and I could see Douglas's collection of books looking down at me from their shelf. *Field Guide to Insects of North America. The Observer's Sky Atlas. From Atoms to Infinity. Half Magic*—

I was moving my eyes along the shelf, reading each title, and I heard a young man's voice say, very distinctly: *You mean he's sleeping in there right now? In Douglas's room?!* Or so I imagined. I pulled back the covers and slipped on the same jeans and T-shirt that I had worn when I left St. Louis.

I didn't want to stay in bed while they were awake—thinking I was a lazybones. And although I wanted to take a shower I didn't want to be naked in the house with all of them out there, talking about me. And so I found my way down the stairs, following their voices, and around the corner from the foot of the staircase I could see the yellow wallpaper of the kitchen and a young man, a teenager, sitting at the kitchen table. I could see through the doorway his tennis shoe and the ham of his calf and his hand reaching down to scratch the sock on his ankle. This, I would learn later, was Rob Higgins.

...

Rob Higgins was eighteen years old that year. Only six years older than me—though the distance between twelve and eighteen is very far, maybe the longest six years we ever travel. Spying on him from around the corner, I guessed that he was in high school. He looked like one of the boys that went to the Catholic high school near the group home back in St. Louis, a certain kind of face that I associated with bullies. Reddish hair under a baseball cap. Freckles. Small, upturned nose. A sort of wiry quarterback build. I thought of the names that such boys would call after us as we hurried back from our school to the blocky, narrow-windowed cluster of buildings where we were kept. "Retards!" they called. "Faggots! Niggers!" And though these words didn't even apply to us, they were still scary—they had a blunt force, the ugliest, dirtiest names that these dull-witted high school boys could think of. That was what we were to them.

Maybe at one point in his life, Rob Higgins might have been one of those types, with their boisterous, unimaginative confidence, but he wasn't that way any longer. Even then, I could see that something about him had been subdued and broken down, and I relaxed a little.

Rob Higgins was having a hard time, Mrs. Dowty told me later. *A tough life,* she said, some of it his own making, some of it just bad luck. Whatever cockiness had been a natural part of him had withdrawn and would probably never really return to him.

He was Mrs. Dowty's nephew, her sister's son, and he and Mrs. Dowty had grown close since the death of Rob's mother and Mrs. Dowty's son in the same year. They had bonded, Mrs. Dowty said, and Rob had started to spend a lot of time at Mrs.

Dowty's house, though this didn't turn out to be a cure for anything, necessarily. He continued to have problems—issues with drugs and depression, I gathered. Trouble getting along with his teachers. An intense and destructive relationship with a girlfriend.

He was sitting there eating cereal and he looked up and regarded me when I came in. It was the kind of look that you would give if a small animal—a squirrel or a stray cat—walked brazenly into your house and stood in the doorway of your kitchen while you were bringing a spoonful of Corn Pops to your mouth.

"Well! If it isn't young Robert Potter!" Mr. Dowty said. He was at the stove making some scrambled eggs in a skillet and he was the first one to speak. "I was just about to come and wake you up!" he said.

"Oh," I said.

"Are you hungry, sweetheart?" Mrs. Dowty said.

Rob Higgins said nothing—but he kept his eyes on me steadily, a kind of mild hostility emanating from him. A drop of milk fell from his spoon and he blinked.

I was telling this to Cassie one night when we were first getting into our mode of marathon telephone conversations.

"Wow," she said. "That's a great story, Robbie!" She had been making appreciative sounds the whole time—"yes," "mm-hmm," "right," "oh—I get it . . ."

And of course when you are in the presence of a good listener you can start to feel as if you actually have something interesting to say.

"I don't know why you say that you can't remember anything," she said. "That all seems pretty detailed to me!"

"I guess so," I said. "My memory has actually been pretty good since I came to Cleveland. Or at least it seems like it is." I considered for a moment. "I guess the big problem is that I'm not always sure about whether anything is accurate."

"Hmm," she said. "That's a problem for everyone, sweetie."

Sometimes I thought about asking Mrs. Dowty.

She came up to my room above the garage, looking for unwashed glasses and dirty dishes, and I sat there in bed, in my underwear, embarrassed. It was two o'clock on a Saturday afternoon.

"Hey," I said. But she was in a mood. She picked up one of my socks from the middle of the floor and looked at it gloomily.

"You don't have to do that," I said. "I'm going to do it."

"Then you should have done it already," she said. "What were you doing up at all hours last night? I saw that light of yours was still burning at four in the morning!"

"Nothing," I said, though for a moment I wondered if she had been able to see me through the window as I talked with Cassie on the phone. I should just tell her, I shouldn't lie, I thought. "I was just . . . thinking about stuff, I guess," I said, and she gave me The Eye.

"If you're having problems with the insomnia, you should go talk to Dr. Bloom," Mrs. Dowty said. "She could probably give you some medication for it."

"Mom, I'm fine," I said. "Geez. I haven't seen Dr. Bloom since I was fourteen."

"She did you a lot of good," Mrs. Dowty said. "You were in

pretty rough shape when you came to us. You know that, Robert. And Dr. Bloom got you calmed down, didn't she?"

"I guess so," I said, though the truth was I hadn't thought of Dr. Bloom in years. I didn't recall that she'd done me that much good. Mostly, it seemed to me, the two of us just sat around and played cards for an hour every week, and then she would write me a prescription for something.

Well," Mrs. Dowty said, "you're a grown-up now—you have to make your own decisions, don't you? I can't force you to do anything."

"I just like to stay up late," I said. "That's all."

Mrs. Dowty sighed and nodded a little. She held three drinking glasses in her right hand, clustered between her fingers like bells, and for a second it seemed as if she were offering them to me. I held my hand out awkwardly. The pads of her fingertips inside the rims of the glasses, the formation of

flesh pressed and wet against a

"You can't go on like this forever," she said.

She peered out the window, down at the driveway and the basketball hoop that she and Mr. Dowty had set up for me when I first came to live with them. For a moment, maybe we both thought about the kind of kid I'd been back then, picturing me down there dribbling and shooting, twelve years old, small for my age, dribbling and shooting, smaller than anyone else in my class, seventy pounds, maybe, circling in the driveway and dribbling and shooting, and I could remember that so much more vividly than anything in my life up to that point that it seemed as if I must have spent seven years in that driveway and only a few long summer afternoons in various foster homes, instead of vice versa. What was the name of that family I lived with before I was sent to the Dowtys?

Lamb? Lambert? Something like that. I sat there, sending out feelers into my memory, tracing it back past the Lamb/Lamberts and it was like trying to place stepping-stones down from one bank of a creek to the other side

The group home in St. Louis and

The Lamberts

And the Holroyd sisters

And that lady Darlene, who was my mother's cousin

And those ones who were religious.

Morrison?

I had never been a very good rememberer. That was one of the downsides of being in contact with Cassie. It reminded me of the things I didn't like about my own mind, the problems with the ways in which it worked and didn't work.

I knew the basics of my own life story, of course. I was five when LaChandra and Nicholas were murdered, and then there were several foster families, one after another, each one farther away from my old home. I came at last to rest in the home of Mr. and Mrs. Dowty when I was twelve, and that was where I went to school from seventh grade on to graduation. I began to work for my cousin Rob's house-painting business during my freshman year at the community college, the year that Mr. Dowty died, and I continued to work for him after I stopped attending classes. I lost the ring finger of my left hand during a fall from a ladder.

Mostly, I thought, I was an average, normal person. I paid my bills. I went out to the bar on a Friday night with my buddies and had a decent time. I liked to laugh at funny shows on TV and I did my work and I tried not to take stuff too seriously.

Still, sometimes I felt worried. On Friday nights, sitting in Parnell's, I'd listen to the other guys talk about themselves, retelling a memory of something that happened to them when they were kids, and I realized that my own brain worked differently from the way theirs did. Their minds were built up of stories—Tony, with his sagas of girlfriends and breakups, or Tino, with his rambling supply of misadventures in which he was always the prankster or the victim, or even Rob Higgins, who had his life sorted and categorized into a catalog of best and worst moments.

I loved the way that they could maneuver through their pasts so easily. I loved the way the events in their lives had beginnings and middles and ends, the way their stories had *points* to them—morals, or punch lines, or twists.

But when my turn would come around, I never knew what to say. *I can't really think of anything,* I'd tell them. *I don't really recall,* I'd say, because I didn't know how to describe the place I went when I sat home at night, when I sank down in the old claw-footed bathtub with my eyes closed, when I stared at the mirror, watching my reflection run its fingers across its face. I'd ask my mind to remember simple things: the house where I lived with my first foster family, for example; or the Christmas of my eleventh year; or my oldest sister's face.

But what I got was another thing entirely. Even though I'd concentrate, the pictures my brain would send me often didn't make much sense. I'd conjure up a vivid image of a row of brownstone apartments and a cobblestone street; I'd imagine that

I recalled an organ grinder and his monkey on the corner, and people passing by in clothes from a hundred years ago. I'd call forth a farmhouse in the middle of cornfields, and I'd see myself walking on a winding dirt road, looking up as a pterodactyl slowly flapped its wings, passing across the moon. I'd picture a crumpled potato-chip bag, or a snowy tundra, where a woman was pinning white sheets to a clothesline in the wind, or the sound of something scratching on the door in the night. Maybe, I thought, the memory-recording apparatus in my head had been damaged in some way.

But when I mentioned all this to Cassie, she seemed unimpressed. "That's all very poetic," she said. "But that's just whimsy, Robbie. It's not memory. I mean, you *do* know the difference between fantasy and reality, don't you?"

"Yeah," I said.

"You're not a schizophrenic, are you? I mean, you don't really *believe* you once saw a pterodactyl, do you?"

"No," I said. I hesitated for a moment. "No, of course not."

"Well, then," she said. I was sitting there on my narrow bed, picking at my bare feet. It was about one-thirty in the morning. We had been talking nearly every night for months, and this wasn't the first time that I didn't know what to say.

"You don't have to make up stuff to impress me, Robbie," she said. "I love you just the way you are."

"Thank you," I said, and she laughed lightly in that way that usually made me feel a kind of glow but this time did not. I wished I could see the expression on her face.

But I couldn't picture it. Actually, I still didn't know what

Cassie looked like, and that, in fact, was another small point of contention that had developed between us. She had promised on several occasions to send me a photo, but it never arrived.

"What!" she had said, the first time I brought it up. "You mean you haven't got those photos yet? I sent them two weeks ago!"

"Well," I said. "They never came."

"That's crazy!" she said, after another week had passed. "I can't believe your cruddy mail service! They must have gotten lost again!"

"They must have."

"Well, I'll send some new ones. I'll send them certified this time."

"Okay," I said, and waited as June turned into July. But when I asked her again, her voice got a little chilly.

"I really don't like to have my picture taken," she said. It was one of the times when there were weird noises in the background again, as if she were just outside the door of some busy, unhappy place, like a police station or a hospital waiting room.

"Actually," she said, "those photos I sent you were basically the only ones I had. Now I'll have to get some new ones taken."

"Well," I said, "I'd really like to have a picture of you."

"Ha!" she said. "It's probably better if you remember me like I was! I'm basically the same as I was twenty years ago—just older and fatter!"

"Uh-huh," I said. And she didn't seem to understand that when I talked about my memory, I was partially trying to explain to her that I didn't remember anything at all about *her*, not even her face. I wanted to ask if she still had curly red hair, but maybe she never had curly red hair. After all those years of searching for me, she would doubtless be offended, I thought. It would hurt her feelings to know how little of her had held fast in my mind.

Walking home from Parnell's on a Friday night, I'd sometimes think of talking about it with Rob Higgins. Sometimes the nights were beautiful—a little fog, or the moon—and we'd be side by side, two old friends with a lot of beer between us, and it seemed like it should be easy to talk. People called us "the two Robs," and said that we were "inseparable."

But it was difficult. The stuff about Cassie was hard and complicated to explain, for one thing. For another, I had the feeling that Rob Higgins would be upset. He had been slow to accept me, and when he finally did, it was as if he had decided to invent me out of something else—out of Douglas, out of a person he'd imagined.

He was big on the idea of family, and was always telling me how great my foster parents were, and how he'd wished, growing up, that they could be *his* parents. "Yer mom makes the best pickled cucumbers I've ever tasted," he'd say. Or: "I miss yer dad so much," he'd say. "He had the greatest sense of humor—how did he come up with all those jokes?" Or: "Yer parents had the nicest taste in furniture. I used to love going over to your house just to sit in that one recliner."

Every time I would think about telling Rob Higgins about Cassie, comments like these would arise in my mind. He would be stumbling along down the sidewalk, grinning affectionately at me, and I couldn't help but feel that if I told him about all the time I spent talking to Cassie, I would seem like kind of a traitor. He had always just assumed that I had melded completely into my adoptive role, as if I didn't even realize that I wasn't a blood relative. He would joke that we probably seemed kind of trailer-park-esque to people, two cousins with the same first name—as if he'd forgotten that I had already had the name of Rob before I became part of his family. He even told me how much I looked like my foster father.

"I see him in your face," Rob Higgins would say, after Mr. Dowty had died. It was a compliment, but it was also a little weird and uncomfortable. Despite our years of friendship, there was always a certain level of pretending going on between us.

I couldn't help but consider it when I got home that night from Parnell's. *A certain level of pretending,* I thought, as Mrs. Dowty's face appeared in the little window above the kitchen sink. She was waiting up for me, and I waved to her and smiled to show that I was on my way to bed. It was touching that she worried about me, I thought, but I also felt aware that it was complicated for her. Even though I'd called her "Mom" for over ten years now, there was also a part of me that still felt like a stranger, a certain part that she didn't know.

"Of course she'd be a little nervous," Cassie said. "I know I would be. You're the son of a killer! And let's face it, Rob: You're not the average twenty-five-year-old guy. You're a little weird, you know? I can imagine her sitting there in the morning with the newspaper: *"Oh, look. Here's an unsolved murder. Here's a rape over at the community college. I sure hope Robbie isn't involved . . ."*

"Thanks a lot," I said.

"You know what I mean," she said. "Partially I'm joking."

But partially, I guess, she wasn't. We had talked for a while about the idea of meeting, maybe Cassie coming to Cleveland for a visit. But Cassie never felt like it was a good idea.

"I don't think any of us are ready for that kind of thing yet," she said.

From the beginning, she had been very firmly opposed to me telling Mrs. Dowty about our conversations. "It's better," Cassie repeatedly said. "It's better if you don't bring it up," and as I struggled to get my key into the door, I knew that Cassie was probably right. There were times during the week when I'd feel so natural with Mrs. Dowty that it seemed like she *had* been my mom for my whole life. I'd eat oatmeal at her table in the morning and she'd gently, affectionately put her palm on the back of my neck. We'd watch television in the evening, gossiping about the characters on our favorite programs; we'd shop for groceries together on Sunday afternoon, and I'd fix the things around the house that needed fixing.

Sometimes I'd try to imagine how it might be. "Hey, Mom," I could say, one afternoon while we were playing chess in the kitchen, and Mrs. Dowty would lift her round, thoughtful head. "Do you remember those other kids . . . the brothers and sisters I had? The biological ones?"

And she would say: "Oh, honey, that's in the past. You don't want to think about that anymore."

And I would say: "Well—actually, there is this woman who called me. Named Cassie. And she says she's my older sister. I've talked to her. A couple times now."

And I thought that we could have really had a conversation

about it—she would have been interested in it, I thought, and she'd have been happy when I expressed a few concerns about Cassie's honesty. She would have some solid advice.

But then I'd come home from the bar and I'd know that Cassie was right. I could feel the moonlight of Mrs. Dowty's gaze on me as I fumbled with the key and the jagged mouth of the keyhole. Remembering what Cassie had said—*the son of a killer,* she said—I could now imagine the lapping of Mrs. Dowty's worries and doubts passing over me.

Robbie is a good boy, I imagined Mrs. Dowty thinking. *He's like my very own son,* she was thinking. *Just like my own flesh and blood! He's a good boy, a good boy.*

I don't know. Maybe I was only projecting such thoughts onto her. *Projecting:* That's the term that Cassie used.

"It's natural for you to be concerned about these things," Cassie said. "We've all of us got to come to terms with it. Whatever is in our genes. You'd be foolish not to be a little scared."

"What do you mean?" I said. "I don't know what you're talking about, Cassie," I said. I was sitting at the little table near the window that looked out onto the driveway, cleaning paint off my skin with a rag and a little bowl of turpentine. I didn't like the direction our conversations had been taking lately.

"You *know,*" she said. "You remember how Karen used to get. All those lies and her little fake hallucinations and trances and stuff. Before the little ones—"

I was silent for a moment, the phone held in the crook between my ear and my shoulder, and I rubbed the little freckles of paint off my forearm. "Actually," I said, "I don't remember things that well. About what happened."

"I doubt that," she said. "What we experienced, that's not something you just forget."

"Really," I said. "You were older than me, so I think it's probably a lot clearer to you."

"Well, then," she said. "I envy you your forgetfulness."

"I guess," I said.

"I've had nightmares every single night of my life since it happened," she said. "God! All of us have. Poor Cecilia Joy said that she was contemplating suicide for a while, before she met her husband. She thought about killing herself, just to get away from the bad dreams!"

"Oh," I said. Hesitantly, I touched the stump where my finger used to be. In my mind, something almost remembered itself, but the fumes of turpentine were making me a little lightheaded; whatever memory was on the verge of coughing itself up was gone even before it materialized. Out the window, I could see a squirrel was stumbling erratically around in circles underneath the old basketball net. Then I realized that it wasn't a squirrel; it was a brown paper bag.

When Cassie said things about *craziness, mental illness, schizophrenia,* that sort of thing, I couldn't help but feel a bit self-conscious. Concerned. I thought about the way the world played tricks on me—squirrels, for example, that transformed into paper bags, phone calls that seemed half whited out when I woke up, memories spotted with imaginary pterodactyls and organ-grinder monkeys and glacial lakes—little things that perhaps

                                                                        added up.

Such things might give a person pause.

Nearly every week I would come across some little thing: a car parked alongside the road, a tree with its branches held up in some kind of sign language, a pattern of wallpaper or a certain color of hair that brought tears to my eyes like an old remembered lullaby—just minor things that would startle me as if I recognized them. *What is it?* I would think. *What is it?* Even worse, I'd notice things that should have been there but weren't—Rob Higgins and I would drive by a park and for a moment I'd be certain a brownstone apartment ought to be there, a building where a pregnant girl should be sitting on the porch steps with her dog. I'd open a drawer in the kitchen and expect to find it full of pennies and postcards and costume jewelry when in fact there was only silverware inside.

The day I lost my finger was something like that. One minute I was on the ladder, three stories up, painting along the frame of an old round window near the peak of the house; the next minute a swimmy feeling trickled up my spine and into my brain. The window was empty and then the face of a woman floated up like a transparent reflection on the surface of water, moving toward me, pressing up against the glass, a face like someone who had loved me once, leaning over my bed at night to kiss my hair. I don't even remember falling, though I recall the feeling as my ring caught against a nail, the finger separating from my body, not so much pain as a kind of gasp. I hit the ground and the wind knocked out of me. For a second I thought I felt my soul, my spirit, bounce out of me and fly up a few feet before fluttering down and settling back into my body.

Rob Higgins and Tony and Tino teased me afterward about it, how they thought I was dead when I hit the ground, the way I sleepily opened my eyes as they rushed over to gather around me. "Where am I?" I said, like a sleepwalker, like a coma person or blackout drunk, and they all laughed with relief. "You were like a little kid waking up from a dream," Rob Higgins said. "Ha! Like you just woke up from a refreshing nap!"

I didn't tell them what I'd seen up there, through the window. The bathroom, the bathtub filling up with water, the naked lady with her long red hair, arms held out to me, gliding swiftly toward where I was peering in.

This wasn't something I told Cassie about, either. It was too—what?—*upsetting*, probably. It would take things too far, I thought, and I could sense that she was growing bored with me. Frustrated? I imagined that maybe there was something the other brothers and sisters had that I lacked.

"What would you do if you saw her again?" Cassie said, almost casually, almost dreamily, the last night I talked to her.

"Saw who?" I said.

Cassie made a soft sound, like swallowing. "Oh, Robbie," she said. "Don't be ridiculous. You know who I'm talking about."

"Oh," I said. It was probably about three-thirty in the morning, and I hadn't turned on the light, so Mrs. Dowty wouldn't know that I was up. "Right," I said.

"Well?" she said, and she coughed lightly. There were some strange echoing sounds in the background—as if she were in a busy public space. An announcer or a conductor was speaking sternly; it sounded as if a nearby child was making a whining request, and a mother responded irritably. But Cassie didn't seem to notice any of this noise. "It's a simple question," she said.

"I don't know," I said. I had to be up in the morning, Rob Higgins would be pounding on my door and jiggling the knob. But it had always been hard for me to go to sleep. I brushed my eye with my thumb, rubbed my feet together beneath the covers.

"No, really, Robbie—" Cassie was saying. "Really. What would you do? Do you think you would talk to her?"

"I guess so," I said. Then I thought of that face in the window on the day that I fell off the ladder. "I don't know for sure," I said. "Maybe I wouldn't."

She sighed. I think I must have sounded bored and evasive, though really I was just tired. I would have tried harder, I guess, if I had known that it was the last time I would talk to her.

"I can't believe you haven't considered it," she said. "Of course you have. What kind of person wouldn't think about it? What kind of person wouldn't remember?"

It was a good question, I guess, but by that time there had accumulated a lot of good questions that were competing for my attention. *What kind of person*, Cassie said, and I wondered about that.

What kind of person was I? This was yet to be decided.

It had been a particularly hot summer, with a lot of thunderstorms. The power was always going out, and sometimes I would wake up in complete darkness—no bedside lamp, no streetlight, no moon. The fan no longer turning, so the air grew close and still. I could hear the cicadas in the boughs of the trees, a vibrating, held note that sounded like hissing.

Of course I thought of *her* then.

                                        Our mother.

...

I looked out from the window of my apartment above the garage and I could see Mrs. Dowty moving through her kitchen carrying a candle. She had a brass candlestick that one of her ancestors had brought across the ocean when they immigrated, and now Mrs. Dowty went padding barefoot through her kitchen, holding her light aloft. Her heirloom.

I myself had a flashlight, which I kept in the drawer of the night table, along with some packages of alkaline batteries. Even through the walls of sleep I'd sensed the lights going out, the electricity shutting off—*that face floating down, I could feel it, moving toward me in the dark, the kiss of the breath, that sweet voice that sounded as if she were smiling, the face looming down as she lifted me from the bed, the sound of water running in the bathroom wake up sleepy head wake up my little one*

—Oh yes I remembered I remembered and I jolted up and grabbed for my flashlight even before I was fully awake.

To Psychic Underworld:

Critter was standing outside the public library with his one-year-old daughter in his arms when he saw a dollar bill on the sidewalk.

It actually came fluttering by, right next to his tennis shoe, carried by the wind along with a leaf.

He hesitated for a moment. Should he pick it up? He adjusted Hazel's weight. She was straddled against his hip and watched with silent interest as he bent down and snagged it.

He'd had the feeling that it wouldn't be just a normal dollar and he was right. There was writing on it. Someone had written along the margins of the bill in black ink, in a clear, deliberate handwriting that he guessed might be a young woman's. *I love you I miss you I love you I send this out to you I love you please come back to me I will wait for you always I—*

This written all around the edges of the bill, and he was standing there studying it when his sister Joni came down the steps of the library toward them. He had come to pick her up. That was one of the conditions of his current circumstance. He used Joni's car during the day so long as he was there at the library to pick her up from work.

"Hello, soldiers," Joni said brightly. "How goes the war?"

"Mm," Critter said, and Hazel stared at Joni sternly.

"And what have we here?" Joni said, indicating the dollar bill he was still clutching awkwardly between his fingers. "A little offering for your dearest sister, perhaps?"

She took the lovedollar from him and looked it over. He watched as she read the writing on it, one eyebrow arching. "Ye Gods!" she said.

"I just found it," Critter said. "Just right here on the sidewalk."

Their eyes met. She was still his older sister, though she was also a tiny librarian woman with short hair and a pointy face, and he was an unemployed Sasquatch of a man a foot and a half taller than she.

She handed the dollar back to him. "Yikes," she said. "Geez, Critter, you're quite the magnet for freaky notes lately, aren't you?"

. . .

He was, yes. *A magnet,* he thought, as they drove back to Joni's house. That was one way to look at it.

He'd found the first note a few weeks after his wife's funeral, on the sidewalk not far from his apartment. It was written in spiky block letters on an index card:

> TO PSYCHIC
> UNDERWORLD:
> STOP ASTRAL
> TRAVELING TO
> MOLEST/DECEIVE
> OTHERS (ANIMALS TOO).
> ANIMALS ARE NOT
> MADE OF HATE.
> CEASE AND DESIST.

"Jesus," Critter thought. This was when he was still in Chicago, still in the old apartment that he and his wife, Beth, had been living in when she died, still thinking that he would probably be able to pull himself together. He was pushing Hazel in her stroller, they were on their way to the park, and he looked around to see if there were any noticeably insane people nearby.

But there was nobody. It was Sunday morning, and the street was quiet except for a jogger a few blocks up. A pigeon rustled at the curb, pecking at the bone from a discarded chicken wing.

Back in the days when his life had been normal, Critter might have been kind of pleased to find such a note. Beth had loved this kind of thing. So had Joni, for that matter. Beth had been a middle school science teacher and Joni was a librarian and they both had collections of weird stuff they had found. Bizarre, misspelled letters written by lovelorn eighth graders. Obscene Polaroids left in between the pages of library books. They used to call each other on the phone to share their latest discovery, and Critter had always remained a little off to the side, never feeling quite as sharp or ironic as they were. Critter was an electrician, primarily home repair, and so he didn't usually come across anything except bad wiring and faulty lighting fixtures.

Several days after he found the first note, he was sitting in the pediatrician's office with Hazel—he was feeling kind of proud of himself for remembering to keep the appointment—when another note fell out of an old copy of *Sports Illustrated* that he was perusing. This was a piece of light-blue unlined paper, and written on it, in the careful cursive handwriting of a ten- or eleven-year-old, was a little list:

1. Go for a walk with someone
2. Go out somewhere with someone
3. Talk to someone
4. Watch TV
5. Go on the computer
6. Play PlayStation 2
7. Go to the cemetery and talk to my mom
8. Listen to music
9. Go in my room

For a moment, Critter thought he might completely lose it. It was, he thought, possibly the most heartbreaking thing he had ever read, and he heard himself make a soft, involuntary sound.

Across from him, a young woman with a sleeping infant looked up sternly. Here was Critter, thick beard and shaggy long hair, making snuffling sounds, and the little mother didn't like the look of him at all. It would not be appropriate for him to start weeping in the pediatrician's office, obviously, he realized, and he lowered his eyes and tightened his jaw and he felt a repressed tear run out of his nose and into his mustache.

Shit, he thought. He needed to get a grip on himself—this was ridiculous.

Nearby, Hazel was sitting in the play area, among some wooden blocks. She gave him a thoughtful expression. Then she lifted two cubes in her hands and touched them together carefully, as if they might give off sparks.

"Boom," she said.

He had been having a fairly hard time of it. Which was natural, he supposed. His wife had been killed in a car accident and he was living alone with his baby daughter and he hadn't been to work since the funeral; customers would call with their electrical needs and he would just let the answering machine pick up, he hadn't even checked the messages in almost a month—there was in fact a sticky note still posted above the telephone in Beth's handwriting:

Mrs. Palmarosa
555-7622
Says her doorbell gives a shock!

Which was the last thing on earth that Beth had written to him before she died.

"Listen," Joni had said. "I want you guys to come and stay with me for a while. Just for a visit. Get out of that apartment for a while. Get out of Chicago. And—you know what?—you might find that you actually like Toledo. You can be an electrician any-where."

"Mm," Critter said. He was sitting on the couch with the por-table phone, staring at the muted TV. "I'll think about it," he said.

"You don't have to do this all by yourself, you know, Critter," Joni said. "There are no prizes for being stoic. You realize that, right?"

"I know," he said.

And so now here he was. It was September, and he and Hazel had been living in Joni's apartment for more than two months, and he guessed that he was basically kind of losing his mind.

Not completely, obviously. He continued to do a decent job as a father, he thought. He kept an eye on Hazel as she toddled around, he kept her diapers clean and made little plates of food with cut-up fruit and cheese and crackers, he took her to the park in the stroller, and they never watched any television that had sex or swearing in it.

He was not yet ready to start looking for a job, but he was helping a little bit with various chores. He rinsed off the dishes and put them in the dishwasher. He took some letters to the post office, and put gas in Joni's car, and went grocery shopping with a list that Joni had made up—though there was a moment where he became kind of frozen in the aisle of condiments and crackers; it was another note, a shopping list stuck to the cage of the shopping cart:

Roach Spray
Batteries
Water Mellon

Which, really, what was so surprising or disturbing about that? Nevertheless he didn't know how long he had been standing there looking at the scritchy, pathetic handwriting when a middle-aged lady had spoken to him firmly.

"Sir, I need to get access to that ketchup, if you could please move forward."

And Critter awakened from his trance with a little shudder.

It was foolish, he knew, to feel so unnerved by such stuff. He had never been a superstitious person, and in any case it wasn't as if there was anything particularly uncanny at work. He was living in a city—of course there were all kinds of flotsam drifting around.

But he hadn't noticed it before, that was the thing. Beth used to tease him, in fact, about how inattentive he was, she was always pointing out the weirdness of the world that he was missing—hot-air balloons in the sky over the park; the woman in the bear suit sitting on the el train a few seats in front of them, her bear's head in her lap; the pool of blood in the foyer of their apartment, right there underneath the discarded catalogs and junk mail. "Oh my God!" Beth said. "I can't believe you didn't see that!"

But now, suddenly, he did. Now, suddenly, it seemed that there were notes everywhere, emerging out of the blur of the world. Something had happened to him now that Beth was gone, he thought—there was an opening, a space, a part of his brain that had been deaf before was now exposed, it was as if he were a long-dormant radio that had begun to receive signals—tuned in, abruptly, to all the crazy note-writers of the world.

"Please," someone had written on a napkin and left it on the table in McDonald's, where he had taken Hazel for a little peaceful snack, a casual Toledo afternoon, but now here was this other voice poking its head through the surface of his consciousness like a worm peeking up out of the ground. "Please," in ballpoint pen on the napkin. And then "Please" on the napkin underneath it, and "Please" again on a third. Someone either very polite or very desperate.

Probably it wasn't such a big deal. When he had first come to live with Joni, he had shown her some of the notes that he had found, expecting, he supposed, that she would find it as eerie as he had—the accumulation of these strange little documents, popping up wherever he went, all of them sad or desperate or slightly creepy. She was the type of sister who had liked to tell him ghost stories when they were younger, back when she was a teenager and he was eight or nine. He'd figured that she, too, would see some kind of omen in the array of notes. But she didn't.

"These are awesome," Joni said. "I love the 'psychic underworld' one."

She had a scrapbook full of stuff that she had come across at the library, and she showed it to him as if she had discovered that they shared the same hobby. As if they were stamps or coins or some such thing.

"Oh, you have to see this one," Joni said, and opened the scrapbook to show him a note written on powder-blue memo paper with pictures of kitties on it:

> Hi, I
> had cyber
> sex!! With
> a guy named
> eric! I love sex!!

"I found this next to one of the computer terminals on the second floor," Joni said. "Can you believe it? The handwriting looks like she's about—what?—twelve?"

To Joni, he guessed, it was something a bit like gossip. Mildly titillating. Something like a glimpse into a window across the street, or an overheard conversation at a restaurant. How weird people were! Her eyes got a kind of conspiratorial glint.

"I love that it's written in pink ink!" Joni said. "It's probably one of those strawberry-scented markers!"

"Yeah," Critter said. "Ha ha."

They were sitting at the kitchen table together, and Joni had opened a forty-ounce bottle of beer, which she poured into two highball glasses. He had a bed in the guest room, and they had set up a crib for Hazel against one wall.

He lifted the glass to his lips. How to explain that he was afraid? How to explain that it felt as if these notes were like the stories she used to tell him about ghostly hands that reached up to grasp your wrist when you weren't expecting it, hands that tightened and wouldn't let free?

"What?" Joni said. "What are you thinking?"

When Beth was killed, she was reading. It was around four on a Thursday afternoon, school was done and she was on her way to pick up Hazel at day care, hurrying down the sidewalk toward the bus stop. Walking and reading, which he always warned her about, her feet moving automatically beneath her as she flipped through a stack of quizzes that her students had taken in preparation for their sixth grade proficiency test.

What is a hypothesis?
What is the relationship between a food chain and a food web?
What holds the solar system together?

And then she'd taken a step out into the street without looking. That is what the police said. Stepped out into the street without looking both ways. The practice tests fanned out, flew up, fluttering, and were carried away, wafting into the gutters or caught in fences or flattened against the side of a building.

He started to imagine this, and then he made a choice not to imagine it any longer.

...

He had always prided himself on being a steady sort of person. Not prone to anxiety. Stable. Even a little intimidating because of his size.

People always assumed that he was called "Critter" because of how he looked. The mane of red-brown hair and heavy beard and eyebrows, which he'd had since his late teens, the bear-paw hands, broad chest, imposing gut. Very few people knew that his real name was Christopher, and that he had become "Critter" because as a child he'd had such a speech impediment that he had a hard time pronouncing his own name. "Chri'er," he called himself. "Cridderfer," he said, and even now he had a hard time pronouncing "Christopher." Even now, at age twenty-nine, he stumbled over the syllables, there was still a slight lisp and sputter as he spoke his own name, "Chrithdopher Tremley," even when he pronounced it slowly. He dreaded the various official encounters—banks and government offices, doctors, policemen, the man at the funeral home—which was always the worst time to try to force the hated name out of his mouth. It was a terrible, exposed sort of feeling.

He was a very private person. Beth used to tease him; she thought it was funny, all the things that he felt uncomfortable about, all the stuff he thought of as *personal*. He disliked being barefoot, he hated to talk on cellphones when people could over-hear him, he didn't like to sit in the window of the el train, where people from the street could see him as he glided past. *My poor shy man,* Beth murmured, and he blushed when she kissed him in public.

He would never, ever, have written a note for people to find lying around the library or the sidewalk. It would have seemed grotesque to him. Maybe that was what bothered him so much about these things that he kept coming across. He had the image of his own personal thoughts softly detaching and being carried off by the wind like dandelion seeds, floating through the city. That was one of the things that grief felt like, he thought. *Astral traveling*, he thought.

And now, as if the notes themselves were not enough—

Lately, he had begun to imagine that he saw notes that weren't even there. They weren't hallucinations. Not exactly. Just little misfires, he guessed.

Like, for example, one day he and Hazel were walking to the grocery store to get a few things that Joni had listed for him, he was pushing Hazel's stroller down the shady block and she was quiet, fingering her teething ring, and then he hesitated. Stiffened. He could see a piece of paper that had been stapled to the side of a tree.

YOU SUCK! it said in big capital letters.

And then when he got closer he realized that he was just imagining things. It actually said: YARD SALE!

And then there was another time when he thought he saw something written in the mud outside of the library where Joni worked. He glanced down to the bare corner of the lawn where the grass had been worn off and it looked for a moment as if someone had printed something there. IM . . . WATCHIN . . . YVV. That's what it looked like at first. And then when he looked closer he saw that it wasn't words, after all. Not English words, at least. Some kind of Chinese characters? he thought. But no, it wasn't that, either. It was just the tracks of birds, pigeons, probably. Their three-toed feet marking a line across the wet ground.

He was surprised by the disappointment that settled over him. Nothing, he thought, and his throat tightened. Nothing, nothing.

If the world was trying to send him a message, what was it?

It was a little after midnight, and he sat there in his room in the dark, in the guest room in Joni's apartment, staring out of the window, while against the opposite wall Hazel was asleep in her crib, her face leaned gently against the wooden bars.

There was nothing to look at outside the window, but he kept looking. The sky was starless and purple-gray, and the silhouettes of tree boughs reached up into it. Through a gap in the trees and buildings, he could see a sliver of a busier street, the red taillights of cars sliding past and then disappearing.

If you have a message for me, he thought, what is it?

There were the strings of high wires that ran from the buildings and connected to poles and then to other buildings and then to poles again—you could hear how they hummed to themselves if you were near them and quiet; there were the gestures of tree branches and the smattering of fallen leaves running together down the middle of the street in a formation; there were the little whispery, wordless sounds Hazel made as she dreamed and stirred.

You might be able to read such things, maybe. Someone might: not him.

He wondered. He was not the man he had been anymore. He thought: *You are still you, but changing fast.*

It seemed so obvious, once he thought it, but still the idea sent a little shudder through him. He would never be the same person. He would never be able to go back.

He could imagine himself the way that he had once been just five or six months ago. What would he have thought, driving by down there on the street, glancing up to see a big bearded man sitting at the third-floor window of an apartment building. A grown man, almost thirty years old, peering out at the street, mumbling to himself.

He would not have recognized himself, bent over a dollar bill that he'd spread out on the sill of the window, carefully writing with a pen.

What a weirdo, he would have thought, as the man held his note out in the air, letting the wind take it from his fingers.

Back then, he probably wouldn't have even noticed. He wouldn't have been looking up toward the windows, and he certainly wouldn't have seen the dollar bill lift up in a gust of autumn wind, carried off with a few leaves and scraps.

Off to join the others in their conversations—all the little messages that the world was bearing away.

St. Dismas

That summer, not long after he turned twenty-three, Pierce kidnapped his ex-girlfriend's son, Jesse. Actually, Pierce thought, it wasn't so much a kidnapping as it was a rescue—Jesse had come with him willingly enough—though there was also, Pierce had to admit, an element of sheer vindictiveness, a desire to wake her up and make her suffer. In any case, after a couple of weeks on the road with Jesse, Pierce had begun to realize that he had probably made a mistake.

They had been traveling west without any real plan in mind, and they had arrived at last at Pierce's father's house in St. Dismas, Nebraska. St. Dismas was one of those old dried-up prairie towns, not even worthy of being called a "town," not even a settlement anymore. There were a few empty old houses and sheds, and a gas station, long closed, and an abandoned grain elevator alongside the railroad tracks, and a few straggling cottonwood trees sending their snowy seeds through the empty streets. Beyond the little cluster of buildings were long stretches of fields—wheat, sunflowers, alfalfa—and a two-lane highway that led off toward the rest of the world.

Pierce was dreaming of St. Dismas when he woke up that morning. He could picture the town as seen from above and the tangle of dirt roads that led away from it, and the highway. He was sleeping in his father's old room, and Jesse was across the hall in the room that Pierce and his brother had once occupied when they were kids. Everything in the house was more or less as it had been since his father died, over a year before—couch and lamp and ashtray, dishes and canned goods in the cupboard and a refrigerator that he didn't dare to open, dressers and pillows and blankets. A lot of dust and mildew.

Pierce opened his eyes and he could hear Jesse talking to himself.

—All right, he was saying. Thank you, thank you, you're a great audience, he said, and Pierce knew that he was probably hopping around in front of the mirror, "capering," as Pierce's father would have said. Telling himself his little secret jokes, making faces and then laughing at the expressions he created. Pierce and Jesse had shared any number of motel rooms, and Pierce had often opened his eyes from a deep sleep to find Jesse deeply involved in one of these private performances.

In general, Pierce thought, Jesse wasn't a bad kid, and there were a lot of things that he actually really liked about him. He was an entertaining liar and a natural-born thief, which had proved useful, and he was always eager to please. It hadn't taken any persuasion at all to get him to turn on his mom, to show where she'd hidden her money and her drugs, and then he'd cheerfully climbed into the car with Pierce and driven away.

He was an impressive acrobat, too. He could walk on his hands just as naturally as if his palms were the soles of his feet, and he could climb up a tree and in through the window of a house with the ease of a monkey.

But Pierce wasn't sure what to do with him. Jesse had recently taken to calling him "Dad," even though Pierce obviously wasn't his father, Jesse was only twelve years younger than Pierce himself. But what could you do? His mother was a nasty piece of work, very neglectful, a temperamental drug addict with a meth lab in her basement, and Pierce assumed that the kid had never learned right from wrong or good from bad and probably didn't have a clear concept of what the term "Dad" even meant.

Pierce had been mixed up with Jesse's mother for over a year. She had been a regular at the bar where Pierce had worked, and at first, honestly, he had been flattered by the attention of an older woman, he'd been impressed by her apathy and amorality, which had at the time seemed very worldly and cool. She had been a drug addict for as long as he'd known her, but in those last few months she'd somehow tipped over the line that separated an interesting, sexy druggie from a boring, nasty one. Honestly, it seemed like she'd become less and less human—her teeth had begun to fall out and she got these strange, measlelike bumps on her face that she couldn't stop picking at, and the tendons on her neck stood out as if she were always straining to sing a high note. Though she was only twenty-seven, she had begun to look like a little old lady, and he pictured her as a zombie, a dead thing clambering out of a grave with a femur clenched in her teeth, her eyes glazed.

It was almost a joke, by the end. When Pierce and Jesse would see her come stumbling out of the bedroom, hunched and moving her tongue around in her gap-toothed mouth in that slow, lizardy way, the two of them could barely keep from laughing. How repulsive she was, Pierce could hardly believe it, and at first it had made him feel happy to think that not only was he rescuing Jesse from her filthy household, but he was also shafting her at the same time. He loved imagining the tortuous inner debate she must have gone through, trying to decide whether to call the cops out to her house. To go into the police station, maybe. How enraged she must have been! The idea had tickled him.

Still, he hadn't really planned ahead—he certainly hadn't imagined that Jesse would still be with him, his responsibility, all this time later.

But what to do with him? How to dump him? He was a liability, he called attention to himself with his odd, hyperactive behavior, he made people look at them and ask questions. And remember their faces.

Pierce rose up out of bed and padded down the hall. Jesse was there in his old bedroom, facing the full-length mirror that was attached to the door. He was saluting himself and marching in place with a look of fierce triumph, like a soldier tramping through the streets of a smoldering enemy town.

Pierce paused and regarded him for a moment until he stopped moving and put his arms to his sides.

—What's up, Pierce said.

—Nothing.

—Well, you better think about getting packed up, Pierce said. We're going to leave pretty soon.

The boy looked at Pierce in that blank, fake-innocent way that he had, glancing sidelong at the mirror again, as if his reflection were an old pal he shared some little secret with. It had occurred to Pierce recently: Jesse was the kind of person who could betray his own mother.

—Can we steal some stuff? he asked.

Pierce gave him a stare.

—It's my house, Pierce said. You can't really steal from your own house.

—Hmm, he said, and he bent down and picked up a feathered Native American headdress, which Pierce guessed he must have dug out of a closet or a drawer, some old souvenir that Pierce's father had once bought at some long-ago roadside attraction or another. The old room was still full of this kind of stuff from Pierce's childhood, junk, Pierce thought, that his dad hadn't ever bothered to throw away.

—I guess I can keep this, then, Jesse said.

He was a real pack rat, this kid, Pierce thought. Every motel room they stayed in, Jesse made up a collection of the free soaps and shampoos and lotions, and sometimes took along the television remote for good measure. And then there were the houses he and Pierce had broken into.

There was that little place in Champaign-Urbana, the occupants away for the weekend, where Jesse had carefully combed through their CDs for stuff he liked: Creedence Clearwater Revival, The Shins, Young Jeezy. In another place in Wisconsin, a vacation house on a lake, he'd been crazy for the tackle box and the little plastic worms and frogs with hooks in them, the metal spinners with pieces of feather fluff attached, the weights and bobbers. Then there was that farmhouse outside Des Moines, where he'd been so enchanted by the collection of figurines on the shelf in the living room—little china elves and fairies and dwarves and goblins and such—that he hadn't even seemed to notice the fact that the house was occupied. Pierce went into the bedroom, looking for things to steal, and was surprised to discover that there was a little old man asleep in the bed, his gaunt head sticking up out of the covers and his mouth open, drawing small breaths.

Maybe I should kill him, Pierce thought, but he wasn't quite ready for that kind of thing yet. He backed out, slowly, closing the door quietly behind him, and Jesse was busily packing the knickknacks into his already overstuffed duffel.

—Let's go, Pierce whispered. I thought I told you to check the bedroom. There's *people* in here, you fuckin' jag-off.

—Wait a minute, Jesse said, in his high, nasal, rat-boy voice. I'm not finished! He spoke stubbornly, loudly, and Pierce couldn't help but think, *Jesus Christ, this kid is going to get me sent to prison.*

—Shh! Pierce said, but Jesse only looked at him, his eyes gleaming. He held up a little knickknack knight, holding its sword aloft.

—This is so awesome! Jesse said. Can you believe this?

Still, all that plunder they'd gathered was as nothing compared to the treasures he was finding in Pierce's old bedroom. Jesse's eyes were wide with excitement and greed. A shoebox full of plastic dinosaurs and farm animals, another of Matchbox cars, yet another with plastic robot dolls that Pierce and his brother had both loved. It was hard to believe that all of it was still here, Pierce thought, untouched for years, and of course he couldn't help but feel kind of sad to see it all spread out once again in the open air.

Back in the day, they had been a pretty nice little family— Pierce, his brother, and his father—and actually, when you thought about it, it didn't make sense that they hadn't turned out better. Pierce's dad had been a housepainter by trade, which meant that he could arrange his schedule to be around whenever they needed him. He was always taking them to school in the morning, or picking them up after basketball practice, or making dinner so they could eat together, the three of them. He didn't make any kind of big mistake that Pierce could remember, he didn't do anything wrong, but the kind of familial attachment that you read about or see on TV, that didn't stick. For whatever reason, they just didn't love him that much. When he had died, Pierce and his brother had both gone on with their lives— Pierce's brother was in Seattle, managing a restaurant, and Pierce

himself had quit his job as a bartender to spend more time with
Jesse's mother and her meth lab in southern Michigan. It was impossible to take time off for a funeral, too expensive and too far
away and so on.

The cremation ashes arrived by parcel service a few weeks
after his death, and one Sunday afternoon not long later, stoned
and feeling kind of ceremonial, Pierce took them out on a boat
and poured them into Lake Erie. He peered down at the surface
of the lake as the ashes soaked up the dark-green water and slowly
dissolved. That was it. There were a couple of exchanges of
emails, but, as it turned out, neither Pierce nor his brother ever
managed to get back to St. Dismas to clean out the house and put
all their things to rest. There wasn't anything of value in there,
and even the property wasn't worth the cost of the upkeep and
yearly property taxes.

So mostly their home was still here, just as they left it, a delin-
quent house that maybe the county owned now—Pierce didn't
know for sure. Maybe nobody owned it now, and it was just going
to melt into rot and ruin and vanish into the soil.

Out in the garage, Pierce found the shovel neatly stored
among the tools where it had always been, and he took it out into
the backyard to look for a place where possibly a hole could be
dug. The garden was high with weeds, and flocks of grasshop-
pers flicked themselves ahead of him as he walked through the
old plot. When they were growing up, Pierce's father was proud
of his tomato plants. They had pumpkins, zucchini, radishes, potatoes. None left, of course, but the soil was still soft enough to
dig a hole into.

. . .

Jesse was still sitting on the floor of Pierce's former bedroom, wearing that crown of Indian feathers, sifting through another box, and he didn't even look up as Pierce stood there in the doorway.

Jesse had found a little trunk under the bed, and Pierce guessed that the kid thought it was going to be something really special—pirate's treasure, gold doubloons and necklaces of jewels; who knows what he imagined. Pierce could picture the greedy look that Jesse's mother would get, hovering over her little Baggie full of clear, chunky meth crystals.

But when Jesse opened his treasure chest, there were only blocks. Wooden building blocks—red rectangles, blue squares, green cylinders, orange triangles. Jesse picked one up out of the trunk and examined it. Smelled it. He began to sift through the wooden pieces, thinking that there was something better underneath.

Pierce shifted a little. Of course, he knew what was in that little trunk, but he was surprised at how vividly a memory arranged itself in his mind.

He had an affection for blocks as a kid—he didn't know why. You have the soul of a carpenter, Pierce's father told him once, but his father was wrong about that, Pierce thought, as he was with most things he imagined he knew about Pierce's soul.

In fact, there hadn't been any particular artfulness or skill in the constructions Pierce made. That didn't really matter to him. Still, standing there at the edge of the room, listening to the xylophone rustle of wood as Jesse sifted his way toward the bottom of the trunk, Pierce could picture the game he used to play with them.

It was something to do with making a city, Pierce remembered. For a moment Pierce could distinctly recall the feeling of
being alone in the center of this old room. Stacking blocks into
skyscrapers. Clustering the skyscrapers into cities. How good it
felt to be alone, stacking blocks. That's what came to him again, a
kind of weight solidifying in his chest: how much he had loved to
be alone—to be outside of his own life, a giant, sentient cloud
looming over his imaginary city, hovering above it. There was a
certain kind of blank omniscience that felt like his true self, at last.

But then his father stood in the doorway, peering in at him,
and he looked up. The feeling flew up out of him like a startled
pigeon.

—What are you making? Pierce's father asked. He was smiling a little, hopefully, imagining his son with the soul of a carpenter, his son the builder, the architect, but Pierce's shoulders
tightened and his eyes grew flat, that joy of aloneness ruined.

—Nothing, Pierce said. His hand moved, as if innocently,
and the skyscrapers came down easily, spilling over into a scattered pile of disordered shapes.

—Oops, Pierce said.

I should just kill him, Pierce thought. *That would be the simplest
thing, if I was smart,* he thought. He imagined the gangster-type
people you saw on TV; they probably would have put a bullet in
the back of Jesse's head right then, while he was kneeling there,
pawing through the blocks. It would solve a lot of future compli-
cations.

...

Jesse must have heard the car start, because he came running out of the house just as Pierce was turning out of the driveway. Pierce had nearly forgotten the sort of dust plume that a car pulls up on those old dirt roads, and he could see Jesse in a cloud behind him, waving his arms.

—Hey, Jesse was yelling. Dad! Pierce! Come back!

It was the kind of devotion that Pierce's father would have been moved by. The kind of devotion he had deserved. How Pierce's father's heart would have broken, to see one of his sons wailing with sorrow, tears streaming, calling after him as he drove down the driveway.

There was about five miles of dirt road up ahead before Pierce got to two-lane blacktop, and then another twenty miles or so to the next town, another grain elevator tower rising up out of the prairie, with a little scattering of little houses around it, and then eventually the interstate and some cities and something. He could picture himself from above, from a distance. The landscape a series of geometric blocks. His car no bigger than a flea, and Jesse even smaller, running and shrinking, running and shrinking.

Thinking of You in
Your Time of Sorrow

The baby dies and there is a little funeral. Okay, try to insert yourself into that moment. Stay calm, stay cool, stay sane. No one else is crying. Everyone probably thinks it is for the best. After all the tortuous debates—abortion or no abortion, adoption or no adoption, marriage or no marriage—now suddenly everything can go back to the way it was. Meg is an ex-mother and you are an ex-father and she can go to college like she'd planned before she got pregnant and you can do whatever it is that you're going to do. That's right.

Through your sunglasses, you can look at Meg privately; you can observe the solemn congregation, your basketball buddies with their hands folded in front of their groins like they're posing for a team photo, your mom with her jaw set, some of Meg's relations. It's hard not to imagine a guilty sense of relief rippling across all their faces. You can see it as they bow their heads, and you clasp your hands in front of you. "Of dust thou art," the preacher intones, and Meg looks at you for a second, the kind of glazed look of someone who has just been startled awake, and then your younger brother, Dooley, who is all bloodshot and damp-faced, staring at you with his mouth quivering. You turn your head away and there are the waves of July heat flickering like holograms over the alfalfa fields beyond the cemetery.

You can be rude if you want—no one will blame you. You can skip the gathering afterward, where the women will bring covered dishes as if for a picnic and the men will sit in the yard near the beer keg your dad has bought, and maybe one of your friends—Jerry, probably, the quiet, sensitive one—will be sent out to scout for you. What you're doing is acceptable. You can drive the interstate with all the windows down, the music so loud it's distorted in the speakers, going twenty miles over the speed limit, and no one will say you're wrong. Everyone is thinking of you in your time of sorrow, everyone's heart goes out to you.

Where to now? People always say you have your whole life in front of you, but then again, doesn't everybody? You know what they mean, of course: that now you are free, you can get out of town like everyone else your age with any brains, you're not stuck anymore. That's what they're really saying, and you can appreciate it, though it takes some adjustment. For a while now, you've been getting used to another sort of life in your mind. In your imagination, you've been building houses, buying baby stuff, finding some sort of trade, like carpentry or plumbing. It was even beginning to seem like something you might even grow to like, though you know it wouldn't have worked out. Take a look around: The town is full of dumb clods who got their high school sweethearts pregnant. See how happy they are?

You haven't talked to Meg in a while. You risk seeming like an asshole in that regard, but what is there to say? The last time you saw each other, really, was when she was still in the hospital, right before the baby died.

The baby was born with a severely malformed heart, and there was nothing they could do except make it comfortable for its brief time in the world. It was a boy, who had to be given a name for the birth certificate, and death certificate. While Meg was still sedated, you chose "Caleb," because you thought it sounded cool, and sturdy, like a cowboy who could survive anyway when they told him he was going to die. But when you told Meg she looked at you with her high verbal SAT stare and said, "I wish you would have waited to ask me." Caleb meant "dog" in Hebrew, she said, and you felt awful. The baby was in a little plastic case; you couldn't even see what it looked like, really, with all the machinery and the white papery tube taped over its mouth.

Meg wouldn't go to see it. Him. She just stayed in her hospital bed with her face turned toward the wall, an IV dripping fluid into her arm, which was very gross, you thought. Her mother sat with her day and night, though when you would come in her mother left the room, trailing icy silence that echoed with a deeply godful prayer for you to die and suffer for a long time beforehand.

Meg said nothing. "Hey, baby," you said softly, and then were sorry. You should erase the word "baby" from your vocabulary, you dick, right along with "Caleb." When you touched her, she flinched. She knew that you were the one who put this deformed child inside of her. Everything inside both of you was separating and pulling apart, and already you were both calculating ways to get away from each other as quickly as possible. The two of you stood there, side by side, and the tectonic plates of your lives began to shift and resettle, continents separating. This is one of your younger brother's fascinations. Dooley is thirteen, and he likes to think about such stuff—he can tell you about the great landmass, Pangaea, which existed before the continents broke apart, and he can tell you the names of the insects and bacteria that will live long after mankind is extinct, and he can tell you of a time in the future when the sun will grow so hot that the earth will burn into a piece of charcoal. It puts things in perspective, Dooley says sometimes.

When you come home the night of the funeral, Dooley is still waiting up. He sits on the sofa, watching a Saturday night horror movie in which some old actor is running through the future, screaming. "Soylent Green is people!" he cries.

Dooley looks up, glazed, when you walk in. He stares at you, full of aching.

"What are you watching," you say quietly, and Dooley shrugs.

"Nothing interesting," he says, and stands awkwardly. "Everybody was wondering what happened to you," he says, and gives you his grim eyes. He believes in propriety.

Dooley is a homosexual. He hasn't really admitted it, but you know that he will become a gay person: It is already in the cards. There has always been a hint of it in his demeanor, but now you are more or less certain. A few months ago, you happened to come into the bedroom the two of you shared. He thought he'd locked it, but you'd given an irritable shove and it opened; there he was, kneeling by the bed, with pictures of half-dressed men taped to the wall in front of him. "Get out! I'm getting dressed!" he'd cried, trying to move quickly, but it was too late. "Sorry," you said, trying to pretend you'd seen nothing—though really you'd been noticing stuff for a while, so this came as no surprise. You've noticed the secret looks he gives your friends, the way he stiffened and backed away, panicked, when Jerry tried to wrestle playfully with him. You understood what Dooley's stricken, frightened look meant: He had a hard-on, and he was afraid that someone would notice. You can't help but think that life will be tough on him, unfairly tough, and that makes you sad. He's got a better heart than most people.

Like now. He feels the grief you should be feeling more keenly than you do, with the kind of dignity and self-possession you've never been able to manage. "You probably got out at about the right time," he says. "It got ugly."

You nod thoughtfully. "How bad?" you ask, and he shrugs.

"About medium," he says. "They got into a fight and everybody left. Mom's really pissed, though. She's going to nail you bad when she sees you."

"Asleep?"

"So far. Dad's passed out in the garage on a lawn chair. He's not going to wake up until morning. Did Jerry find you?"

"No," you say. "I was just out driving around."

"Well," Dooley says, and purses his lips diplomatically, "he was out looking for you, so maybe you should call him or something. I don't know, maybe you should stay over at his place, because Mom is . . . you know." He clears his throat. "Did you go see Meg?" he says hopefully, and when you shake your head his mouth grows smaller, more judicious. "Well," he says. Then his eyes widen in warning.

And you turn. Your mother is standing in the doorway, observing the two of you, her nightgown spectrally pale and billowy in the dark.

She's taken something, some pill, and she puts her hand on the door frame for support. "Look who's home," she says.

Brace yourself.

She is an angry woman, your mother. There are reasons for that, reasons that you might feel more or less sympathetic toward, if you had time to think about it. But there isn't time. There is only space enough to dodge what she is throwing at you—a cake of soap, which bounces harmlessly onto the sofa.

"Do you think of anybody but yourself?" she says, as if it is a real question, as if she just wonders. "I don't think I've ever met a person like you," she says, and she's gritting her teeth like she does when she's trying to keep calm. "Do you realize that people were out hunting you? There were fifty people at this house and they came to pay their respects to that baby and to give you their condolences. But you didn't even have the common decency to show up. You don't think about others. All you think about is me, me, me."

"Listen," you say. "I'm sorry! I was upset, that's all." Which is true—but her words get under your skin, and your face feels flushed. You can't think of how to explain. "I just needed to get away," you tell her. "I didn't think it would matter that much. Why should anybody care what I do? I mean, my God, it was my baby, not theirs!"

"Your baby!" she says, and you see that she will snap this up like a weapon, the way she is prone to do. "Let me tell you something, mister. That wasn't *your* baby. That was Meg's baby. All you did was have sex with a girl. That doesn't make you a father by a long shot, I'll tell you that right now. It doesn't give you the right to play the prima donna. What do you suppose people think of a person who decides a baby's funeral is a good time to put on a big show? How do you think they feel about such a person?"

"They think such a person is an asshole," you say. Why not? It's true.

"Exactly right," she says. "I couldn't have said it better myself."

"I'm sorry," you say, and she looks at you with such disdain that you lower your eyes. "I thought . . ." you say.

"No you didn't," she says. "You didn't think about anything. You just acted on a shitty little whim. That's your problem, sweetheart—you don't know what thinking *is*."

"I deserve that," you say, hoping to disarm her, but you don't.

"Yes you do," she said. "And probably worse than I can give you."

And then she is quiet, glaring at you, waiting for you to answer, though she knows she's won. You are speechless. You are a
big boy—six-one, 210 pounds—so you know that bawling won't
help, but it comes out of you anyway, a thin line of tears and snot,
not sorrow, but frustration and hate and shame. "I can leave,"
you say to her, and Dooley says, "Come on, come on," placing
himself between the two of you, because it can get worse—much
worse. It has before.

"I'll be so glad when I can get out of this place," you whisper.

And she grimaces with disgust. "Is that supposed to be a
threat?" she says. "You need to learn a new trick, sonny boy."

After that, you can't go to sleep. You sit there with Dooley, who
is silent in the waves of grimness you are emanating. The two of
you sit side by side as Dooley flips slowly through the channels—
music videos, home shopping networks, old black-and-white
movies, static.

"So," you say after a while, "do you think I'm an asshole?"

"No," Dooley says. "Not really." He looks at you sidelong,
gauging your reaction. "You should call some people," he says.
"That's what I would do. People will understand." He stares at
the screen thoughtfully, clicks forward. Women in sequined bath-
ing suits are dancing. "I think you should call Meg, too."

"Yeah," you say. "I know."

You wonder what is the worst thing that can happen to a person. How far from where you are is the very worst? You make
some calls in the morning, sitting at the kitchen table where your
mother can hear you apologize if she wants, though she pretends
she isn't paying attention. You go through the cards and call the

people—your relatives, your parents' friends, your coach. Your own friends can wait.

"I just wanted to let you know," you say. "I just wanted to say that I appreciated the card, and that I'm real sorry I wasn't able to see you last night. I went out for a drive to clear my head and I kind of lost track of things and didn't get back as soon as I should have. So I just wanted to apologize . . ."

Everyone is nice about it. Their voices are soft and considerate, and even their hard questions—How's your family holding up? Have you spoken to Meg? What are your plans now?—you can gloss over pretty well.

Dooley is in the living room on the sofa, watching cartoons with his blanket over his legs like a little kid, though he is also reading from the book he's been carrying around all summer, which is *A Brief History of Time* by that famous crippled scientist, and he's also raising his head occasionally to listen to you. Dooley is a whiz in this regard. He can juggle three or four things in his mind, though he often can hardly walk without tripping over himself.

You keep talking to people, repeating some of the lines, until your mother mumbles, "Mr. Smooth," under her breath, staring at you like you are a fake. And you have to wonder: Are you a fake? You don't even know, do you? You can't even hear yourself speaking anymore.

Jerry calls to cuss you out. He got the worst of it, not the rest of them, who sat around and drank beer and had pie and coffee and munched from a relish tray surrounded by funeral flowers. Jerry was out looking for you.

"What the hell, man?" Jerry says. He is the type of person who will always be your friend, for as long as you can stand to keep disappointing him. But the truth is, you're already starting to imagine a world without Jerry, who, in his loyalty, has begun to seem like a moron. People like Jerry, or even Dooley, for that matter, seem to lose IQ points every time they turn their faithful eyes toward you. You feel ashamed for them.

"Why didn't you call me, man?" Jerry says now, plaintively. "Everybody was, like, worried and freaked out for you. Like, who knew what could have happened to you? You should have just told me—I would have covered for you or whatever." He is silent for a moment, waiting for your apology, your explanation. "I mean, where did you go, man? I drove up to Meg's place, I drove down Union Ave., I drove down the interstate . . ." And he wants to hear that he was close, that he missed you by inches, by moments. That's all he wants, but for some reason you can't even bring yourself to give him that.

"I was just around," you say, "just around and about," you say, lightly enough that his quiet grows brittle with hurt. "Look," you say, "I'm sorry. I apologize," knowing that this probably wounds him more than anything. You can feel the edges of the friendship begin to crumble in the pause at the other end of the phone.

Burn, bridge, burn.

You have yet to call Meg. There are other people to call. The navy recruiter, for example. Imagine yourself aboard a ship, headed for other countries. Imagine yourself stupid and numb, yelled at by some abusive sarge, doing push-ups and marching while chanting stupid call-and-response rhymes. Try to insert yourself in that situation. It might not be so bad.

There are college brochures to look at. There is a fishing boat in Alaska that you read about in the back of your father's *Outdoorsman* magazine, six months and fifty thousand dollars, no healthy man turned away. There is your car and the open road, the fabled lure of random adventure. You stand at the verge, and you could become anything. Your future shifts and warps with your smallest step, your shitty little whims. The man you will become is at your mercy.

Already, one man you might have been is dead, and you should take some time to clear his cobwebbed bones from your mind. His house, his garden, his dull, loser job. His baby. And Meg—your former future wife—you should clear her out of your mind as well, before you speak to her, you should get rid of the wife you were already kissing good morning and fucking and loving into imagined decades. Wave good-bye to that alternate dimension, that other life. Dismiss that, and then call her and finish this—you'll be fresh and new as a squeaky baby leaf, unfolding.

But Fate intervenes. You hang up with Jerry and the minute the phone is down it rings. It's her: She's calling you, and you see Dooley lift above his cartoons and books; your mother freezes, like a deer in a forest before a bullet hits it.

"It's me," Meg says when you say hello, and that's all she needs to say.

"Hi," you say, and she clears her throat.

"Are you okay?" she says. "I heard that you went missing last night and I was worried. I mean, I heard a lot of shit. You're okay, aren't you?"

"Of course," you say. "I just went for a drive. You know."

"Yes," she says, and her thoughtful pause stings, needlelike, inside of you.

"Do you want me to come over?" she says, and your heart pinches like a nerve. You shrug against the phone.

"It doesn't matter," you say. "If you feel like it. It's up to you."

She is silent: hurt, maybe. "Okay," she says, coolly, uncertainly.

Why do you even bother? What can you do that isn't wrong?

What? Your dad is awake now, arising from his lawn chair in the garage and perambulating through the house in stocking feet, his footpads arousing your mother to the various sorrows of her own life. Dooley lays his open book on the arm of the sofa.

"Was that Meg?" Dooley asks, and you shrug at him.

"Yeah," you say, after a moment, and your mom and dad look at you, too. Your screwed-up family mobilizes their screwed-up attention.

"She's not coming to see you, Dooley," you say, and your eyes manage to wither him back into his sunken spot on the sofa. Jesus Christ, why are you so mean? Why do you act like such a rotten person?

Your mother could perhaps answer this for you but when she opens her mouth to speak your father says, "Leave him alone, Angie." He mutters, shaking his head at her. "Let him be, will you?" Good old Dad.

• • •

You're not a bad person. In fact, it was not so long ago that it seemed like you were the only one in your family who was doing anything right. People liked you in school, despite your weird family, you were good in sports—football, basketball, track—you got decent grades, you were dating a girl whose beauty and niceness were an honor to you and your family. Wasn't that enough? Wasn't it enough that you were willing to give your future to Meg and the baby? Didn't that prove something?

Maybe not. Maybe they can see something about you that you can't, and that's why you should be leaving. Go somewhere, someplace where—if you keep a low profile—people will assume that you are an all-right guy. An upstander, as Jerry says.

You are thinking about these things when Meg's car pulls into the driveway. You are standing on the porch, and in the background your parents are fighting again, and Dooley comes to the window from time to time, peering out at you with hopeful sorrow. You've put them behind you. Now you have only Meg to get through, and you'll be on the other side.

She's still beautiful, even after everything, that round heart-face and deep eyes, the perfect, fleshy, short-girl ass that would of course have become fat if she had married you, the hint of sadness in her face that you'd loved as if it were your own sadness, your self-pity made honest and real, and it does break your heart to see her as she opens the door and climbs out. You might have grown old with her, but now, this might be the last time you see her. Okay, insert yourself calmly into the scene: the clunk of the car door shutting, her tennis shoes scrunching on the gravel driveway, her eyes hooking into you.

"Hey," she says, and the syllable hangs in the air. You walk across the grass to meet her, and you recall that once there had been a babble of easy conversation between you, schoolbooks and gossip and future plans, all meaningless.

"Hey," you say, and the two of you face each other. Oh, please: if only you could give her what she wants, if only you knew what it was. Then it would be over and you could go.

"How are you doing?" you say.

"Okay," she says, and gives you a kind of smile—the kind of smile she might give Jerry, famously gullible Jerry, with his quotable dumb questions. You recall, out of nowhere, a Jerry-question the two of you used to laugh about: "Do fish freeze in the ice in the winter?" he'd asked, and she knew how to smile at such things. It is probably true, as you've often thought, that girls are wiser than boys, and having her smile at you like that makes you feel sorry for everything all over again.

"Sorry," you say.

"Don't be," she says. "I'm sick of people being sorry. I don't even know how I feel about it anymore."

"I know," you say, and you do understand, at least a little bit. "Me, neither."

"I just came over to see how you were doing," she says. She shudders a little. "I was worried."

"Why?" you say. You try to touch her for a moment, and she lets you, she lets you put your hand on her arm, but you can see that she really doesn't want you to; she moves back after a second: off-limits. She looks at you again, sighing heavily.

"People were saying that you died last night, did you know

that?" she says. She waits a minute, seeing that you didn't know, then shrugs. "That's what was going around. They said you killed yourself. You got drunk and drove into a tree. You know how it goes."

"Jesus," you say. "Who told you that? That's just sick! Who said that?"

"Oh, come on," she says, and flinches irritably. "I'm sure all your friends heard the story, and all my friends heard the story, and I'm sure they all passed it around among themselves. Like whispering down the lane. I mean, I don't even care where it started. They can't help themselves. It's all one big TV show to people."

"Well," you say. You let this sink in for a moment. What do people really think of you? "Well, I guess I'm still alive," you say at last. "Are you glad?"

"I don't know," she says. And that's not what you want to hear. But she only shrugs, doesn't look at you. "You know, the first thing I thought when I heard it was, like, 'Good for him.' I mean, I thought—at least you did *something*. Do you know what I mean? I guess I always thought it would be bigger, when a terrible thing happened. Didn't you think so? Doesn't it seem like the houses ought to be caving in, and lightning and thunder, and people tearing their hair in the street? I never—I never thought it would be this small, did you?" She wipes a hand over her nose, shutting her eyes tight. She looks small and fierce standing there, though everything in the neighborhood is quiet. A car passing in the distance is playing Top 40 music loudly, and sprinklers are ticking away on lawns, and an airplane is drawing a white line across the sky. She is not crying. "I'm glad you're all right," she says. She looks up at you as you stand stupidly. "I mean, you *are*, aren't you? You aren't going to kill yourself, are you?"

"Not unless you want me to," you say, and it's only half a joke—you don't know what the rest of it is. But she doesn't answer anyway, only puffs out her cheeks in a tired sigh.

"So," she says at last, "what are you going to do now?"

You notice, of course, that she doesn't say "we." That can't be helped, though it also tends to make your reply pretty much meaningless. You wave your hand vaguely. "Haven't decided yet," you say, and she nods.

What if you said, "We could still get married"? What if you said, "I still love you. We could have other kids." There was a time, before Caleb died, when you could have said it. You prayed to God, actually. Dear God, you said, please don't take my baby. I'm sorry that I ever bitched about Meg getting pregnant, I truly repent every negative thought I ever had, and I swear that I'll be a good father and a good husband and I'll be happy with my life. Please, God, you said, hunched outside the glass case of Caleb, his poor little monkey body drawing another breath, please, God, I made a mistake. I take it all back.

But you can't tell her this, either—your maudlin prayers would only hurt her, would only draw you both back to the baby's eyes, opening, raking across the incomprehensible world. That empty, terrible look: She knows it, too, though she never went to look at him like you did. You can see it in her expression as she shifts from foot to foot. There will be no more marriage, no more babies.

"Well," you say, "I would have married you, you know. I would have been happy."

"I know," she says. She is quietly thoughtful for a moment, but she is leaning away from you. You won't touch her again, or kiss her, and it's even hard to look her in the eye.

"Do you think we'll always be sort of in love with each other?" she says, and smiles at a sad thought she's thinking. She doesn't blame you, exactly, though she knows you should have been a different person. "Do you think we'll be always connected?"

You just shrug. "I don't know," you say. "I haven't lived that long."

Dooley comes out after she leaves. He's been watching, of course. He wants to know if something beautiful or tragic has happened, because he believes in beauty and tragedy. And though you don't want him near you, you don't have the heart to drive him away. At least he loves you—that's something. Watching the car pull away, you think of him at the window, watching Jerry playing touch football with you. You think of him offering up a complicated, scientific answer to one of Jerry's stupid questions, and Jerry widening his eyes in that earnest, good-natured way: "Whoa, you're brother's kind of a brainiac, isn't he?" and Dooley glowing at him. Watching her car turn left at the stop sign, you imagine that you and Dooley could understand each other perfectly, if you wanted. "Get this," you say, as he stands there expectantly behind you. "Rumor has it that I got drunk and drove myself into a tree last night. People are saying I killed myself."

"Geez," he says.

"People will talk," you say, and he nods. The fag of the school, he already knows this.

"But she wanted to know you were all right," he says hopefully.

"Yeah," you say. "She was thinking of me."

Your tone of voice makes him silent, and you both listen. The argument indoors has mellowed; there are no voices. They've gone to separate rooms, probably, or they might even be making up. This happens sometimes: There is evidence that they were once wildly in love. They got married young, as young as you and Meg are, and maybe if they hadn't had kids right away they would have been okay. You really don't know.

"They've quieted down," you say, and he tilts his head doubtfully.

"So far," he says.

But you wonder. If Caleb had lived, would Meg have hated him as much as your mom hates you? Would you have become an old drunk, like your dad? Does everything perpetuate itself?

Who knows? You and Dooley are here now—there's no turning back. You sit there together, and Dooley's fingers pick at one another nervously, as if he's trying to pluck words out of them.

"Did you guys make up?" he asks in a small voice, and you give him a hard look.

"What are you talking about?" you say, and you feel his big eyes turn on you—earnest, sad eyes, hoping for approval.

"You could still get married," he says. "You could have another baby." It's a squeak, a whisper, but of course it goes right through you like a thin arrow.

"No," you say. "That's not going to happen."

"But . . ." he says. And then, terribly, he starts to cry. "It's not fair," he says, and you stand there, frozen in place, as he snuffles stiffly, as kids are riding their bicycles on the sidewalk and the fourteen-year-old girl next door is setting out her towel on the front yard to sunbathe. "I miss the baby," Dooley tells you solemnly, wiping his eyes. "I know it sounds weird, but I would have liked to be an uncle. It would have been fun." He clears his throat. "Just that," he says, "it could be so different, that's the weirdest thing."

"It could have been so different," you repeat. What do you say to that? "Dooley," you say. "Let me tell you something. Look at your books. Look at *The Great History of Time,* or whatever the fuck it is. One person doesn't mean anything. There are how many people in the world? Five billion? Six billion? How long did you say it would take to count to a billion? You know, you told me once. Like a hundred years or something? One baby doesn't amount to a hill of beans, Dooley," you say, and when he gives you that stricken, red-eyed gape, you have to go on. He has to know, doesn't he? He's not a child anymore.

"Listen to me," you say, and you give him a hard shake, holding him tight by the scruff of his shirt. "Does it ever occur to you that you need to start thinking about yourself, Dooley? Does it ever occur to you that you don't fit in here, and you'll never fit in here, and that if you are ever going to be happy you are going to have to stop worrying about how different things could be and get out of this rotten place? That's what I'm going to do, and that's what you should do, as soon as you can. Does that ever occur to you? Or are you a total moron?"

Oh, horrible—to see him bawling like that, to feel him jerk away as you try to catch him. "Don't touch me!" he cries. "You don't know me! You don't have any idea what would make me happy, you asshole, you asshole," he cries. And you can hold him in your arms, you can restrain him. You can hug him, rocking.

But there's something in his eyes that frightens you.

What if it's more terrible than you think? What if Dooley knows more than you? What if you have to carry this dead baby with you forever? What if you have to linger with this for the rest of your life?

That wouldn't be fair, would it?

Slowly We Open Our Eyes

1

O'Sullivan and his older brother, Smokey, have been driving in silence for a long while when the deer steps out of the darkness and into the middle of the road.

For a second, it seems as if the world is paralyzed. They can see the deer with its hoof lifted, taking a delicate step into their path, dreamy as a sleepwalker. They can see the enormous skeletal bouquet of antlers as it turns to face them. They can see the truck's headlights reflected on the blank black surface of its eye.

Then they hit it. The thump of the body blow comes almost simultaneously with the shatter of the windshield, the blinding swash of blood across the glass. "Watch out! A deer!" O'Sullivan cries belatedly, and Smokey says, "No kidding, motherfucker," and he yanks the steering wheel to the left and right. The truck lurches sideways toward the ditch. It seems likely, O'Sullivan thinks, that they will flip over and roll down the embankment and burst into flames.

So when they don't—when, instead, they come to a stop at the side of the road and the dust uncoils its slow eddies into the tangle of headlights—it almost doesn't seem real. The two of them sit there, speechless for a moment, until finally Smokey turns on the windshield wipers. The wipers twitch like the last gasp of an insect leg and smear an arc through the grue.

"Oh my God," O'Sullivan says. "Yuck."

2

Things had turned bad for O'Sullivan in Chicago, and he had decided to make a new start of things out west. O'Sullivan liked the sound of this sentence, its muscular clarity. *Things went bad for O'Sullivan,* he thought, as Smokey's eighteen-wheeler truck pulled up in front of his apartment. O'Sullivan also liked the idea of people calling him "O'Sullivan," though for most of his life he had been known by his first name, Donald, or Don, or Donnie, all of which struck him as rather small and petty. To say, "Donnie had decided to make a new start of things out west," sounded somehow more pathetic.

He hadn't yet decided what the "new start" would involve. In actuality, O'Sullivan and Smokey were on their way home for their grandmother's funeral, and O'Sullivan had not yet told his parents that he planned to stay on indefinitely, that he was hoping that he could live in his old room for a little while, that he was not only broke and without a job and a month past due on his rent, but he had also managed to amass a fairly significant credit card debt.

It had been their mother's idea to have Smokey pick O'Sullivan up as he passed through Chicago, because O'Sullivan of course couldn't afford a plane ticket home for the funeral. She had been nonplussed by this admission, she almost seemed like she didn't believe him. O'Sullivan was, after all, a college graduate, the first person in his family to reach this pinnacle, and his mother was so far blissfully unaware that her son had no marketable skills whatsoever—yet another liberal-arts major who found himself struggling to hold down a job in the service industry. Waiter: fired. Bartender: fired. Hotel room service: also fired.

Smokey, meanwhile, had dropped out of high school and had been driving trucks for a good ten years now. *Makin' great money!* he said. And there was, O'Sullivan felt, a certain level of aggressiveness in the way that Smokey parked the big semi truck outside O'Sullivan's apartment building and blew the big foggy lighthouse horn until O'Sullivan came to the fourth-floor window to peer out.

It would have been nice, he thought, to leave with some dignity. He would like to say: "O'Sullivan swung his duffel bag into the cab of his brother's semi and they sped away, toward the silver strip of interstate, heading into the horizon." But the fact was that O'Sullivan had three suitcases and several large plastic garbage bags full of his stuff and one box of books that had to be shoved and argued into the narrow storage area in the back of the semi cab.

"What the fuck?" Smokey said. "Looks like you're taking your whole goddamn apartment with you!"

"Not exactly," O'Sullivan said.

There was an awkward silence. The apartment building disappeared in the rearview mirror and the truck crawled out of Evanston and into Skokie, inching, stoplight by stoplight, toward the interstate. The cab of the truck smelled like motor oil and pine air freshener and male body odor. They were suddenly vividly aware of how little they knew of each other, how little they had in common. How long had it been since they had actually spoken to each other? Two years, maybe?

"So," O'Sullivan said. "What's been going on with you?"

Smokey sighed, and the air brakes sighed too as the traffic light turned green. "Oh, not too much," he said. "Just workin'."

"Yep," O'Sullivan said. He nodded masculinely.

Some time went past. O'Sullivan became aware that there was, in addition to the other odors, a very strong smell of diesel fumes, which made his forehead feel like it was slightly expanding.

"So," O'Sullivan said. "Too bad about Grandma and everything."

"I guess," Smokey said. "She was pretty old."

"Yeah," O'Sullivan said.

"And she'd gotten pretty mean, too, in those last months," Smokey said without taking his sunglassed eyes from the road. "She really gave everybody a hard time."

"Huh," O'Sullivan said. "I guess it had been a while since I talked to her, actually."

"Lucky you," Smokey said.

He handed O'Sullivan a flask of peppermint schnapps, and O'Sullivan took it and drank without comment.

3

Smokey is driving a semi truck whose primary purpose is the transport of medical and other hazardous wastes. This is Smokey's specialty—he has a particular license and various authorizations to drive such a vehicle, which is somewhat scary, O'Sullivan thinks. "So what is medical waste, exactly?" O'Sullivan had asked after a long stretch of silence had unraveled, and Smokey filled him in with far more detail than he probably cared to know.

So now O'Sullivan has a pretty good idea. There are probably used needles and tongue depressors and cotton balls; also rubber gloves, empty intravenous bags, bloody bandages, culture dishes, scalpels, swabs, lancets . . . no doubt a few pieces of people as well, tonsils, placentas, appendixes, malignant tumors—whatever kinds of goop might be contained inside the human body. It grosses O'Sullivan out quite a bit; he thinks of it all stuffed and sloshing in the yellow plastic "hazard" drums that are stacked up in the trailer they are pulling.

As they sit on the edge of the highway after the deer incident he is faced with the image of the semi jackknifing and the barrels bouncing along the asphalt and cracking open. He pictures amputated human arms flopping like fish down the center of the road; syringes floating on beds of liposuctioned fat; gelatinous human eyeballs wiggling merrily as they roll down the highway; and so on. He could continue to imagine other such grotesque stuff, but chooses not to.

"Jesus Christ," O'Sullivan says, and Smokey looks at him, blinking slowly, as if he's just woken up. "Jesus," O'Sullivan says. "Did we kill it?"

"We didn't even hit the thing, I don't think," Smokey says, and then lets forth a colorful string of truck-driver curses. "We must have missed that son of a whore by the most gossamer of hairs."

O'Sullivan is silent. Nonplussed. The truck is tilted a little on an embankment, and the headlights illuminate a tangle of oddly slanted trees and shadows.

"Well," O'Sullivan says, "we must have hit something. I definitely heard a thump." But when they get out to look, there is nothing there. No twitching hooves, no rack of antlers, no mangled body. Upon inspection, the gore on the windshield looks like it might be reddish mud. There's a crack in the glass, but it isn't shattered, after all.

4

"These pills are mostly a mixture," Smokey said, handing O'Sullivan a plastic Ziploc baggie. "They're just ordinary pharmaceuticals, but they'll still get you happy in various ways."

"Isn't it dangerous?" O'Sullivan said.

"What?"

"Mixing pills and alcohol. Isn't that dangerous?"

"Of course," Smokey said. "But you're twenty-four years old! Where's your sense of adventure? You're supposed to think you're immortal."

"That's true," O'Sullivan said, somewhat apologetically. He put a pill carefully into his mouth, then swallowed another drink of the schnapps they'd been passing back and forth. "Brr." He shivered.

"You'll feel better after a time," Smokey said. "Don't be a pussy."

"I'm not," O'Sullivan said.

"You want to hear a joke?"

"Okay," O'Sullivan said.

"So there's three guys, right? A Frenchman, an American, and a Russian. And they're sitting out in the woods, in a cabin, having a drinking competition, which is, first you have to drink a bottle of vodka, and then after you drink every last drop you have to go outside and shake hands with a bear, and then, finally, they have to make mad, passionate love to a beautiful woman."

"Wait," O'Sullivan said. "I thought they were in a cabin. Where'd the beautiful woman come from?"

"Never mind that," Smokey said irritably. "She's just there."

"Oh," O'Sullivan said.

"So anyways," Smokey said, "first thing, the Frenchman drinks a half a bottle of vodka, but he passes out before he finishes."

"A pussy," O'Sullivan said.

"Just like you," Smokey said. "Now it's the American's turn. He drinks the whole bottle of vodka, but before he can get outside to shake hands with the bear, he gets stupefied and passes out, too. Right? Now, finally there's the Russian. He drinks down the whole bottle of vodka, no problem. Then he marches out into the woods. You hear a lot of roaring and thrashing around out there, but finally he comes back inside. He's a little messed up, breathing hard, clothes a little ripped, but he's still standing, and he looks around the cabin.

"'Where is beautiful woman?' he says. 'I have to shake hands with her, and then I am winner!'"

O'Sullivan was silent for a while. He considered.

"I don't get it," O'Sullivan said.

5

They had been driving for a long while, and as the afternoon waned it had begun to seem to O'Sullivan that they were traveling along the same identical fifty miles of interstate over and over, the landscape scrolling past the windshield as if it were a film strip looped and repeated—fields and farmhouses, exit signs and fast-food oases. Lots of roadkill. Dogs, cats, deer, raccoons, skunks. Even once a fox, which made him inexplicably sad.

Things always seemed to go bad when O'Sullivan was around, he thought.

He had been trying to put this thought out of his mind, or at least to get things into perspective. He hadn't killed anyone, he reminded himself. He had only stolen a little from his various employers, most of whom deserved it in any case; he had sold drugs, but only briefly, because he was desperate for money; he had lied—a lot, it was true—to nearly everyone he knew, and had taken advantage of friends' generosity until they ceased to be friends. He had—in the three years since graduating from college—accumulated mountainous debts, not even including his student loans, and there seemed no escape from it, nothing but an endless stream of bad jobs that made him depressed so he charged something on the credit card to make himself feel better or he drank too much at night and couldn't get up the next day to go to work . . . clearly it was a bad cycle, something had to be done.

O'Sullivan had decided to make a fresh start out west, O'Sullivan thought. *The interstate unreeled beneath the eighteen-wheeler's rumbling bulk*

Things had gone bad for O'Sullivan in Chicago and as he sat in the cab of his brother's semi truck he stared fixedly out at

What now? O'Sullivan thought as he stared moodily out at the unreeling interstate highway

O'Sullivan didn't know what lay before him but a vague sense of dread hovered as he stared out at the unreeling

Shit.

He would have to throw himself on the mercy of his parents, he thought. He would have to beg them to help him. To save him from the inevitable fuckup from which he couldn't escape. And they might even find it weirdly satisfying, both of them high school dropouts, they might be secretly pleased to discover that college was nothing but a scam, a big Ponzi scheme being perpetrated on the hopeful youth of the nation.

He sighed. Out the window, O'Sullivan could see that a motorcycle was passing on the right-hand side, and when the motorcycle rider saw O'Sullivan looking down he gave a big grin and a jokey, two-fingered Boy Scout's salute. All afternoon they had been leapfrogging each other down the highway, Smokey's semi and the motorcycle, one passing the other, then slowing and being passed in turn. O'Sullivan watched as the motorcycle advanced past them, swerving around several slower-moving vehicles and skating onward toward the horizon, the silver spokes of its wheels glinting in the sunlight, the rider's long hair flapping like a pennant.

O'Sullivan swung onto his motorcycle and gunned the engine. He had nowhere to go, no responsibilities, nothing held him down. The great unreeling expanse of the highway opened before him and he grinned, his long mane of hair unfurling behind him in the wind of velocity and his

Unfurling?

Undulating?

His long hair undulating behind him as he sped toward

6

The semi truck has come to rest on the berm on the edge of an embankment. A corrugated metal guard rail runs parallel to the highway, and beyond the guard rail is darkness. Trees. A cliff, perhaps?

What now? O'Sullivan thought

Outside of the cab, illuminated by the blinking of the semi's orange hazard lights, O'Sullivan scratches his head. He is still having a hard time believing that they didn't hit anything.

Behind him, Smokey has unzipped his pants and is taking a whiz alongside his truck. O'Sullivan can hear the sound of pee pattering on the tire.

Up ahead, he can just barely see a thin white shape in the darkness. He thinks maybe it's a tree, or the skeleton of a road sign. For a second, it might even be the shape of a person standing there.

"Hello?" he says.

He takes a couple of steps down the road. The blinking light from the semi has a mild strobing effect, so that the figure appears to move forward and then draw back into the darkness, forward and back in the steady pulsing hazard lights. *Is that a scarecrow?* O'Sullivan wonders. He squints.

About fifteen yards down, O'Sullivan sees a white cross.

It is a little bit shorter than O'Sullivan himself is, and it is wearing a hat. Or—rather—a hat has been attached to the top of the cross, a baseball cap. At the base of the cross is a pile of brightly colored objects. There are some plastic flowers—pink roses, yellow daffodils, white lilies—and a green Christmas wreath, and a cluster of stuffed animals, bunnies and teddy bears and duckies, and ribbons, which wave lethargically in the light breeze. There is something written on a banner, but he can't make out the words. As they've driven across the country, he has been noticing that there are a lot of these little roadside memorials dotted all along the highway. A lot of people die in car accidents, obviously.

But it seems like there are more of them these days. Or maybe it is just that they are more elaborate. When did people begin to decorate these accident sites as if they were shrines?

"Hey, Smokey," he says. "Check this out."

And then he notices another one, just a few yards farther down. He can only barely make it out in the darkness. Another cross with a circle of offerings beneath it.

7

They were pulling into an interstate oasis, and the sudden reduction in speed slowed the conversation into an ellipsis.

". . ." O'Sullivan said, and Smokey shook his head silently.

"I've got to get some gas."

When they stopped, O'Sullivan got out of the cab and walked quickly toward the bathrooms and vending machines. He was hoping to quickly throw up and then buy himself a Dr Pepper and a candy bar to cut the taste of vomit. It had occurred to him, suddenly, as his feet touched the asphalt, that he might die. His heart was pulsing alarmingly against his rib cage, and as he stumbled woozily toward the restrooms, the distant door frame began to waver. The solid rectangle appeared to quiver gelatinously, and an irregular twitch started up under his left eye.

Am I having a heart attack? he wondered.

Then he was in the stall, holding the metal-gray graffiti-scratched walls as he retched.

Then he felt a little better. He stood there at the sink, cupping cool water in his palms and pressing his face into it. He looked at himself, drawn and sallow in the mirror, and dipped back down.

"Are you okay, man?" said Smokey, behind him.

"Sort of," O'Sullivan said, but then, when he lifted his head, it wasn't Smokey. It was actually some other guy who he didn't quite know, and the guy was now standing at the row of fluorescent-lit sinks beside him. O'Sullivan felt certain that he recognized this person from somewhere. He had the uncomfortable presentiment that it was one of the many people he had wronged in his life.

"Hey, man," O'Sullivan said familiarly, as if he completely recognized the person. "What are *you* doing here?"

Then he realized: It was the motorcycle guy. They'd passed each other probably a dozen times in the past three hundred miles. Once, he'd seen the guy pumping gas at the same gas station where they were pumping gas. Later, the guy was throwing away his trash at a fast-food place just as O'Sullivan and Smokey were walking in.

"Dude," the guy said, "you have a little fleck of puke on your chin."

"Oh," O'Sullivan said. He brushed at the spot with his fingers. "Thanks," he said.

"No problem," the guy said. He considered O'Sullivan's face

for a moment, not unkindly. "Get some fresh air, man. I've been there before myself."

"Yeah," O'Sullivan said.

"You'll be all right," the guy said. He patted O'Sullivan on the back with his black-gloved hand. "I hope you're not driving," he said.

"I'm not," O'Sullivan said.

"That's good news for the rest of us," the motorcycle guy said, and gave a grin, the same grin he'd had when they passed on the interstate, the one O'Sullivan would see in his mind a while later, when he thought back to this day, when he thought about the bad things he had done in his life.

O'Sullivan lowered his face into the cold water. When he raised up, the guy was gone.

Then O'Sullivan found himself standing outside the rest stop, holding an RC Cola and a Reese's peanut butter cup, taking in the sharp late-autumn air. His brain felt unusually empty, and when Smokey finally came up behind him, he was standing near the dog-walking area, trying to remember the names of constellations he should've been able to recognize, after a full semester of astronomy.

Sagittarius? Pegasus?

Centaurus?

"Jesus Christ," Smokey said. "I thought you died. Where the hell have you been?"

"Right here," O'Sullivan said.

"Well, let's go, then! This isn't some fuzzy-chinned college-boy yankabout. I'm a working man."

"All right," O'Sullivan said.

"It's time to hop," Smokey said. "I hope you don't mind if I *put the pedal to the metal,* as they say in truck-driving parlance."

"All right," O'Sullivan says. "Let's hop."

8

Smokey comes walking down the berm toward the roadside memorials, where O'Sullivan is standing.

"What have you found, little brother?" Smokey says, wiping the high beam of his flashlight down O'Sullivan's face and across his chest. Then he stops.

He shines his flashlight into the darkness beyond the memorial, and O'Sullivan notices another one, just a few yards farther down. He can only barely make it out in the darkness. Yet another cross with a circle of offerings beneath it.

He catches his breath. Because just beyond *that* cross is another one. And another. Five. Six. Seven crosses! Clustered there at the edge of the road.

And then—O'Sullivan stands frozen in the flashlight beam—he sees the deer, coming slowly toward him. The deer is stepping delicately through the little forest of memorials—*clip clip, clip clip,* the sound of hooves slowly approaching over asphalt—

"Well," Smokey says. "There's your fuckin' deer, I see."

The deer, the buck, is standing about fifteen yards away. It pauses for what seems like a long while, peering at them alertly, and then bolts abruptly. O'Sullivan has a glimpse of its sudden, jagged startle and leap, and in a moment it is gone, in a moment it is little more than a dark shape, a flicker, vanishing into the trees; there is a shudder of leaves and the shadows in between them.

"Oh," O'Sullivan says. It's funny, because all of a sudden, okay, now he gets that joke. The Russian guy had mixed things up. He'd fucked the bear and then was going to shake hands with the beautiful woman, instead of vice versa.

He doesn't know why the memory of that joke should make him shudder. He doesn't know why the sight of the living deer should fill him with such dread, such a weird sense of

What now? O'Sullivan thought as he stared out at the unreeling

Such a weird sense of something missing, something unremembered—a stove burner that you might have left on, an alarm clock that didn't go off. Instinctively, he puts his hand to his front pocket, to feel for his keys, but he has no keys. No car. No apartment.

He gazes at the cluster of crosses, the blank face of a stuffed bear, a silver pinwheel revolving slowly, glinting with the red of Smokey's emergency lights, the shuddering rustle of plastic flower petals, a ragged bit of ribbon flapping, undulating like long hair blown back in a breeze.

It will come to him in a moment, O'Sullivan thinks, though actually he doesn't want it to. It's that awful, inevitable feeling, the sound a bicycle makes when it is on its side, as the wheel's spinning slows and comes to a stop. The ticking of a roulette wheel as the marble finally settles in place.

"Oh my God," O'Sullivan says.

Shepherdess

1

This girl I've been seeing falls out of a tree one June evening. She's a little drunk—I bought a couple of bottles of hopefully decent Chardonnay from Trader Joe's on my way over to her house—and now she's a little drunk and a little belligerent. There is something about me that she doesn't like, and we've been arguing obliquely all evening. It's only our fifth real date, and though we've slept together once—it was the week after my mother died; pity sex, so it doesn't exactly count—we don't know each other that well.

For example, I just found out that she has an ex-husband who lives in Japan, who technically isn't an ex-husband since they haven't officially divorced.

For example, I didn't know that she thought I was a bad kisser: "Your kisses are unpleasantly moist," she says. "Has anyone ever told you that?"

"Actually, no," I say. "I've always gotten compliments on my kisses."

"Well," she says. "Women very rarely tell the truth."

I smile at her. "You're lying," I say cleverly. But she doesn't seem to catch the interesting paradox. She looks at me blankly and downs the last bit of wine in her glass. Then she turns her attention to the tree that rises up alongside the railing of her deck, her eyes following the trunk upward to where it branches out. She locates her cat, Mr. Niffler, about ten feet above us, where he has fled to escape the terror that is me, his claws affixed tightly into the bark, an expression of dyspeptic alarm on his face.

"Mr. Niffler," she calls. "Kitty, kitty, kitty. What are you doing up there?" And then she gets up and goes to the base of the tree. She hoists herself up on the two-by-six ledge of the railing and stands there, teetering for a moment.

"You know," I say, "that doesn't seem like such a good idea."

2

My mother appears in the doorway, silhouetted in the morning light. Her dark hair stands up stiff, like a shrub. Smoke from her cigarette curls up. I'm half awake but I can see how bony she is, a skeleton in a nightie, barely ninety pounds. She's not much heavier than the two Brittany spaniels that hover behind her—Lady and Peaches, my mother's dogs, watching as she wakes me, alert and so quiveringly shy around men that they sometimes pee a little when I speak to them. I can feel their tension as I stir in my bed.

"Okay," I murmur. "I'm up, I'm up." But my mother and her dogs just stand there. My mother is a few weeks away from her sixtieth birthday and I am nearly forty, but for a moment, here in my old teenage room, we replay our roles from the past. She knows that if she leaves, I will roll over and go back to sleep. Lazybones.

So after a moment, I sit up. I'm an adult, and I wipe my fingers across my face. "What time is it?" I say, though she can't hear me.

She's been deaf for almost five years now. A freak infection shut her ears down despite various attempts at intervention by various doctors—but the truth is that in half a decade she hasn't done much to help herself. She stopped going to her lip-reading classes early on, and forget about sign language or anything like that. She refuses to hang out with other deaf people.

Mostly, to be honest, I don't know what she does with herself. I don't know who her friends are or where she goes or what she does with her soundless days. The dogs make little anxious noises as I pull the covers off myself, and I watch as my mother turns, as her bare, crooked feet slide across the carpet toward the kitchen, where she will make me coffee and breakfast. It's about six in the morning, time for me to drive back from Nebraska to Los Angeles, where my fairly successful grown-up life is waiting for me.

I am in between my second and third date with Rain at this point, and I'm looking forward to seeing her—things are going well, I think. "I've met a girl I really like," I tell my mother. At the time, I have no idea that she will fall out of a tree. I have no idea that she thinks I am a bad kisser.

3

In the emergency room, there is a Plexiglas barrier between me and the receptionist, whose name tag says VALENCIA.

"I'm here with Rain Welsh," I tell her, and she asks me how to spell it. I have the purse and the billfold and I put Rain's driver's license and insurance card through the little mouth hole at the bottom of the glass wall.

"Are you the husband?" Valencia asks me, and I shift awkwardly, looking at the stack of neatly rowed credit cards in Rain's billfold.

"I'm the boyfriend," I say. "I don't really know that much about her. She fell out of a tree."

"Please take a seat in the waiting area," Valencia says. She gestures toward the couches just beyond. A series of five Mexican children—boys and girls, aged approximately two to nine—are sitting politely together, watching a sitcom on the television mounted on the wall.

"Do you know how long it's going to be?" I ask Valencia. But that's not the right question. "Is she going to be all right?" I say, and our eyes meet for a moment. I am usually pretty good at these kinds of encounters—I have the face of a nice person—but Valencia doesn't approve. "Take a seat," Valencia says. "I'll let the doctor know that you're waiting."

4

I've been talking to myself a lot lately. I don't know what that's about, but my mother was the same way. She hated to make small talk with other people, but get her into a conversation with herself and she was quite the raconteur. She would tell herself a joke and clap her hands together as she let out a laugh; she would murmur to the plants as she watered them, and offer encouragement to the food as she cooked it. Sometimes I would walk into a room and surprise her as she was regaling herself with some delightful story, and I remember how the sound would dry up in her mouth. She stood there, frozen in the headlights of my teenage scorn.

Now, as I close in on my fortieth birthday, I find myself doing a lot of the same sort of things. An ant crawls up my leg and I say, "Excuse me? May I help you?" before I slap and crush it. I get up in the morning and narrate my way through the rituals of awakening. "Okay, we're taking a shower now," I whisper, and I mumble shampoo into my hair and toothpaste into my mouth and stand mesmerized in front of the coffee machine. At times, the procedure seems heartbreakingly complicated—grinding the beans into dust, separating the filter from the packet (which requires the same kind of fine-motor skills as threading a needle), bringing water from the sink to the reservoir of the automatic coffeemaker. My God, it's like building a house every morning, just to get a cup of coffee! I stand there at the counter holding my mug, waiting as the water burbles through its cycle and trickles into the pot. "Okay," I encourage softly. "Okay, go—go!" At times I get very urgent with my coffee, as if I am watching a horse race that I have a lot of money riding on. Now, in the emergency-room parking lot, I am having a very involved talk with the contents of my girlfriend's purse. "I cannot believe this is happening," I mutter to the handbag confidentially. "This is ridiculous," I say, and then I find what I'm looking for. "Well, hello, beautiful," I say, to a crumpled pack of extra-long, extra-thin, feminine cigarettes: Misty, they are called.

5

My mother collapses on the floor of her bedroom. She is perhaps on her way to the bathroom or to let the dogs out. I am sleeping in a motel outside of Provo, headed back to L.A., and she lies there with her face pressed against the carpet, unconscious. The dogs are anxious, pacing from the bedroom to the back door in delicate circles, nosing my mother with their muzzles, whimpering introspectively. They lower themselves down beside her and rest their heads against her side as her breathing slows and she goes into a coma. They lick her salty skin.

She is still alive when her neighbor friend comes by the next morning. The dogs have relieved themselves in the kitchen, unable to control their bladders any longer, and they hide in shame under the bed as the neighbor friend calls my mother's name. "Mary Ann! Mary Ann!" the friend, Mrs. Fowler, calls. Even though my mother has been deaf for as long as they've known each other, Mrs. Fowler nevertheless continues to speak at her— loudly, steadily determined, oblivious. When she sees my mother on the floor, she screams like a maid in a murder mystery. When I get back to Los Angeles, there is a message waiting for me on my answering machine. "Charles," Mrs. Fowler will recite in her most declamatory voice. "This Is Mrs. Fowler. Your Mother's Friend. I Am Sorry To Have To Tell You That She Is In The Hospital, And Very Ill."

After I've listened to the message a few times, I get on the cellphone and call Rain. "Listen," I say, "it looks like I'm going to have to cancel our date again. You won't believe this but I have to fly back to Nebraska. My mom's in the hospital! It must have happened practically the minute I left!"

"Oh, my God," she says. Her voice is soft with concern, actually very warm and—though we've only dated briefly— seemingly full of genuine tenderness. I imagine her touching my hand, stroking my forearm. She has beautiful dark-brown eyes, the ineffable sadness of a girl who drinks too much—I'm drawn to that.

"Actually," I say, "I think my mom's going to die. I just have this feeling."

"Go," Rain says, firmly. "Just get on that plane and go to her," Rain says. "Call me when you get there."

6

I know that she is going to fall, but I'm not sure how to stop her. I stand there, with my hands clasped awkwardly behind my back as she shimmies unsteadily up the tree toward her cat. "You know," I say, and clear my throat. "Rain, honey, that doesn't seem like such a good idea." She pauses for a moment, as if she's listening to reason; and then, abruptly, she loses her hold on the branch. I watch as her body plunges down like a piece of fruit, not flailing or screaming or even surprised, but simply an expressionless weight coursing to earth. She hits the edge of the deck's railing, knocking over a plant, and I say: "Oh, my God!" And then she lands on her back. "Oh, my God," I say again, and finally have the sense to move toward the flower bed where she has come to rest.

"Are you hurt?" I say, leaning over her, and for a moment she doesn't open her eyes. I take her hand and squeeze it and a tear expels itself from beneath her eyelid and runs down her face.

The wind has been knocked out of her, and at first her voice is hinged and creaky. "I'm so embarrassed," she whispers, wheezing. "I'm such an idiot."

"No, no," I say. "Don't worry about it."

But she begins to cry. "Ow," she says. "It really hurts!"

I bend down and kiss her on the mouth, comfortingly. "It's okay," I murmur, and run my hand over her hair. But she flinches, and her eyes widen.

"What are you doing?" she gasps. "I can't feel my legs." And then she begins to cry harder, her mouth contorting with a grimace of sorrow like a child's. "Don't touch me!" She cries. "I can't feel my legs! I can't feel my fucking legs!"

7

Another hour passes. The five children and I sit in the waiting area and watch the television together, and I keep my eye on them. These children seem to know what they're doing, whereas I have never been in a hospital waiting room before. Rain's purse sits in my lap and the children laugh politely along with the pre-recorded laughter on the soundtrack of a comedy show.

I am not really sure how I am supposed to behave in this situation. I can't help but think that I should be sitting at Rain's bedside, pressing her damp hand between my palms. I should be arguing vehemently with doctors, demanding results, I should be surrounded by people who are bleeding and screaming and shocking one another with defibrillators. I sit there for a while longer, imagining this romantic pandemonium, and then finally I go to stand in line at the reception booth again.

When I sit down in the chair opposite the bulletproof glass, Valencia stares at me grimly. "Yes?" she says, as if she has never seen me before.

"Hi," I say. "I was just checking on the status of Rain Welsh. I've been sitting here for a while and I hadn't heard anything so I thought . . ."

"And you are . . . ?" Valencia says.

"I'm the boyfriend. I'm the one that called the ambulance. I've been sitting right over there waiting because you said . . ."

But she is already looking away, staring at her computer screen, which faces away from me, typing a little burst of fingernail clicks onto her keyboard. Pausing, pursing her lips. Typing again. Pausing to consider. Typing again.

"She's in X-Ray right now," Valencia tells me at last, after several minutes.

"Well," I say, "do you have any idea how long it's going to be? I mean, do you have any idea what the situation is? I've been sitting here patiently for a long time now, and I'd just like to know . . ."

"That's all the information I have, sir," Valencia murmurs firmly, and gives me a look that says: *Are you going to give me trouble? Because I know how to handle troublemakers.*

"So I guess I'll just wait," I say. "I'll just wait right over here."

8

NO SMOKING ON HOSPITAL GROUNDS, so I head out to the bus stop on the sidewalk just beyond the parking lot and stand there to smoke one of the nasty Mistys that I found in the purse. It has a kind of perfumey, mentholated flavor, like a cough drop dissolved in Earl Grey tea.

I had no idea that Rain smoked, and in some ways this makes me like her more. The fact that she was shy about it, that she wanted to hide it from me. That's kind of sweet.

I've always liked the idea of smoking more than I liked the actual smoke. Watching someone smoke in movies, for example, is a lot more pleasant than waking up after a pack of cigarettes and coughing up a yellow-green slug of phlegm.

Nevertheless I have a predilection for it. My mother was a fiercely committed smoker, and, growing up, I probably ingested half-a-pack-a-day's worth of secondhand smoke. I've always found cigarettes comforting, a taste of childhood, the way some people feel about Kellogg's cereal or Jell-O or Vicks VapoRub.

I'm just about finished with my smoke when I look up and see three women coming toward me. The women are being led out of the emergency room in their gowns and slippers, pushing their wheeled IV stands down the sidewalk. The IV stands look like bare silver coat racks; a clear plastic bag full of clear liquid hangs from each one, and a tube runs from each bag to each woman's arm. They walk along, single file, followed by an orderly who is talking on a cellphone. When they get close to me, they all stop, take out packs of cigarettes, and light up.

It's pretty surreal, I guess. I didn't realize that such things were allowed, but apparently they are desperate enough for nicotine that someone (the orderly, smoking himself) has decided to take pity on them. Has sneaked them out the back door for a quick fix.

This isn't, after all, the fanciest neighborhood in the world, nor the nicest of emergency rooms. The women are all poor to working class, grim-faced, clearly having a bad day, and I can't help but think of my mother—who wouldn't go anywhere unless she could smoke. Had, in fact, once left a hospital in outrage because they refused to give her a "smoking room."

I stand up, gentlemanly, and nod as the women approach.

"Hello, ladies," I say. "Beautiful evening."

Having grown up kind of poor to working class myself, I can't help but feel a kinship with them. "You really romanticize the white-trash period of your life," Rain once said to me, which I thought was a little hurtful but perhaps true.

There is, for example, this blond woman who reminds me of my mother's side of the family—all sharp cheekbones and shoulder blades and sinewy muscle, a body built for hardscrabble living—and I smile companionably at her as she breathes smoke into the night air. She is gazing off toward some cheap apartment buildings in the distance, the vertical rows of identical balconies, and I stare out with her. Together we look up and see the moon.

9

As expected, she's dead by the time I get there. By the time my plane touches down she's being moved from the hospital to the funeral home, and her friend Mrs. Fowler calls me on my cellphone as I'm standing in line at the rental-car place.

"Charles," Mrs. Fowler says. "Would you go and sit down somewhere for me, honey? Sit down in a comfortable chair." And then her voice breaks. "I have some terrible news."

About two hours later, I pull into the driveway of my mother's house in my rented car and it still hasn't sunk in.

The death of a parent is one of those momentous occasions, one of the big events of your life, but what do you *do*, exactly? My father died when I was three, so I barely even remember it, and my ex-wife's mother passed away during the early, happiest years of our marriage, and I hardly had to do anything at all; I just stood by looking sympathetic and supportive and people would occasionally nod at me or pat me on the shoulder.

So: sinking in. I sit there in my car, idling in the driveway, and I try to remember exactly what went on at the funeral of my late ex-mother-in-law but my mind has gone completely blank. Here is the door of my mom's house, well-remembered childhood portal. Here is the yard, and a set of wires that runs from the house to a wooden pole, and some fat birds sitting together on the wires, five of them lined up like beads on an abacus.

I left home when I was eighteen—more than twenty years have passed!—and though I came back dutifully every year the connections that held us together grew more threadbare as time went on.

I can remember being about five or six and running around and around that lilac bush in the front yard, chased by Mother. Laughing, joyous, etc.

I turn off the ignition in the rental car and after a minute I take out my cellphone and call Rain.

I don't know why. We seem to have connected, she seems like a very bright, sensitive, caring woman.

"This is Rain," she says. She is in the midst of directing a commercial, a public-service announcement about teen suicide, and her voice has an official snap to it.

"I need some advice," I say. "I'm not sure what to do."

"Charlie?" she says, and I love the way that she says my name, a matter-of-fact tenderness.

"My mom's dead," I tell her.

10

A little past midnight, the television has been shut off and the children in the waiting room are huddled together in a row on the chairs, leaned up against one another, smallest to largest, sound asleep.

How long are people expected to wait in these places? No one seems to know the answer, though as time has passed I've tried to engage some of my fellow waiters in conversation on the subject.

"I've been waiting here for five hours," I disclose, and people regard me with varying degrees of commiseration. "Does that seem normal?" I ask them. I don't know why I do this: why, after all these years in Los Angeles, I still have the Nebraska-like urge to banter with strangers.

I seem vaguely familiar to people, which is frequently a kind of advantage, particularly in Los Angeles. They are always asking: Do I know you from somewhere? And I shrug modestly. Probably they have recognized my voice from television commercials, or—especially if they have children—from one of several popular animated series such as *Fuzzy Fieldmouse and Friends*. One of my specialties is the earnest, disarmingly boyish voice. "I don't know if I can do it," Fuzzy Fieldmouse often says. "But I know I can try!" Anyone who watches children's programming on public television has no doubt heard me utter this phrase.

Which is not to say that this gives me any particular leverage in a situation such as this one. It's not as if I can throw my weight around with Valencia: "Do you realize that I am the voice of Fuzzy Fieldmouse?" doesn't exactly open too many doors.

Though I have to admit that I am used to being a little better liked than I have been tonight. Valencia glances over at me once, but when I give her a little hopeful wave her face goes still and her gaze sweeps past. When I finally manage to catch her eye, she emanates a serene kind of inhospitality, like Antarctica or deep space.

And so another hour has passed when a man comes out of the AUTHORIZED PERSONNEL area to wake the children.

"Little ones," the man whispers, and I watch as, head by head, they lift their sleepy faces. "Do you want to go back and see Mommy?" the orderly says. "Your mommy wants to see you guys."

It's kind of heartbreaking how delighted the poor kids are, how excited they are to see the mommy. *Yes! Oh, yes!* They beam, and the girl of about four actually does a little hopping bunny dance, and the orderly gives me an indulgent look. "Cute," he says.

It occurs to me at that moment that no one will stop me if I follow along behind them. I can just walk right through along with them, just shadow them past the AUTHORIZED PERSONNEL sign, past the security guard who stands holding the door open for them, following along as if I might be some kind of guardian, an uncle, perhaps, a neighbor or family friend.

Amazingly, no one says a word. I just line up behind the tiniest child and march right through; the security guard even smiles respectfully at me as if to acknowledge that, hey, I'm a good guy, to be watching over these children. I glance over my shoulder at Valencia, and she's chatting with someone on the phone; she isn't even looking.

11

Shortly before she falls out of the tree, I think Rain is getting ready to break up with me. We have been circling around that sort of conversation all evening long.

She has been telling me about her husband. "Your ex-husband?" I say, and she says no, actually, they are still married—it's just that he has been living in Japan for the past year and they're going through a period of questioning. Deciding what to do, letting things drift, and so forth. "You know what I mean," Rain says, and takes a long drink from her glass of Chardonnay.

"Um," I say, and consider. "Hmm," I say. Did I know what she meant? Up until the moment that she told me about the husband, I'd thought things were going pretty well between us—so perhaps not.

"I'm a little surprised," I tell her. "About the husband thing."

She sighs. "I know," she says. "I realize that I should have told you. But—you know. All this stuff with your mother and so on. You seemed like you were in a very fragile state."

"Fraj-*ile*," I say, pronouncing it the way that she does—as if it might be a popular tourist destination in the Pacific, beautiful Fraj Isle, with its white sandy beaches and shark-filled coves.

It's the kind of conversation that reminds me of my own former marriage, which fell apart abruptly, perhaps similarly, with a series of emotional signals that I had completely failed to interpret.

"Surely you realized how unhappy I've been for the past few

years," my ex-wife murmured, and I recall this as Rain tilts another few ounces of wine into her glass.

12

The rooms where the patients are being kept are not exactly the way they appear on television. Everything is very subdued, people huddled individually in their little warrens with the flimsy curtains pulled partway closed.

I fall back as the children are led toward the cubicle where their mother is awaiting them—no one has stopped me or even seems to notice that I'm here, and it appears that actually once you make it past Valencia that's pretty much all there is. Still, I'm feeling a bit wary. I slow my pace, let the children pitter-patter away. I try to peer surreptitiously into the little curtained roomlets, looking for Rain.

I can't help but think of the pens in an animal shelter, the stricken, doomy look of the strays as you pass by, that sense that it's a bad idea to make eye contact or pause.

I drift past several dreadfully intimate tableaus, trying to avert my eyes. Behind one curtain is the melancholy glare of a bleeding, tattooed hip-hop guy, emasculated by a cotton smock with a periwinkle pattern; behind another is a skeletal old person in an oxygen mask, male or female, whose gaze of biblical despair trails along beside me as I pass.

"Hello," I say, at last, to a woman with a clipboard—my heart is beating very fast at this point, I'm feeling as if I'm having a kind of panic attack; wouldn't that be a laugh? "Hello," I say, whispering exaggeratedly, as if the nurse were an usher at a matinee I'm interrupting. "I'm looking for a woman named Rain Welsh—"

And then—as if I have been led directly to her curtained doorstep—there she is; I see her only a few yards away. She is sitting propped in her bed, wearing a neck brace and a metal halo that encircles her forehead, frozen there into an alert, attentive posture the way statues of empresses sit in their thrones.

"Charlie?" she says, and she watches with a kind of dreamy abstraction as I come toward her. It's not clear if she's glad to see me, but I hold up her purse like a treat: Look what I brought for you!

"Hey, sweetheart," I say, still in my whispery voice. "How are you?"

"Meh," she says. It seems like it takes her a lot of effort to compose a sentence. "I don't know. They've got me on pain meds, so I can't really tell."

"But you're okay," I say encouragingly. "You're not paralyzed or anything, right?" I say this and then I realize that it has been a fantasy hovering in the back of my mind: What if she's paralyzed? Would I be courageous enough to stick with a wheelchair girl? Would I be amazingly, fiercely loyal, would she love me for it, marry me, etc.? I can feel this scenario passing again briefly through my future, and my smile stiffens.

"Charlie," she says. "What are you doing here? It's two o'clock in the morning."

"I don't know," I say. "I couldn't exactly leave you."

"Oh," she says—her voice a dreamy, medicated sigh. "Oh, Charlie. I told them to tell you. You should just go home."

"Well," I say, "I'm just trying to be, you know. A good guy."

"I appreciate that," she says, "but——" and her brain seems to drift along down the stream for a ways before she lifts her head. "But honestly, I've been thinking. This is," she says, "really not working out between us. I've been meaning to tell you for a while that . . ."

She closes her eyes for a moment, five seconds, ten seconds, and when she opens them again it seems that she has lost her train of thought. She smiles up at me fondly, as if I'm an old dear friend she hasn't seen in a long time. "Did I tell you, Charlie? My husband is flying back from Japan! I'm going to be in traction for a few weeks and he's flying home to be with me."

I consider this for a moment. "Wow," I say. "That's wonderful," I say.

"Oh, I'm so sorry," she says, and I watch as she closes her eyes, blissful as a sleepy child. "I wanted our last night together to be . . ."

I wait for her to finish her sentence, but now she appears to be completely unconscious, and her expression slackens and sags. "Rain?" I say, and I adjust the blanket on her bed, straighten the wrinkles underneath her hand. For a moment, I imagine that I could just sit here and talk, the way Mrs. Fowler used to talk to my mother, my mother sitting there deafly, the two of them watching TV, Mrs. Fowler chatting away.

I have this concept going around in my head. I would love to try to get it off my chest, but when I start to talk she makes a little sad face in her sleep. She moans lightly.

At last, I set Rain's purse down on the bed at her feet. Her cigarettes are still tucked in my pocket.

13

This is one of those things that you can never explain to anyone; that's what I want to explain—one of those free-association moments with connections that dissolve when you start to try to put them into words.

But I consider it for a moment, trying to map it out. Look: Here is a china knickknack on my mother's coffee table, right next to her favorite ashtray. A shepherdess, I guess—a figurine with blond sausage curls and a low-cut bodice and petticoats, holding a crook, a staff, in one hand and carrying a lamb under her arm—a more mature Bo Peep, I suppose, and when I am eleven years old I will notice for the first time the way her porcelain neckline dips down to reveal the full slopes of her porcelain breasts. Years later, when I am nearing forty I will notice a woman in a hospital gown and slippers walking through the parking lot of an emergency room, holding her IV stand like the crook a shepherdess carries, and I will lean over my sleeping ex-girlfriend and try to explain how I found myself in a Mobius strip of memory, traveling in a figure eight out of the parking lot and cruising past the glimmering sexual fantasies of an eleven-year-old noticing the boobs on a porcelain figurine and then curving back again to find myself in my mother's house, a few days after her funeral, hesitating as I'm about to drop the shepherdess into a plastic trash bag full of my mother's other useless belongings.

Alone in my mother's house, I am ruthless with her possessions. I live in an apartment in Venice, California, and I don't have enough room for my own stuff. For example, what should be done with an old cigar box full of buttons and beads that she has inexplicably kept? The collection of whimsical salt and pepper shakers? The cards and letters, the dresses wrapped in plastic in the closet, unfinished needlework, clippings from newspapers, her high school yearbooks, her grade school report cards, a doll she loved when she was two, all the accumulation she stuffed into drawers and boxes and the corners of closets? What can I do but throw it away? Though at last I spare the little shepherdess; I stick it in my pocket and eventually I'll find a place for it on my own coffee table.

The dogs, Lady and Peaches, are not so lucky. They hide from me most of the time that I am cleaning out the house. They sleep underneath my mother's bed, crouching there as I haul bag after bag of junk out into the daylight, as I dismantle furniture and leave bare rooms in my wake. At last, almost finished, I tempt them out of their lair with a trail of luncheon meat that leads to a dog cage, and when I close the metal door behind them, they gaze out through the bars at me with a dull, grief-stricken stare. They are older dogs, and it seems cruel to take them to the pound, to try to find some new home for them after all the years they spent with my mother. Still, I don't look at them in the face again. I do not stick around as the veterinarian "puts them to sleep," as they euphemistically say, one after the other, with an injection of sodium pentobarbital. I drop the dogs off at the veterinarian's office and drive away, back toward California, and, driving along the interstate, I realize that this is something I will probably never tell anyone, ever.

Perhaps such things will accumulate more and more from now on, I think. More and more there will be things I can never explain to anyone. More and more I'll find myself lost in parking lots at four in the morning, stepping through the rows upon rows, a long sea of vehicles spreading out beneath the canopy of halogen streetlights, and me with no idea whatsoever where my car might be. I'll find myself pressing the teeny button on my car's automatic anti-theft alarm system. "Where are you?" I will whisper to myself. "Where are you?" Until at last, in the distance, I will hear the car alarm begin to emit its melancholy, birdlike reply.

Take This, Brother, May It Serve You Well

Sitting in the bar of the Heathman Hotel in Portland, Oregon, early May. Here is Dave Deagle peering from the foggy window as a chill rain falls on the metal patio furniture outside and a skinny red-haired kid in a Beefeater costume, apparently the doorman, is opening a taxi and extending an umbrella to an alarmed-looking businesswoman.

What's up with the Beefeater costume? Dave Deagle wonders, and decides that he will allow himself two glasses of beer. He is lonely and so he decides it is okay to bestow a little indulgence upon himself. This is one of those situations, he thinks, fairly dire situations, in which the Deagle of the past, the former Deagle, is to be allowed a certain amount of leverage.

The Deagle of the past is the Deagle who managed to become the victim of a heart attack at the age of thirty-nine. It was a minor heart attack, but still it hurt quite badly and he collapsed to the sidewalk outside his building while having a cigarette with some secretaries. Totally humiliating. And of course it was scary—the proximity and approach of death, etc. He found himself in the hospital, where his bad habits were cataloged with grave disapproval. He was a lifelong smoker, for example, and a heavy drinker and a glutton. Along with his poor heart, his lungs were blackened; his liver was growing fatty; he was, in general, out of shape and "obese" (the word used by a very smug and judgmental prick of a doctor).

Nevertheless, the prick MD had a point. The Deagle of the past recognized that changes needed to be made, and so thus, in fact, the Deagle of the present has tackled these issues head on. Without a complaint, it might be added.

Still—the beer is a pleasant treat! Deagle pats his perspiring brow with a napkin, then lips the foam off the rim of the glass.

He feels lonely. He knows no one in Portland, and upon the streets there appear to be nothing but fairly unpleasant-looking people. There is a kind of keep-on-truckin' West Coast vibe at work here, and he has listed in his notepad a few passersby: aging hippie man, possibly stoned or homeless, wearing a stocking cap over long braids; Asian woman with a small flower tattoo upon cheek; fifty-ish motorcycle babe in red heels and black leather escorting guy who appears to be in the middle stages of multiple sclerosis; three slightly overweight young women with long hair, somewhat "punk" in their dress. Do people use the term *punk* anymore? He crosses out the word and then rewrites it with three question marks after it.

There are a great number of what appear to be teenage runaways, but in Portland it seems that even the elderly dress as if they are teenage runaways, in hoodies and kerchiefs and ragged jeans, stinking of patchouli and dirty feet, and one tattooed old man even rolls by on a skateboard.

My God, Dave Deagle thinks, he is lonely, there are no friends only strangers wherever he goes, and it seems a little impossible for him to try to fit in anywhere at this point. Age forty, already a widower, already the victim of a heart attack.

He stares down into the golden reflecting pool of his beer, upon which floats the final remnants of foam.

He really wants a cigarette.

In the drugstore down the street, Dave Deagle finds himself pondering the evolution of the American pharmacy. Once there was the venerable corner drugstore, now there are nothing but these massive chain stores, Walgreens, Rite Aid, Eckerd, etc. How, exactly, did we as a country arrive at the concept of the sort of place that he is now standing in—this brightly lit bazaar of random items, vast warehouse crammed full of aisles, each aisle with its own "theme": Cold Remedies; Lady's Toilette; Shampoos, Soaps and Hair Products; Baby Needs; Tooth Care; Maladies of the Foot; Problems of the Bowel; Candy; Weight Loss; Seasonal Items (in this case, Easter, though past, is still being represented by rabbits, chicks, eggs, etc.). No doubt someone could research this phenomenon and write an interesting article.

"What kind of cigarettes do you have here today?" Deagle asks the unsmiling young woman behind the counter and she raises her sullen gaze as if her eyes are weapons she is training upon him.

"All kinds," she says. Hateful Portlandians! Can't anyone give a poor lonely middle-aged fat man a friendly smile?

"What's the favorite of the day?" Deagle continues, teasing hopefully. "What's the best-tasting?"

She does not answer. She just looks off to the side, peers around over Deagle's shoulder, and he is aware that if there were someone behind him in line, they would have been beckoned forward, he would have simply lost his place.

But there is no one else in line, and so they stand there for a moment. Impasse! Who will be the first to blink?

"I guess," says Deagle, finally, "I'll just have a pack of Marlboro Lights. That's what I used to smoke when I was human."

The girl doesn't respond to this, either. She merely turns and lifts a pack of cigarettes from the rack behind her. She sets the pack upon the counter and recites a mind-boggling price.

"For one pack?!" exclaims Deagle.

"Yes," the girl says.

"I'm outraged," says Deagle.

"Do you want the cigarettes or not?" the girl asks.

"Yes," Deagle says. "Yes, I do."

He should have bought an umbrella in the drugstore, he realizes when he gets outside, for now the rain is coming down more determinedly. But he doesn't want to give any more of his money to the unfriendly drugstore and their sour employees.

He undoes the cellophane wrapper on the cigarettes and then has a terrible realization. No lighter. No matches.

"Aargh!" he cries aloud, and his anguished cry echoes against the sides of the buildings, the sound bouncing back and forth and shrinking at last to a whisper imperceptible to human ears.

Down the block the road dips downward from the Heathman Hotel toward some neon signs that are very likely to be bars.

A good place to find matches.

And so Deagle begins a kind of lumbering run in this direction, down the hill, very undignified, his large shiny black oxford shoes slapping through puddles on the sidewalk, his heart quickening. How many years since he actually *ran*—now there's a question. By the time he gets to the door of the bar, his glasses have steamed up from heavy breathing.

Inside it's surprisingly empty, but does the bartender turn to look at Deagle with an expression of welcome, a cheerful countenance? Shockingly, no. The bartender turns to Deagle with a face as blank as a thumb.

"Beautiful weather you people are having," Deagle says. He tries to smile, though he is sopping wet.

"Yeah," the bartender says. He observes as Deagle approaches a barstool, as Deagle struggles heavily onto the perch. Out of breath. God, he's so overweight, it's very unfair.

"Is this a way to treat visitors to your city?" Deagle complains. "Torrential rain?"

"Sorry," the bartender says. "I actually don't make the weather." He regards Deagle with his neckless, thumblike head, a balding young man perhaps thirty years of age.

"Well," Deagle says, "how about a free drink, then?" He is

trying to get a comic sort of banter started with this person, though already he sees it is likely to be pointless. "I'm a dying man. I don't have long to live."

"That's too bad," the bartender says. "But, um—we don't serve free drinks."

"Of course you don't," Deagle says. He takes out his wallet and puts a damp twenty on the surface of the bar. "How about a local beer," he says. "And maybe a glass of Scotch on the side."

He glances around. Besides himself are perhaps five other patrons. All men. He imagines briefly the possibility of a lady, a kindly, haggardly woman with a drinking problem sitting there smoking and hoping for a guy to come by and purchase a beverage for her, but there is no such person.

My God, he is lonely! Even a woman with a harelip or other deformity would be suitable. Anyone with an ounce of kindness, an ounce of compassion, such is all he asks. Is that so much?

He sits there humbly upon the barstool and watches the hand of the bartender deliver a drink before him. He raises it to his mouth. Closes his eyes. Swallows.

Cheers.

"A shot," Deagle says. "Bartender? May I have a shot of tequila, please?"

He lifts his head and some time has passed and the bartender has distributed a few more shots. For a time Deagle was moodily engaged in some memories. His frugal childhood in rural Minnesota, his growth as an intelligent and ambitious high school student, triumphant college years, top 25 percent of his class at law school, his wedding and the birth of his two beautiful children, his career sort of taking off and advancing at an acceptable pace.

All of this fairly much ruined and rendered meaningless, now. *Nel mezzo del cammin di nostra vita mi ritrovai per una selva oscura ché la diritta via era smarrita.*

Et cetera, et cetera.

There is a stage you reach, Deagle thinks, a time somewhere in early middle age, when your past ceases to be about yourself. Your connection to your former life is like a dream or delirium, and that person who you once were is merely a fond acquaintance, or a beloved character from a storybook. This is how memory becomes nostalgia. They are two very different things— the same way that a person is different from a photograph of a person.

As time has accumulated—one year since his heart attack, two years since his children went away, went to live with his sister in Mankato, three years since his wife's death—he has been aware of a certain degree of suicidal ideation. He will fly out on these trips under the auspices of Saunders, Dearman & Dorr, he'll arrive at the hotel, keep his receipts with an awareness of his per diem, and yet there is also the thought that he might not return. There is a round-trip ticket, but what if he doesn't appear at the airport on the day he is supposed to go home? What if he is never seen or heard from again?

What would remain?

He can't help but think of the Hobblers. When his wife was sick, when she was in her last days, he used to see them moving down the sidewalk past his house, the dreadful old couple out for their evening constitutional. They must have been in their eighties or nineties, easily forty years older than Deagle and his wife, and by the time they made it past the neighbor's driveway to the Deagles', some of the leaves on the trees had turned from green to red.

"You're so mean," Deagle's wife said. "Don't make fun," she said. "I think they're sweet."

Deagle didn't say anything. Maybe they *were* sweet: inspirational in their way. But he still didn't like them. That Hobbler wife with her bowed, osteoporotic back, staring downward loomingly; the Hobbler husband, dazed and batty-looking in his tweed jacket over a pajama shirt, his hand on his wife's elbow as if escorting her to a formal dance. Deagle's wife had heard that he was an emeritus professor. Physics? Psychology? She couldn't remember.

You could say that they were sweet, or you could say that they were something out of a horror movie.

This was September, and his wife was dying pretty rapidly. She had about a month or so to go. The cancer had started in her ovaries, but now it was everywhere, and she had reached the stage where her lungs kept filling up with fluid, a kind of slow-motion drowning, and every few days Deagle and his wife would go in for a lung tap, which provided a little short-term relief. Deagle's wife could still make it up and down the stairs, though it took a while.

They were having a lot of quiet time together. Deagle had taken time away from work, and their children were spending the fall at his sister's house, and in some ways it was like a kind of vacation for both of them. The days had begun to waver and lose their shape. Looking out the window, reading books aloud. He drove down the hill to buy her some lemon gelato. He cooked a chicken in a pot and brought the broth to her in a small bowl. Here was one of those wonderful spoons that they had stolen from a Chinese restaurant, and he lifted it to her lips.

She didn't make it long enough to see the first snowfall, and by that time the Hobblers had vanished as well. The sidewalks were probably too slick for them, too treacherous, the cold air too hard on their old bones; it would run right through them and they'd feel as if they would never be warm again.

Sitting there, Deagle thought that perhaps they'd emerge again in spring.

Late April.

Early May.

Tulips and daffodils and lilacs and budding trees.

He wondered if that would make her happy, to know that the Hobblers were still around. Down the block and back, down the block and back, getting a little exercise. Maybe—probably—she would like it. "Sweet," she would say.

As for Deagle, he didn't know what he would prefer. He would sit at the window, peering out, and he didn't know whether he wanted to see them, or if he hoped that they would never come again.

Outside the pathetic bar, under an awning, Deagle lights a cigarette and takes out his notepad, examining his notes. "Beefeater," he has written, and "keep-on-truckin' West Coast vibe" and "punk???" and "history of American pharmacy" and now he takes out his special pen and writes "Hobblers?" and circles it. Was there a way to make sense of it? he wondered. Or was it, like so many of the things he thought about, just another random flight of fancy?

A fat raindrop falls from above and makes a splattered Rorschach out of the word "punk," and so he is compelled to quickly close the notepad and tuck it into the pocket of his suit jacket. He focuses again on the cigarette. He'd forgotten the way that the filters of Marlboro Lights would adhere to the skin of your lips, but the smoke itself is a pleasant sensation and it expels itself into the Portland air, which is as heavy and dewy as fog.

Back in Minnesota, when he was an undergraduate student, Deagle had taken a class in poetry writing. The teacher was an evil, judgmental old hippie with a long neck that she swathed in scarves, and her lessons were disconnected rambles that usually ended with some liberal parable about the plight of women, people of color, etc., and her comments about his poems had been vaguely rude and dismissive. Nevertheless, he had enjoyed the semester-long assignment she had given, which required them to carry a notebook with them everywhere. "Record your observations," she said. "Nothing is small enough to escape the poet's notice!"

And here he was: still carrying his notepad, after all these years. His wife used to like reading the notepads, once upon a time, though sometimes she would shake her head over a particularly acidic observation. "You shouldn't be so cynical and morbid," she told him once. "It's not good for your health."

Though of course her optimism had done her little good—no

wise or hopeful thoughts came to her at the end, only a kind of pained, puzzled, childlike mumbling, last words that even he can't bring himself to write down.

Maybe someday, he thinks, he might eventually expound on these little notes; and maybe someday after his death his heirs will uncover this cache of unwritten poems and somehow interpret the jotted fragments, the raindropped blurs, somehow finding buried within the essence of Deagle. The stubbed-out nub of himself.

Such maudlin thoughts are not his usual mode.

That is the Deagle of the past, he reminds himself. The former Deagle used to read sad poetry at night, drinking Scotch and weeping distractedly and accidentally dropping lit cigarettes on the carpet of his study, luckily not burning the house down; the former Deagle would buy canisters of cake frosting and eat them while sitting alone in his car in a parking lot; the former Deagle popped little ten-milligram Desoxyn pills in between meetings with clients and then drove home and faced his unnerved Uruguayan housekeeper and then broke down while reading *The Runaway Bunny* to his children at bedtime, tears rolling down his face while the kids sat frightened in their pajamas. Falling down the stairs a couple of times in the night, drunkenly peeing on people's flowers as he walked home from the bar, once nearly running a slow driver off the road and giving her the middle finger as he roared past. Smoking his way steadily toward his heart attack, toward the grim, pharisaic face of his sister in his hospital room. "Those children can't be living with you," she was saying. "My God, David, there's a difference between grief and monstrous selfishness," she said, and he agreed with her. "Absolutely," he said. "You should take them—that's a great idea!"

"Just until you get your act together," she said. "You've got responsibilities," she said. "Do you think this is how Laura would have wanted you to behave?" she said. "Don't you think she would have expected more out of you? I think she believed she married a decent human being."

"Yes," he said. Obviously, he had to remake himself. Obviously, a new Deagle had to be born; his life and his pathway through it had to be rethought and reimagined and rewired.

There are little wisps of jelly in a living brain. Deagle knows this well: neurons, transmitting signals—and the soul, so to speak, is somewhere in those flashes. He heard once on a science program that the spindle cell—present in humans, whales, some apes, elephants—may be at the heart of what we call our "selves."

What we recognize in the mirror—that thread we follow through time that we call "me"? It's just a diatom, a paramecium, a bit of ganglia that branches and shudders assertively. A brief brain orgasm, like lightning.

In short, it's all chemicals. You can regiment it easily enough: fluoxetine, sertraline, paroxetine, escitalopram, citalopram—the brain can be washed clean, and you can reset yourself, Ctrl+Alt+Del. You don't have to be a prisoner of your memories and emotions.

Vials of such curatives can be found back in the Heathman Hotel, in a room, in a suitcase, in a zippered plastic bag, though that seems very far away at this point. In a distant alternate universe, there is a good Deagle who takes his medication with a glass of water, who slips between crisp, bleached sheets and rests his head on an ergonomic pillow, who sets his alarm in preparation for the next morning's arbitration hearing, and awakens bright-eyed.

Still, he has to admit, being this drunk is a pleasant treat. It's been well over a year since the last time he was this loaded, but he slips into it easily, like a nice pair of galoshes and an overcoat. He had always been something of a lush, for most of his adult life, and his wife hadn't minded it, really—had tolerated it, at least, in the way she tolerated his smoking, and had even sometimes found him endearing or amusing when he was a little lit up.

Of course now things are different. Now, drinking is a private activity—Deagle, party of one!—and when he's drunk or high it seems as if he expands somehow, there is a kind of self-communion, as if he's grown a second head, a Siamese twin who will laugh at his jokes and commiserate with his sorrows and chat agreeably about his cynical and morbid observations.

Or else it's the opposite. Maybe it's simply that drunkenness reduces some unwanted piece of himself—irradiates it, like a malignant growth.

In either case, Deagle eases down the sidewalk, enjoying the gloam of long-absent alcohol through his blood and visiting another unfriendly bar and then moving along—ever hopeful—toward the next.

Which, irritatingly, does not appear.

He walks a little farther, and then after a few more blocks he pauses.

God! How long has he been out here on the street? In the rain. Talking to himself.

It actually seems as if he has been walking for a while. His shoes and socks are full of rain, and his hair drips in tendrils down his face, and clusters of wet humanity regard him as he goes. "Back," says Deagle, when a shambling pile of rags rises up on two legs from out of the shadows to ask him for a cigarette. "Back," he says, and makes a cross with his two index fingers.

And in the meantime, he has no idea where he is. On his BlackBerry cellphone, he has a program with a Global Positioning System and satellite-guided maps, but it appears that the battery on the phone is dead. When he tries to turn it on, it plays a sweetly melancholic bar of notes, the sound of polite regret. Then it goes black.

When he looks over his shoulder, the landscape is utterly unfamiliar. How far in the distance is the Heathman Hotel? In what direction? He has no clue.

"This is a predicament," says Deagle to Deagle, and he stands there, frowning, cursing his reliance on technology and his own poor sense of direction. He scopes the dark street for signs of a common pay phone. He can't recall the last time he actually used one, and they may, in fact, be extinct—he's not sure. Certainly there is no sign of one on this block—where the darkened buildings have the blank, unwelcoming faces of people on a subway train. No lights but the street lamps, spotlighting the tangled lines of rain.

"Hello?" he calls, the way you might call into a canyon to hear

your echo. Would it be possible, he wonders, to backtrack, to re-
discover the bar—which, he suspects bitterly, is now closed, in
any case? He looks over his shoulder.

"Hello?" he calls again, and it is a bit startling—even
alarming—when a female voice responds.

"Hello," the female voice says from somewhere in the darkness beyond. Casually—the way a shopkeeper will greet you
when you enter his store.

As much as he's wished for it, the ghost of his wife has never
appeared to him. He has never even, despite all the drinking and
drugs and medications, been the victim of a hallucination—her
face bending down to kiss his forehead? Shaking her head in disappointment? No, nothing—not the barest phantasm.

So now he walks toward the sound of the voice with hopeful
trepidation. It has occurred to him that the ghost of his wife
might be rightfully pissed off at his behavior since her death.

The figure appears at the mouth of an alleyway. It is a woman
with long hair and a long raincoat that reaches almost to her an-
kles, like a gown. Spread open above her head is a large and ancient black umbrella.

"Hey there, Drunk Man," she says, in a clear, girlish voice—
she might be nineteen or twenty. "What're you looking for?" she
says, and gives him a musing smile. "Whatever it is, you're in the
wrong neighborhood."

She doesn't resemble Deagle's late wife in any significant
way. Still, there's the lingering of suggestion, and he stumbles
toward her as if he recognizes her.

"I beg your pardon," Deagle says. "You wouldn't happen to
have a cellphone that I could borrow, would you?"

She lets out a little laugh, as if he's told her a charming joke, and Deagle chuckles, too—though he's not sure, exactly, what is funny. Still, it's the first time all night that someone has been amused by something he's said.

"You're soaking wet—do you know that?" she says. "How much have you had to drink tonight? A lot, I'll bet."

"Do I know you from somewhere?" Deagle murmurs, and she cocks her head.

"I don't know," she says. "*Do* you?"

The girl's name, she says, is Chloe, and she has lived in this city for six years, and she has never heard of the Heathman Hotel.

"It's the one with the guy in front of it," Deagle tries to explain. "He's dressed in a costume? A Beefeater—you know, like the ones that watch the Tower of London?"

"You realize that you're in Portland, right?" she says. She smiles softly, puts her gentle, thin-fingered, skeletal hand on his shoulder. "Maybe you should come with me."

Were Deagle not so drunk, and so melancholy, this might give him pause. He peers uncertainly into the alley she has emerged from: a dim and narrow brick corridor, the walls decorated in brightly colored, uninterpretable graffiti. The rain spatters thickly against black plastic garbage bags and rusting Dumpsters. A puddle contains a discarded hypodermic needle and an oozing packet of fast-food mustard. Is that a doorway in the distance?

"Do you want to get out of the rain, or not?" Chloe says, as Deagle tries to make the wobbly alley shadows come into focus.

"I . . ." Deagle wavers. Then he sighs. He accepts the space she offers him under her umbrella, huddling close enough to her that he can smell her scent of dry grass and copper pennies. "You're a good Samaritan," he says.

"Not really," she says.

He follows along unsteadily until they reach a doorway. He stumbles when they come to a stop and she reaches out to keep him from falling, a hand on the small of his back, and my God, it is startling, such a simple kindness—Deagle is quite moved.

"Is this," he says—indicating the filthy, rusted door she is wedging open—"is this your home? You're very generous to invite me into your home."

"It's my office," she says.

"Ah," he says. "Are you a lawyer?"

"No," she says. She regards him. "Are you?"

"Yes," Deagle says. "Unbelievably." And he pauses, realizing after a moment that this exchange is a bit non-sequitur, that his hold on the train of thought isn't very firm. He gives his swimmy head a shake.

"What is it that you do?" he inquires politely.

"I'm a psychic," Chloe says. "I also practice tarot and palmistry." She pulls the umbrella closed with an athletic, javelin thrower's thrust, and the metal door makes an exclamation as she pushes against it.

"Sorry about the mess," she says.

The space that opens before them appears to be a small abandoned warehouse. It might, at one point, have held some shabby office cubicles; it might, at another point, have been a sweatshop of some kind. Now, though, it is more or less an indoor junkyard, piled with stacks of scrap metal, some ancient broken computers, fax machines, dot-matrix printers, old filing cabinets, loops of copper wire, rotting furniture.

In the center, a fire is flickering in a metal barrel. Some wheeled office chairs are arranged around it, and Chloe gestures him forward.

"Have a seat," she says. "It's warm and dry, at least," she says, and Deagle wavers over a cardboard box filled with cobwebbed 3x5 floppy disks. It is the sort of place that he should describe in his notebook, he thinks, and he fingers his pockets uncertainly. He finds a damp packet of Marlboro Lights, and his dead Black-Berry, and a pen.

"Do you have a phone in here?" Deagle says. "I'd like to call a taxi."

Chloe says nothing. She shakes the rain from her long hair and walks toward the firelight, which exudes translucent undulations of heat and greasy smoke.

Deagle realizes then that there is another person in the room, a silhouette sitting in a chair near the burning barrel, and when the figure lifts its head Deagle sees that it is a male Caucasian, wiry and shirtless, sporting a kudzu of dreadlocked hair. Deagle's heart sinks a little, he intuits that things may begin to go badly, and Chloe, psychic that she is, gives him a look as if to apologize.

"Have a seat," she says again, and the dreadlocked male leans forward and rests his eyes on Deagle. Deagle imagines that this cavemanlike being will probably use a blunt weapon when the time comes; he imagines that it will hurt to be bludgeoned.

"What's up?" the male says.

Chloe says, "This is Boomer."

"How're you doing, Customer?" says Boomer, and Deagle nods.

"I've been better," he says.

"Haven't we all," says Boomer.

Deagle guesses that shortly there will be a robbery, or other crime committed against his person, but he is still drunk enough that the thought disturbs him only vaguely, like that ticklish, heebie-jeebie sensation in the small of the back, the monitory intuition that something is creeping up behind you. Is there a scientific word for that? Deagle wonders. Something like déjà vu? He considers writing this in his notebook, pats his pocket. But the notebook is not on his person. He feels a little zing of loss, a distant firework arching into the night sky, but what can be done at this point?

It's better, perhaps, to just sit still. He folds his hands, as he sometimes does at the many arbitration tables he finds himself at—flying here and there across the country to arbitrate labor disputes for his clients, usually pointless, but it has made him an expert at folding his hands in a peaceable and significant way, and it has also allowed him to perfect a certain kind of measured and expectant breathing.

Boomer regards his performance with some interest. The two of them sit there in silence for a time, while Chloe busies herself in some corridor of dismantled office furniture. Presently, Boomer withdraws a hand-rolled cigarette and lights it.

"Are you here to get your fortune told?" Boomer asks. "Chloe, she's pretty accurate, pretty accurate."

"That's good to hear," Deagle says, and stares at his hands.

When you are a widower, you're supposed to move your wedding band from the left ring finger to the right. This is etiquette, or something. An old tradition, and when Deagle had removed his own ring, about a year after she died, there was a crease in the flesh below his knuckle, a little belt that didn't go away, though he massaged it and rubbed it with lotion; it seemed for a while that it would be more or less permanent. Now, however, the mark is gone.

Deagle clears his throat. "Actually," Deagle says, "I just got lost. Lost in Portland. That's all."

"Word," says Boomer. "Right on."

When Chloe appears at last, she is no longer wearing her raincoat or her boots. She has on a tasseled shawl, and a long, vaguely ethnic skirt, and her feet are bare. She does not wear a turban, Deagle is relieved to see, though her dark hair has a Gypsy-ish kink to it.

"I thought we might have some of those cheap cellphones," she says to Boomer. "Those pre-paid, no-contract ones, you remember? What happened to those?"

"I dunno," Boomer says. "Did we sell them?"

"Maybe," Chloe says, and then she shrugs her shoulders at Deagle regretfully. "Sorry," she says. "I think you're out of luck, Mr. Drunk Man," and Deagle watches as she settles herself into Boomer's lap, leaning back against him, that thin hand brushing along the length of his bare arm, an absently tender gesture.

"You got fifty dollars?" she says to Deagle. "I'll read your palm for you."

...

Most people would not believe this, but once there were happier times, a territory of years in which Deagle was surprisingly satisfied. He didn't even know it at the time, but there was an entire period in which it seemed he was going to have a nice life.

He loved coming up behind his wife while she was washing dishes, and putting his hands underneath her shirt, to touch her warm back.

He loved to ride in the car together, the ordinary drives to a cheap restaurant or a park, the four of them listening to children's music, or speaking brightly about the things you talk to children about—his wife in the driver's seat, and him beside her, the kids snug in their car seats—

Or to find her in bed, absorbed in a book, her head bent and a small private smile on her face, marking some comment in the margin—a remark to the author? To a future reader? But now indecipherable, a message only to her missing self.

Or the little basket of stones and shells and flotsam she had collected; they had spent hours walking along beaches and riverbeds and hiking trails, and he loved the sweet, dreamy attention she paid to these little objects—because they were "pretty," or "interesting"—choosing one over the other, using some unfathomably subtle calculation—

As mysterious as the part of himself that was chosen and loved by her, the part of himself that was there only when they were together.

There is two hundred dollars left in his wallet, plus the credit cards, which, Deagle suspects, will mean more to them than they will to him. He can feel the warmth of the fire in the barrel as he passes the wallet to Boomer, and Boomer grins, showing a row of nice teeth, the orthodontia some long-ago parents once paid for: only one missing.

In exchange, Boomer offers a thin glass tube, about the size and shape of a cigarette. He extends it, nobly, like a king presenting a sword to a knight. "Take this, brother, may it serve you well," Boomer says, and Deagle places the tube to his lips, drawing smoke when Boomer holds a lighter to it, and he can feel it go branching through his lungs and brain. His heart quickens. The barrel fire glows orangely, its waves of heat like ripples in an old windowpane, and he leans back as Chloe and Boomer curl in their chair together, and he loves the way they touch each other, the way she puts her lips to his ear and the way his nail-bitten fingers absently roll the edge of her skirt up her thigh, their two heads bending over his billfold, examining its contents like children who have opened a gift.

"Sweet," his wife would say, and Deagle closes his eyes.

Maybe there is time for Chloe to see what is left in his palm.

Here it is. He holds it out to her.

The Farm. The Gold.
The Lily-White Hands.

1

Alone for years now, Daddy has settled into his rituals and routines. He wakes up a little before dawn, dresses in the dark: white running shoes and warm-up pants, a plain blue T-shirt. His dog fetches her own leash and stands there, waiting, holding it in her mouth.

It's a beautiful morning, middle of June. Birds. Lawns. Flowers. It's the kind of pleasant upper-middle-class old suburb on the edge of the city where you wouldn't necessarily expect to find a man like Daddy. But he has changed a lot over the years, has transformed himself into the sort of handsome older guy who jogs with his dog early on a Tuesday morning.

Six A.M. and they go winding down the long hill that leads from the Ambleside apartment building, everything green and blooming, the dog, Angeline, trotting and gazing up at Daddy with her black Labrador sort of love, soft brown eyes and a coat the same shiny color as Daddy's hair. His hair still doesn't have much gray in it.

In general, Daddy is in great shape for a man his age, broad of chest and flat of stomach, and even the smoking hasn't done much noticeable damage. He doesn't have the kind of wrinkles you'd expect from a fifty-four-year-old with a pack-a-day habit. His teeth are healthy, a little yellow but no cavities, none have fallen out. His eyes are still that devastating dark.

Does he have a lady friend, someone to have sex with? Probably not, but he could, if he chose to pursue it.

He prefers his solitude. Daddy uses his key card to buzz himself back into the quiet of the apartment building and none of his neighbors notice as he pads along the white fluorescent hallway, leashed Angeline panting demurely beside him.

If he were to disappear, if police went from door to door in the Ambleside apartment building with his photograph his neighbors would shake their heads. I've never seen the guy; oh, once or twice, maybe, but rarely; can't say I've ever spoken to the man

And turns the key in the lock, opens and closes the door. Angeline goes to the kitchen and laps some water from her dish.

Alone for years now, Daddy doesn't usually think about what his apartment might look like to a stranger. The bare walls, the unemptied ashtrays. Easy chair facing a television in the middle of the undecorated living room, jar of spare change on the counter in the kitchen, mattress on the floor of the bedroom, the sheet and blanket braided together by Daddy's restless feet as he sleeps.

He tries not to think of how it would all look if he died, for example, and the building super had to unlock the apartment with his master key and they found him there on that mattress, floating on the surface like a fish belly-up in an aquarium, eyes and lips slightly parted and the ceiling fan turning and dirty ice cream bowl with a cigarette put out in it, and so on.

He tries not to think of these kinds of things and yet it is true that such thoughts sometimes circle around in his head and he finds it difficult to fall asleep, he wakes up in the middle of the night gasping, sleep apnea, sometimes choking or crying out. Angeline, also startled, will rise up from her curled position beside him on the mattress and begin to bark warnings at the dark opening of bedroom door.

Usually he doesn't remember his dreams but there was one last night in which he woke and his eyes were still closed and he could sense someone bending over him. A face was pulling close to his own face, the exhalation of breath touching his lips, feathery brush of lashes against his forehead. A face like someone from childhood, an adult who had once loved him, leaning over his bed at night to smell his hair.

He was paralyzed. He had stopped breathing.

He had stopped breathing for a moment and then he sat up abruptly with a glottal choking sound as if mucus were caught in his throat.

The dream disappeared, and yet a little scrap of it hung above him,

like a little ragged
strip of cloth caught
on a barbed-wire fence
like the lyrics to an old song or story from childhood.

The farm.
The gold.
The lily-white hands.

He couldn't quite put his finger on it.

And now it is morning and Daddy is still troubled, still something nagging at him. He opens a can of dog food and spoons it into Angeline's red dish; she waits with a dignified paw lifted, like a lady in olden days offering her gloved hand to be kissed.

He makes coffee, opens up the newspaper and turns to the funny pages where he puzzles over Sudoku and brings a cigarette to his mouth. He looks at the space on his left hand where his finger used to be. Considers.

2

Years before, he was working as an independent contractor: carpentry, house-painting, cabinet installation, doing pretty well for himself. He owned his own business and even had a guy on the payroll, a buddy, Skully, who worked with him on most jobs.

And yet we still crossed his mind. Despite the ten years passed and despite himself he would find himself dialing the old home

number (disconnected), looking through some boxes of old papers, bills mostly, thinking he might come across a photograph.

He was going through a little gloomy period, not depression
necessarily though there was some insomnia involved, difficulty
concentrating, that sort of thing.

But he got up that morning as usual. As he did every morning,
no matter how blue he was. Coffee, funny pages, cigarettes. He
packed himself a lunch, and when Skully honked in the driveway
Daddy came out smiling; he laughed at Skully's dirty-joke-book
jokes as they set up the ladders and spread the tarps and set up the
circular saw. He had never missed a day of work in his life.

They were listening to a rock-'n'-roll station on the radio.
Bruce Springsteen, Creedence, rock-'n'-roll oldies, the DJ said,
and Daddy was uncomfortably aware that he was almost forty-
four years of age. Forty-four! The recent birthday, that was a part
of his moodiness, probably, though he would never admit it. He
imagined the wry way his ex-wife might call these moods a
"midlife crisis," and the notion made him actually blush. Crisis: a
neurotic, effeminate word.

For a while after the divorce he had imagined that he might
get married again, that he might have more children, new daughters to replace the ones who he had been separated from for so
long.

So why didn't he? What was stopping him?

From the top of the ladder, he sang softly along with the radio
as he worked and reflected and remembered and suffered hang-
over, "Badlands," he sang, and "Green River," and Skully told
his joke about the rich farmer with the three beautiful daughters,

the red-haired daughters with the pale hands and freckled cheeks, and

yes, there we were. He could see us through the window, he stood on the ladder outside the third-floor window of the empty house and when he glanced through the glass there we were in our bedroom, in our beds, with our pink lamp on our nightstand and our toys put away and the covers pulled up to our necks. Faces sunk into pillows. Eyes closed. Waiting to be kissed.

and one minute Daddy was on the ladder and then almost in the same second he'd hit the ground and

Skully came running

Oh my God,

oh my God, he said, and Skully was actually weeping a little because he assumed that Daddy was dead. Daddy's hand was bleeding, his finger was gone, it must have gotten hooked on something and pulled itself right off his hand, what happened to his finger? Oh my God! Skully took off his T-shirt and bent over Daddy and wrapped the shirt around Daddy's hand where blood was bubbling out steadily.

That was the part of the anecdote that Daddy liked to tell later. Poor Skully crying and then the two of them trying to find that damned finger in the grass. Looking everywhere but finally heading off to the hospital without it. Possibly it was carried off by a dog or a bird or something. He will say this later, half joking, just because it makes a good ending to the story.

On the other hand, he'll never tell anyone about what he'd seen up there, glimpsed, not exactly supernatural not something you would talk about

3

We have been apart for a long time. Eden is a graduate student in Ohio and Sydney lives with her husband in New Hampshire and Brooke works at a restaurant in Portland and the last time we were together was for our mother's funeral.

Is it Brooke who is the most lonely? She sometimes believes so, leaving the restaurant at two in the morning, in the city, in the rain, and the barred metal grates have been pulled down over the front of the nearby liquor store. Her sisters don't miss her as much as she misses them, she thinks, everyone else has things, no one ever thinks about her with this kind of longing, they will not ever be on such a poorly lit side street where every window is dark and sleet taps hesitantly on the canopy of the umbrella.

She only wants to make her way to a decent street where there are cars, where she can catch a taxi back to her apartment but the water has accumulated and she is wearing her nice new shoes. It is such slow going. Such winding, careful steps. In the puddles on the sidewalk are dozens upon dozens of earthworms. Most of them are dead, but some are still alive, writhing weakly, trying apparently to swim. Brooke is staring down at her feet, trying not to step on them.

The wind makes her raincoat fly back and ripple like a sheet on a clothesline. Abruptly, the wind catches her scarf and carries it up into the sky like a leaf or a flap of newspaper.

"Oh!" Brooke cries, with frustration, grasping too late after her scarf. The moment she reaches out her hand, her umbrella is wrenched inside out. "Oh!" she says. "Goddamn it!"

There are more worms now, the sidewalk is thick with them, and she can barely put a foot down. Before she can avoid it, she feels the soft, slick mass of a night crawler squashing beneath the toe of her shoe.

She stands there, motionless, holding her inside-out umbrella as the flecks of icy rain catch in her hair. Above her, some birds are clustered on a telephone wire, looking down. Blackbirds, grackles maybe, ravens?

They seem to regard her for a moment. Then they begin to lift up from their perch, flapping off into the darkened sky one by one until the wire is just a bare line above Brooke's head.

It is not like a premonition of death.

It is as if she died a long time ago, and she just remembered it.

4

Midnight and Daddy was on his way home to kill us all.

We were asleep in our beds and Mother was curled on the couch in the living room with the television going, dozing a little, exhausted after the past week and now a hot humid night in late June, the ceiling fan going on high so that the steady whirring practically covered the voices on the TV.

Mother opened her eyes partway when Daddy's truck crept up the driveway with his headlights turned off, the crackle of gravel beneath his tires, the flutter of sparrows in the hedge, stirring then settling. She closed her eyes and he came through the gate and stood there in the backyard in the moonlight, under the apple tree. He looked up and there was the darkened window of our room

5

In the basement of Sydney's new house is a little room that is about the size and shape of a coffin. Sydney and her husband discover it a few days after they have moved in. There is an old, heavy door that they hadn't noticed when they were touring the house with the Realtor. There is a doorknob, and one of those iconic keyholes like in cartoons, with a real skeleton key in it! They unlock it.

Behind the door is a space just big enough for a little man to stand in. The walls are cement and plaster, the corners are curved rather than straight. It smells like a cave.

"I think this is possibly the creepiest thing I've ever seen," Sydney's husband says, and Sydney looks at him sternly.

"It's a closet," Sydney says.

"No it's not a closet," her husband says. "There's nothing to hang things on."

"Maybe it's a fruit cellar," Sydney says. "They probably kept their sacks of potatoes in there. To keep them cool."

It is cool in there, her husband concedes. "It's like something you'd store a dead body in," her husband says. "That's what it's like."

Sydney sighs. "Look," she says. "This was a great bargain. I hope you're not planning on getting into one of your superstitious things."

"I'm not," her husband says. "I'm just speaking metaphorically." And they both glance over to where the washer and dryer are lined up, mute, open-mouthed, on the opposite wall. They will have to have their exposed backs to this dreadful coffin-door every time they put a load of clothes into one of the machines, they are both realizing.

Metaphorically. And she has an uncomfortable flicker, a little thought that swallows itself before it actually makes it to the forefront of her mind. *"In the farmer's basement was a little room where he kept his gold,"* she thinks briefly, a line from a story she read once as a child. Her mouth hardens.

Metaphorical. And she watches her husband turn the key in the lock of the coffinlike door.

Metaphorical for what?

6

Without him for years now we talk on the phone and there is some agreement that we won't mention certain aspects of the past.

Which one of us said: *Do you ever wonder where he is?*

Which one said: *He's alive somewhere, living somewhere, and I don't know why we shouldn't try, after all these years*

There were a few moments of silence. Our mother rose up out of her grave and stepped delicately through the headstones in the cemetery toward the little pub where we were sitting at a table with our beers, and outside the rain had begun to turn into sleet.

This was the little bar next to the movie theater and we had been planning to go see a film that was a comedy about three sisters who lived in Manhattan and who were all struggling with the vagaries of love and life in a contemporary setting.

The spirit of our dead mother had begun to move swiftly toward us,

gliding now through the night over the fields and interstates and rivers of the Midwest toward the city where we were having our little gathering. Sister Conference, we called it.

And our mother said: He was standing there above your bed with the pistol, and the three of you were asleep and I didn't know what else to do, I just got down on my knees and I said please don't kill them please just kill me, just kill me, they didn't do anything to you, they love you with all their hearts

And he said it doesn't matter anymore, nothing matters anymore

And he pulled the trigger. I thought I would scream, but I didn't. He pulled the trigger and it was your head, Brooke, and the chamber was empty. And then it was Eden. And then Sydney. *Click. Click. Click.*

And then he turned the pistol toward me, as I was kneeling there. Click, at my head. And then he put it in his mouth and pulled the trigger a last time.

Oh God I prayed there would be a bullet that last time, but there wasn't.

Of course we remember all this as we sip our beers, as we sit there, a football game playing on the television above the bar.

We were asleep and in one universe we didn't ever wake up, in one version of the story we died and the rest of our lives was just a long dream in which we grew up and became waitresses and housewives and graduate students, an extended extended extended pause before the bullet entered our brains.

7

Alone in his apartment, Daddy lights a cigarette, and sits in his chair facing the television, and the dog rests her muzzle sympathetically against his thigh. He is not unhappy, not exactly, though sometimes it occurs to him, sometimes he realizes: This is how his life has ended up.

Not really what he would have expected.

He used to spend so much of his time in a state of dreadful anxiety about the future, so worried about the choices he'd made, so terrified

for example, he could have gone to college, he was smart enough, he thought he would just work for a while and then go, but before he knew it, he was caught up in his contracting business, all the tools and equipment and a new truck and the mistakes he'd made with his taxes, he was so far into debt, there was so much overhead, and he remembers that moment when he saw that he'd never never go to college

and he was married to his high school girlfriend, in fact the only person he'd ever slept with, and sometimes the guys he worked with would start bragging, ten women, they'd say, dozens of women, and even though he knew the guys were exaggerating he'd blushed inwardly and it wasn't just being married but there were children, the three girls one after the other and he had adored them in some ways but there was also the sense that once they were born he was trapped. He had built his own future brick by brick around himself but there were no doors or windows, at least that was the way it seemed at the time he had thought to himself, *I am locked in,* it was like one of those ghost stories where you wake up and you are sealed into a coffin

and you begin to thrash around, thinking, I must escape

He peers for a time at the television and rests the palm of his hand on the muzzle of Angeline the dog and she nudges it as if to remind the hand to pet, to continue to pet.

He actually did manage to escape, that's the thing. He extricated himself. He pulled free

8

Eden is the youngest of us, she doesn't even remember Daddy, really, though there are times when she is in the classroom, when she is teaching her class in remedial composition and there is an older student in the back of the room and she asks them to open their books: What are your reactions to the text? Is the work unified, with all the parts pertaining to a central idea? Is it coherent, with the parts relating clearly to one another?

The man is in his thirties, she would guess, dark-haired, dark-eyed, a stillness leaking out of him as she speaks to the class about analysis, interpretation, synthesis of texts and he has the face of someone who is passing a terrible accident in his car, trying not to look. He doesn't seem like someone who is paying attention and so she calls on him: Christopher? she says and he just stares at her with his shaggy tired glare.

I don't know, he says. I didn't get a chance to read it this time, and she feels uncomfortable about her authority in the classroom, and she feels actually shaky and so she speaks sharply, Christopher, talk to me after class, please, and afterward he stands there grimly in his muddy work boots and cheap janitor pants as the other students file out.

"Christopher," she says, "I don't see how you are going to be able to pass this class if you're not doing the reading and you're not turning in your work."

"I'm sorry, Ms. Bell," he says, a broad-shouldered, bearded Yeti of a man, slumped and moody, an odd sort of spittly speech impediment, "I just can't make sense of what you're talking about," he says, "I've got to have this class but this is not my thing, I'm not much for analysis," he says, "I just need the degree or I'm never going to get promoted," he says, "I've got a kid," he says. "I'm a single father."

"I sympathize with your situation," she says, "but you have to do the work," she says, "you understand that don't you?"

"No," he says, and she stiffens, he's not threatening in any obvious way but, "I don't understand. That's the problem. You're not a very good teacher, Ms. Bell, I can't seem to grasp anything you're talking about," he says, there is a thick hostility emanating from him and of course she can't help but imagine the long walk she has to take alone through the parking lot, 10:15 P.M., Monday night, what if he followed her

and even when she gets home she will be in bed and she closes her eyes and she can imagine Christopher in her room, the heavy shadow of him leaning over her and she turns on the light and opens her book. Outside her window she can see the blurry golden smudge of the moon behind a miasma of clouds, the moon sinking in the west and she wonders where Daddy is right now what he is thinking about

9

When he was a boy Daddy's mother lost custody and for a while he stayed with his grandmother and then after she died he was in foster care for a time.

He was placed in the home of an old farmer called Mr. Athen, back in Shenandoah, Iowa, and Daddy was sixteen years old, old enough for work, five in the morning and Mr. Athen was bending down to shake Daddy awake Time to get up Mr. Athen said, not mean but not gentle, either. There was no love lost between them. Mr. Athen took in a foster boy to have someone to work for him for free, an indentured servant, that's what Daddy thought.

This was on a pig farm. He remembered the smell of it, of course, the noise of the hogs snorting and banging against the metal bars of their pens, the sows in their stalls and farrowing crates. The hazy blue eyes of the piglets, their clean wet nuzzling snouts. He put his fingers in their mouths and let them nurse, cradling them in the crook of his arm. It was a kind of love, he realized later, a certain glimmer. To care for something helpless, knowing it was doomed.

That morning he was walking through the barn with the far-rowing crates, this was one of his jobs, to look for the baby pigs that were lost or had escaped or were in trouble. The piglets were fenced off from their mothers by a grille of bars, they could reach the teats but the sow was in a separate pen so that she could not roll over on her children or step on them or eat the ones she was dissatisfied with, and the piglets were always getting stuck as they tried to reach her or finding little gaps in the pens that they tried to squeeze through and he rescued the ones that he could, some-times finding the ones that had broken their necks or suffocated and throwing their bodies in a wheelbarrow that he was pushing along.

That was the morning that his mother died. She hanged her-self in the Iowa Correctional Institution for Women in Mitchell-ville, a convicted drug felon, thirty-four years of age, a little nutty the guards said, always a bit unstable, she had been singing all morning and then the singing stopped.

Daddy looked up.

He was in the barn with the piglet in the crook of his arm with his finger in its mouth and it was as if he heard the melody cut off abruptly as her neck broke. It was as if the noisy barn became suddenly silent.

She was standing down at the end of the barn near the open door and the sunlight made a blur against the dark edges of the wood. His mom. He would never tell anyone about this.

Later, he wasn't even sure that he had really seen it, he thought that maybe he had made it up and it seemed so real in his imagina-tion that it turned itself into a memory.

There she was   She stood there dressed neatly in her jeans and her pretty peasant blouse with the orange flowers on it, and she smiled at him in her kindly, teasing way.

"I couldn't get out," she said, "I wanted to leave but I couldn't get out," she said, and she turned and of course she never spoke to him again.

10

We ourselves have never seen ghosts, though we would like to. Brooke would like to, particularly. She likes to read those stories, *True Tales of the Paranormal and Supernatural,* that sort of thing. Even today, even as an adult woman she watches the TV show about ghosts and mysteries and anomalies, a segment on a two-headed baby on the Discovery Channel as the sleet patters against the window of her apartment, and she looks anxiously at the room reflected on the windowpanes; there is herself in a wingback chair watching television.

She is thinking of that night with the Ouija board, back when we were girls. She was eleven and Sydney was thirteen and Eden was nine and it was a night in October, the three of us in the room with the candles in a circle on the floor and all of us dressed in black and our pale thin girls' hands each on the planchette (the pointer tool), and we hunched there over it waiting for it to move.

There are things that you must never ask the Ouija board, Sydney told them. Never ask about God, she said. Never ask when you are going to die. Never ask where the gold is buried.

"Why not?" Eden said. "What gold? Why can't we ask where it's buried?"

"Because they want to keep it hidden, that's why," Sydney said, and then abruptly the planchette began to move in slow figure eights around the center of the board.

"Brooke, I know it's you moving it," Eden said. Already a little afraid. But Brooke was not moving the planchette. Of all of our hands, hers were held the most loosely, and the most still. Of all of us, her mind was most empty and receptive and willing.

"Spirit," she whispered, her breath a little moth, "are you there?"

YES, said the Ouija board.

Brooke closed her eyes lightly. "Spirit," she said, "who are you?"

The planchette seemed to hesitate for a moment. It trembled a little, then made its gentle figure eight.

W-E, it spelled at last. It began to move very slowly and deliberately, letter by letter, across the board. W-E-A-R-E-Y-O-U, it said.

Eden took in a little breath, and she looked at Sydney, and Sydney shushed her with her eyes.

"Spirit," Brooke said, "what is your name?"

B-R-K, said the Ouija board. E-D-E-N, it said. S-Y-D.

"Brooke, I know you are doing it," Eden said. "I'm telling." But she didn't take her hand off the planchette.

W-E-A-R-E-D-E-A-D-Y-O-U, the Ouija board spelled, very slowly.

YES   YES

"I'm telling Mom!"   Eden said, her voice tight.   "I'm telling Mom you're trying to scare me!"

"Shhh!"   Brooke said fiercely.   "Shut up!"   But by that time Eden had pulled her hand away. She was up in an instant and had knocked over a candle as she ran to get to the light switch.

Sydney had never admitted that it was she who had moved the planchette. She was very calm, though, calmer than Brooke, certainly calmer than Eden, she had been moving it almost subconsciously, that's what she told herself later, though at the time she could barely contain her pleasure, she was happy that the other girls had been frightened, a kind of glow opened inside her as she looked at their faces, her hand still hovering above the letters on the board.

And now, years later, as she stands at the door to the basement holding her basket of laundry, she thinks of the little coffin-door down there with the skeleton key in it and she is almost certain that if she went down there right now and turned the key and opened the door she would find inside the little room her own body

There she would be, she thinks, she can picture it, her own body light as a husk, eyes closed, skin pale as paper, mouth pinched tightly closed

W-E-A-R-E-Y-O-U, she thinks. She remembers that night with the Ouija board: Oh, she should have never done that! She should have never made those words

those spirits.

11

Daddy is on his way home to kill us.

Sydney likes to imagine this, she can't help it. Here: He is driving through the snow in his pickup truck, and the defroster casts its thick wooly smell over him. He is black-bearded, dark-eyed, and his black hair stands up in crooked tufts from the friction of removing his stocking cap. The gun is on the seat beside him, and the wet feathers of snow land against the windshield and the wipers cast them away.

Was it winter when he came for them? She isn't sure. Maybe not.

She has the picture of Daddy and the snowman, one of the few photographs that haven't been destroyed, and naturally this is the image she is drawing on, there isn't any real memory.

What if she were to call him? she wonders. She has thought of it more than once, she has run his name through the search engines on her computer, Sampson Bell, also known as Spike, and there are hundreds of entries but nothing that resembles him. What if she could find him and call him on the telephone?   Would he

In the photograph, Daddy is a big bear of a man, standing next to a snowman that is as tall as he is, and his little daughters are in his arms: laughing Sydney, age three and one half, in her pink parka; baby Brooke in green, too little to laugh, eighteen months old perhaps. Eden not even born yet.

What does it mean that she was once this, this round face

peering out from beneath a pink hood, her wide delighted eyes, her upturned, milk-drinking toddler nose, a little girl with her Daddy. Does it mean anything? Did she, the real Sydney, the Sydney she knows now as herself, exist somewhere inside that child in the photograph? Or was that other Sydney, the little Sydney that Daddy knew and loved, another creature entirely, entirely separate?

She considers. She is fond of this kind of vague philosophical conundrum, and perhaps that is why her life feels sad to her even though she should be happy. She wants to find connections where there are none, meanings and structures that she can't completely discern, that are perhaps indiscernible.

Metaphors   for what?

12

Actually, if you look closely, our ghosts are fluttering everywhere, dispersed and dispersing, smoke and glimmers of ash rising up from Daddy's cigarette, earthworms emerging from the soil when it rains and lifting up with birds to grip the power lines in our claws, we fall as leaves upon a human finger, curled in the grass at the edge of a house and never found, we settle as dust upon a key in a basement door that leads nowhere. We cast down through the sixty-watt lamplight onto the page that Eden is bent over, reading diligently.

"Could anything be more miraculous than an actual, authentic ghost?" she reads. Thomas Carlyle, the nineteenth-century Scottish essayist, how the students loathe him. She reads:

The English Johnson longed, all his life, to see a Ghost; but could not, though he went to Cock Lane, and thence to the church-vaults, and tapped on coffins. Foolish Doctor! Did he never, with the mind's eye as well as with the body's, look round him into that full tide of human Life he so loved; did he never so much as look into Himself? The good Doctor was a Ghost, as actual and authentic as heart could wish; well-nigh a million Ghosts were travelling the streets by his side. Once more I say, sweep away the illusion of Time; compress the threescore years into three minutes; what else was he, what else are we? Are we not Spirits, that are shaped into a body, into an Appearance; and that fade away again into air and Invisibility?

She will read this passage aloud to them, Eden thinks, she will read it with great inflection and feeling and they   some of them

She will look out at the students at their desks and there will be Christopher with his dark sad eyes

Are we not all of us Spirits? And she will look directly at him   right into

13

Let us say that there is soon to be a moment when Daddy wakes up and he cannot breathe; the dog Angeline is sound asleep on his chest and his mouth opens to try to take in air and there is nothing, his throat clenches and his lungs don't fill up and there is that feeling of someone bending over him. A face is pulling close to his own face, and in the dream he is having he is a little girl whose father has come into the room to kill her while she sleeps

and in the little girl's dream she is a woman who is walking down the stairs into the basement, where in a little earthen room she will see a woman hanging from a noose made of knotted sheets, a woman who looks almost exactly like her

a poor fucked-up woman in the Iowa Correctional Institution for Women in Mitchellville, Iowa, a convicted drug felon, the cloth of the sheets tightening around her windpipe and her legs kicking, her hands as if with a mind of their own scratching at her throat, her mouth opening and closing, eyes rolling up and she can see a boy with a baby pig in his arms, standing there watching her

and there is a woman who wakes up suddenly from a dream and she knows that she is still in her apartment in Portland, it is still raining, she can hear the patter and rattle of rain against the windowpane and she thinks

She knows: My father has just died.

Let us say that this, all of this, has a logic to it. We understand each other, don't we? Are we not, you and I, both of us spirits?

Reader, do not ask me who at this very moment is dreaming you.

Do not ask me when you are going to die.

Do not ask me where the gold is buried.

Acknowledgments

Thanks to the Ohio Arts Council and Pauline Delaney Professorship Fund, which offered financial support during the writing of this book. I'm also indebted to my agent, Noah Lukeman, and my editor, Susanna Porter, as well as Gina Centrello, Libby McGuire, and all of the great people at Ballantine/Random House who have made the past decade so remarkably easy—I know I've been incredibly lucky to have found such a warm, friendly, and patient home for my books.

Many people helped me with individual stories, and I owe thanks to the editors of the journals in which some of these stories first appeared, as well as to a great number of friends who indulgently read and commented on these pieces.

Stay Awake

Stories

Dan Chaon

A READER'S GUIDE

A Conversation Between
Dan Chaon and Emma Straub

I was lucky enough to have Dan Chaon as my professor at Oberlin College—we first met shortly before his second collection of short stories, *Among the Missing,* was nominated for a National Book Award in 2001. Dan is one of my favorite contemporary story writers, in part because he believes in the genre itself, in its strengths and its quirks. *Stay Awake,* Dan's third collection, includes stories written between 2002 and 2012, and shows a true master at work. The book is dark without a moment of gloom, hilarious without the need for a punch line. Dan's work is as rich as it comes, and I was delighted to be asked to talk to him about

Stay Awake, one of the best books of the year, and his stunning return to the short story form.

Emma Straub: Many of these stories first appeared elsewhere, as long as ten years ago. How does it feel to have them all together in one volume? Were you surprised at how some of the older and newer stories—I'm thinking specifically of "The Bees" and "Stay Awake"—fit together?

Dan Chaon: I was a little surprised at how constant my obsessions have been over the past ten years. "The Bees" was written in 2002, I think, and the first few paragraphs of that story are even older than that. I was asked to write a story for *McSweeney's Mammoth Treasury of Thrilling Tales,* edited by Michael Chabon. Chabon's project was to combine so-called literary writing with pulp and genre storytelling elements, and I was very much inspired by what he had to say. I felt like "The Bees," was a breakthrough for me, and after that I set out to explore that ghostly/horror story element. I learned a lot from writers like Karen Joy Fowler, Kelly Link, George Saunders, Kevin Brockmeier—and many others—who were doing interesting work with genre-bending. It opened me up to the idea that "literary" didn't necessarily mean "realism." And I started looking at the ghost stories written during the modernist period by people such as Edith Wharton and Elizabeth Bowen and Shirley Jackson. It seemed to me that these stories really spoke to the contemporary condition. I thought: Maybe we need the uncanny to find a way to express the way it feels to be alive right now.

ES: I like your use of the word "uncanny"—I think that gets at a certain unsettling feeling present in many of the stories in *Stay Awake*. How important do you think cohesion is in a story collection? I assume you've written more stories than you've included here—did you pull some out that didn't quite fit?

DC: To me, there are two types of story collections. One type shows off the author's range, and in that kind of story collection the pieces are *really* meant to be separate little cookies. Then there's the other type, which shows off the author's variations on a single theme. This collection, I knew from the beginning, was going to be the latter type. I really wanted it to hold together as a reading experience that felt like it was a holistic experience—the way watching a lot of *Twilight Zone* episodes or reading a lot of Hardy Boys books is kind of a cumulative thing.

I originally had about twenty stories, and my agent, Noah Lukeman, and my editor, Susanna Porter, and I all spent a lot of time trying to figure out which ones fit together and which didn't. And how to organize them so that they built on one another.

One of the weird things was how many times images repeated from story to story. That wasn't planned. My first instinct was to change the details to make these echoes less noticeable. Then, after thinking about it, I began to like the idea that they had a kind of déjà vu quality, that they were forming and re-forming around the same knot of feeling. In the end, as I was revising the collection, I ended up adding even more of these echoes and connections from story to story. The final story, "The Farm. The Gold. The Lily-White Hands.," contains elements of all the previous stories—it's like a mash-up of everything I was thinking about over the course of writing these. As a former DJ, this made me really happy.

ES: One of my favorite aspects of *Stay Awake* is the sense of layering that accrues with each story—what you've just described as déjà vu—after reading the stories back to back, the reader is left with a sense of so much built-up weight. What do you think it is about those motifs—relationships between parents and children, feelings of loss and grief, sibling relationships, in particular—that keeps you circling back around to them?

DC: Of course, all of those themes are very personal, and the stories allow me to explore them and obsess over them in a kind of contained way.

It makes me think of my favorite music. I love the way that certain artists seem to be working out something over the course of a recording, and you can "read" the album in the way that you can read a cohesive story collection. Think, for example, of Joni Mitchell's *Blue*, or Tom Waits' *Frank's Wild Years*, or Beck's *Sea Change*, or The Mountain Goats' *Tallahassee*, or Page France's *Hello, Dear Wind*, or Modest Mouse's *The Moon and Antarctica*—all of which are big influences on me. I'm inspired by the way the accumulation of different songs transports you into a single mood but shows you how it has layers and levels and many rooms. That was my goal here.

The title "Stay Awake" is a lullaby from the musical Disney film *Mary Poppins*. In 1988, a few years after I finished college, Hal Willner put out a compilation of covers of Disney songs on A&M Records called *Stay Awake: Various Interpretations of Music from Vintage Disney Films*. The album contained an incredible and haunting version of "Stay Awake" sung by Suzanne Vega, which stuck with me for years and years. Even as a young man, I knew that I wanted to write about the feeling that the song had evoked in me. So, in any case, whatever autobiographical elements exist, they are trumped by a particular *mood*, which has been with me for my whole adult life.

ES: Are there other stories in the collection that have musical associations? You mentioned your past life as a DJ, and I happen to know that you often find out about cool new bands one to three years before the rest of us.

DC: There are a lot. I love all kinds of music, from disco to jazz to folk, but I have to admit that I have a particular affection for sad songs. My sons sometimes tease me about my taste; they call the stuff I listen to "suicide music." Artists like Red House Painters, Idaho, Jennifer O'Connor, Cat Power. But the thing I love about it is that it's cathartic power, the way that it takes you so fully right inside a strong feeling. And I know that's my ride. There is something about listening to these songs that gets in deep and moves around in a way that is so dark but makes me know I am not alone, there is someone else who is sometimes filled with cold black eels. And, wow, that's an important thing to be able to do. I don't think it's that you set out to make people feel crummy. Instead, it's a certain kind of life preserver you are sending out to the people who are listening. You. Were. There.

ES: This book is full of flailing adults, sensitive and overgrown men, and other characters who don't seem, at first or second glance, terribly heroic. And yet, like Critter in "To Psychic Underworld:," they are the heroes of the story. Do you feel that it's important to shine a light on characters who have been otherwise marginalized? What is it that really interests you about a character?

DC: I don't really like the word "marginalized" because it suggests that I'm writing about people who are oppressed by some societal force. And that's not really where my interest lies, though it may be marginally true for some of my characters. But most of them are "marginalized" by themselves, rather than by The Man.

I'm interested in people who screw up. I like people who have the capacity to misbehave and do wrong things because that seems to have more dramatic potential for me, as a reader and as a writer. People who have done something that they regret in one way or another. I'm curious about people who might be considered "unsympathetic"—in some deep unconscious way, I feel that I am part of their tribe.

Fiction is a particular kind of rhetoric, a way of thinking that I think can be useful in your life. It asks you to image the world through someone else's eyes, and it allows you to try to empathize with situations that you haven't actually experienced. People write fiction in their minds all the time—every time we read a "human interest" news story, or a true-crime tale, we find ourselves fascinated because we're trying to understand why people behave the way they do, why they make the choices they do, how we become who we become. Imaginative empathy is one of the great gifts that humans have, and it means that we can live more than one life. We can picture what it would be like from another perspective.

I'm certainly very influenced by what you would call "contemporary headline horror," stuff that is true crime or for one reason or another catches our attention in the media, those strange cases that we end up obsessing about. I'm always influenced by weird anecdotes and news. For some reason, thinking about the extreme incidents and trying to filter them through my own understanding of the world is a very satisfying way to process my own (much less dramatic) personal experience.

In particular, I'm curious about how people process grief and how they process loss. And I'm also interested in the ways in which an event can have long-reaching consequences and a life over the course of years. I think it's about the ways in which we remain connected even when we're separated by distance. And about the ways in which mistakes will travel through time, and the little choices that you make will travel through time. I guess it's sort of about the presence of the uncanny in daily life, too.

Why should something that happened twenty years ago matter now? Why do I keep thinking about that thing? And what if I had done this or that differently, how would my life be different? Those are ghost questions, you know? Because they're abstract, but they also have this power to rise up in your life. The people that you might have been, or the things that you might have done, or the things that happened that you wish didn't happen—those are the real ghosts.

ES: In "Patrick Lane, Flabbergasted," the title character writes notes on his own skin. In "To Psychic Underworld:," a young widower becomes obsessed with scraps of messages that strangers have left behind. What role does language play in *Stay Awake*?

DC: I started out as a poet—a quite bad poet; nevertheless, I've always been interested in the sound of words and in the power of chants and memes and earworms and those little phrases that circle around in your head for no reason. These interest me in the way that the world of ghosts interests me.

I'm also interested in collage. I like the way fragments work together to create a mysterious and resonant whole. I learned a lot about fragments and collage when I was a DJ back when I was young, and working with sampling and remixing and discovering the ways in which a mash-up could transform and mutate a song. I also learned a lot from my friend Lynda Barry, the novelist and cartoonist, who discovered amazing things with collage in her books *What It Is* and *Picture This*.

There are aspects of our world—our subconscious, our secret image-world—that can't be told as a narrative, but can be accessed through little glimpses of language and fragments. That's fascinating to me.

ES: I love thinking of those scraps of paper as collage, or earworms, tiny little pieces of the outside world that find their way into your brain. Does that idea also factor into the "contemporary headline horror" you mentioned, with abstract images and story lines entering into your work from the media? Are there particular stories that began as tiny kernels that way, ripped from the headlines, as it were?

DC: Almost all the stories started out as small observations that I keep in a notebook that I carry around with me—the kernel was just things I noticed while going about my daily life, or anecdotes that someone told me, or something that I happened to read. If I went through each story I could probably pick out particular parts that were originally just little fragments, like the notes that Critter finds in "To Psychic Underworld:."

But here's one example, from the story "Stay Awake," which is a story that I worked on for a long time. As I mentioned above, the title comes from a song, but the original impetus comes from a real news item. Historically, there have been only ten documented cases of *craniopagus parasiticus* as it is described in the story. Two of the cases were fairly recent, in 2003 and 2005, including a little girl who was featured on *The Oprah Winfrey Show*, and who gave me the original idea. Many of the elements of the story including "The Two-Headed Boy of Bengal," and the research done by Dr. Robert White on rhesus monkeys, are based in fact.

Around the same time, I knew a few couples who were having a difficult time conceiving a baby, and I had a couple of conversations with them about that process, and some of the technical details, which stuck with me. By the way, I do hope that the story doesn't come across as a critique of people who are struggling to conceive, because I understand the longing and desire to have "children of your own" very well, and I hope the story is a sympathetic portrayal.

I have a very particular and personal point of view on this, since I myself was adopted as an infant, and that has certainly made me more cognizant of the ways in which that deep desire for a baby can warp and skew relationships; the ways in which "babies" are much more than just small human mammals, but also containers for these enormous projected emotions and hopes and fears.

So in any case, there were a number of different fragments— from both personal and impersonal sources—which seemed to come together as I was trying to write that story. And I think that in general that's the way most of the stories in the collection were written. They are an accumulation of different kinds of data that are then somehow sown together into something that manages to come alive. Like Frankenstein's monster, I guess.

ES: Children, and young people, are often in peril in these stories—"St. Dismas," for example. That said, there are also hilarious moments here. Do you think that some people miss your humor? How do you feel your sense of humor diffuses the darkness inherent in the stories? Can one really separate the two, or are we just sickos for laughing?

DC: There's a famous essay by the nineteenth-century critic William Hazlett where he asserts that comedy and tragedy, like love and hate, are really two sides of the same coin, and that's something that has stuck with me.

For example, I remember as a kid being very upset by the Warner Bros. Road Runner cartoons, because for some reason I identified with Wile E. Coyote. Those cartoons are truly painful and tragic if you look at them from the coyote's perspective. My God, they are so dark! Or was I just a sicko for not laughing?

I don't know. There is a certain kind of laughter that I don't like, in which the good are rewarded and the evil are punished and ha ha, they deserved it. There's another type of humor that comes from being thwarted and disappointed and recognizing a kind of cosmic joke in it. That's often the kind of comedy I indulge in, and it's fairly subjective, so I don't blame people if they miss it.

I often find that people will come up to me after a reading and say, "Oh, I didn't realize that story was so funny!"—maybe because of the way I present it, or my tone of voice, or whatever, people feel like they are allowed to laugh whereas maybe when they are reading to themselves the voice they hear is more grim. Because, yeah, of course the subject matter is grim, most of the time.

But I was always aware that the situations I was writing about had their funny side, and there are some stories in the collection that I thought of as straight-up humorous, like "Long Delayed, Always Expected," and "Slowly We Open Our Eyes," and "Shepherdess."

ES: "Shepherdess" is the funniest Dead Mother story I've ever read, for sure.

DC: Reviewers often mention how bleak the stories are, and yes, that's true, but it's the humor in the face of bleakness that has kept me going. Even if it's gallows humor.

I admired Cormac McCarthy's apocalyptic novel, *The Road*, but I think there are a few things he got wrong. I think the end of the world will include a lot of great jokes. And singing. Laughter and music are probably the last human thing that will be taken away from us.

ES: That brings me to the idea of genre. I feel like you have deftly avoided getting pigeonholed as a genre writer, but in many ways, these are horror stories. Perhaps with the exception of "The Farm. The Gold. The Lily-White Hands.," which I read as a ghost story, these are not in any way supernatural, but there is an inky, murderous glee running throughout. Have you ever been tempted to go full-throttle on the other side of the fence? Or is there no longer a fence at all?

DC: I think there was a certain period of American Literature—maybe about fifty years, 1950–2000, let's say—where "realism" and "literary" were more or less synonymous, and that had to do with the rise of genre as a commercial category as much as anything. In the nineteenth and early twentieth centuries, many of our canonized writers had no qualms about working with the fantastic—from Hawthorne and Poe to James and Wharton—and my sense is that a lot of the prejudice against fantasy, horror, etc. started with the New Critics in the 1930s and '40s. There's probably a long essay in that, which I won't write.

If there has been a change, a lot of it, I think, was borne of frustration and boredom. By the mid-1990s, the domestic mode was starting to feel like a prison to a lot of younger writers. Many of us had grown up during the heyday of commercial SF and horror in the 1970s, and that was what we read as kids. Personally, I started out as a straight-up horror writer, and it was only when my creative writing teachers told me that they didn't accept "genre fiction" that I began to work in a more realist mode. I would say that the restrictions were good for me, and that I really needed to broaden my emotional range and explore character more fully. At the same time, I think that a lot of the creative energy and impetus in my work comes from the fantastic, the supernatural, etc. I think there's a little glimmer of it even in my most realistic pieces—and when it's not there, the piece doesn't feel as alive to me. But I also don't think I'm exactly in the genre camp, either. I'm sort of caught in-between.

But anyway, it's hard to make sweeping statements about literary culture. Whether we're in a new era, I don't know, but I do think that the fence is easier to cross.

ES: I'm curious if you feel like there is a midwestern sensibility in literature. Are things darker in the middle, like an inverted Oreo cookie, with brittle, light edges and a dark, rich center? What do you think living in Ohio, and growing up in the Midwest, has added to your work? Or do you feel so yoked to place that it's not even a question of adding a layer, that it's simply a part of your worldview?

DC: Part of it has to do with the intensity of feeling you have for any place you grew up. Any place you grew up in is, to some extent, haunted because you're always looking back at the child that you were and there is a sense that that child is kind of a ghost in your life anyway. That's one of the reasons I write about Nebraska and the Midwest so much. Western Nebraska, especially, has a hold on my mood as writer. The landscape is very desolate and it's got a beauty to it, and yet there's a sense that it wasn't really meant to be inhabited. People shouldn't be there. There's a hostility about the landscape that's really appealing to me. Settlers came and made these little elevator towns, but if you look at a 1930s map of Cheyenne County (where I grew up) you'll see all these towns on the map that don't exist anymore. They are nothing but foundation. There's a quality about western Nebraska similar to the famous colony of Roanoke where they disappeared and nobody knew what happened to them. Something about the landscape can swallow people up.

Still, I'm not entirely sure what the terms "midwestern" and "regional" mean. Cleveland, where I live now, and which appears in some of the stories, is entirely different from western Nebraska. Other stories take place in Los Angeles, Portland, Boston, etc. I keep trying to expand my range.

But I do have a particular affinity for characters who have grown up in the middle of the country, and I think that it has to do with a certain kind of sense of being separate from the deciders and the trendsetters and the "center" of culture, which seems to be located somewhere on the coasts. I've always felt like an outsider, and my sympathies have always been with the folks who, for one reason or another, have been forgotten or ignored. Which is not to say that there aren't plenty of forgotten and ignored folks in NYC and LA—only that the blanket seems heavier and perhaps more permanently suffocating as you approach the Heartland.

I can think of two or three stories in the collection that address this issue directly. The story "Shepherdess" is about a man who has found a degree of success in Los Angeles, but who is pulled back, maybe dragged down, by his own midwesterness. Meanwhile, "Thinking of You in Your Time of Sorrow" is about the way that a small town can become a weight and anchor, a paralyzing force. It's funny, because even in the stories that take place outside the Midwest, the region exerts some kind of strange gravitational pull

ES: This is your first story collection since *Among the Missing*, which was nominated for a National Book Award. Did you feel pressure returning to the genre, or do stories feel like a more comfortable zone for you?

DC: As you noted, these stories represent work that I've done in the short story form over the past ten years, since the publication of *Among the Missing*. So it's not exactly like I'm "returning" to the form—I've been working in it all along. It's been accumulating steadily, quietly, over the last decade, in between working on my novels.

Novels, it seems to me, require an exploration of a larger universe—a novel requires a certain kind of world building and also a certain kind of closure, ultimately. Whereas with a short story you have this sense that there are hinges that the reader doesn't see. I would say that all short stories have mystery naturally built into them.

Short stories are a single glimpse into that larger novel world. They give you that thrill of peeping through a keyhole or catching a scene through a passing window. The glimpse becomes larger than the sum of its parts, and it lingers in your imagination; as a reader, you are an active participant in creating the world that exists beyond that brief glimpse, and to me that is an exciting thing. There is a sense that the reader and the writer are collaborating, and that the reader can imagine and create so much beyond the edges of the narrative.

You might say that, metaphorically, short stories are photographs, whereas novels are films or TV series.

And I am attracted to photography. I like the ways that it remains, always, open to interpretation and suggests spaces that you can only imagine, never see. I feel like stories can really possess you, that they can feel like waking dreams, and you don't necessarily know what's going to emerge from them. You just can't do a novel like that. I've tried, and believe me—it just turns into a huge mess.

ES: Your novels have both veered into the same dark, knotty places as the stories. When you have an idea and begin writing, is it clear to you whether that idea will be a story or a piece of a longer work?

DC: It's funny, because most of the time I have no idea what form a piece will eventually take. Both of my novels started out as short stories. And there are three pieces here—"Stay Awake," "I Wake Up," and "The Farm. The Gold. The Lily-White Hands.," which I worked on for a while thinking that they might be novels.

I probably wrote fifty to a hundred pages on each of those before I gave up. For example, there are a few chapters of "Stay Awake" from Rosalie's perspective, as a child and as a teenaged girl, when I imagined the story as a kind of ghostly *Middlesex* sort of book; and there is a long section from "I Wake Up" in which the narrator goes on a quest to meet his long-lost siblings; and there is practically another hundred pages of junk about the three sisters in "The Farm. The Gold. The Lily-White Hands.," from when it was going to be a novel called *Three Sisters*, and each woman lived in an alternate universe.

I ultimately gave up on all three books, and it's hard to explain why they got stuck. The simple answer is that I was more interested in those stories as mystery. The novels all required me to explain things, and the explanations seemed to sap the energy out of the original idea.

ES: Well, luckily, the resulting stories are full of energy. I read *Stay Awake* on the subway, and missed my stop more than once. I know I'm speaking for many other readers when I say that whatever pages had to die to make this book, it was all worth it. I think the stories are mysterious, in both heart-quickening and very sympathetic ways. The world may be a dark and scary place, Dan, but it's less so with these stories in it. It may still be dark, but at least we're not alone.

Emma Straub is from New York City. Her story collection, *Other People We Married*, was published in February 2012 by Riverhead Books. Her fiction and nonfiction have been published by *Tin House*, *The Paris Review Daily*, *The Wall Street Journal*, *Time*, *Slate*, and *The New York Times*. Her debut novel is forthcoming from Riverhead Books. Emma lives in Brooklyn, New York, with her husband.

Questions and Topics
for Discussion

1. In the interview, Chaon talks about the stories in this collection as "ghost stories." Did you read them this way? In what ways are the events of the stories "supernatural"? Or does a ghost story have to have a literal ghost? What is a ghost?

2. Chaon mentions his love of sad music in his interview and says, "The thing I love about it is that it's cathartic power." Do you find that to be true for yourself? Chaon's stories often submerge the reader into a dark situation and then end without an easily resolved solution for the characters. Does this have

the same cathartic power as a sad song? Or is the effect different?

3. Chaon speaks of his interest in people who "screw up," and the book is full of characters whose choices lead to trouble. How sympathetic are they? For example, how awful is January's decision to sleep with her brain-damaged ex-husband in "Long Delayed, Always Expected"? How do we feel about the narrator's decision to run out on his baby's funeral in "Thinking of You in Your Time of Sorrow"? Which characters in the book were most sympathetic to you? Which characters do you most relate to? How would you react in a similar situation?

4. The loss of a child in handled in different ways in the stories "The Bees," "Stay Awake," and "Thinking of You in Your Time of Sorrow." How do these varying facets of grief intersect with each other, and in what ways do they present vastly altered experiences?

5. In some of these stories—"The Bees," "St. Dismas"—characters are trying to change. In others—"To Psychic Underworld:"—change has been thrust upon them. Does either scenario seem to imply that change is indeed possible? Can any of the characters in these stories escape from their situations and transform themselves?

6. Many of the main characters in the book seem to be "stuck" in some way—Robert in "I Wake Up," for example, or Brandon in "Patrick Lane, Flabbergasted." Is being "stuck" a situation of

their own making? What prevents the characters from moving on in their lives?

7. In "Shepherdess," the author uses humor to further explore a character's feelings about his mother's death. Where else is such dark humor used in the collection? Were there points where you found the stories funny?

8. "Slowly We Open Our Eyes" presents a sequence of events featuring Smokey and O'Sullivan, two brothers, but the dramatic action in the story is obscured. Why do you think that is? What exactly happens to them?

9. The main characters in both "Take This, Brother, May It Serve You Well" and "To Psychic Underworld:" are widowers. In what way do you think that informs their actions and behaviors in the stories?

10. What is the meaning of the last section of the story "The Farm. The Gold. The Lily-White Hands.": "Are we not, you and I, both of us spirits?" What does this question mean in the context of the story? What does it mean in the context of the collection as whole?

DAN CHAON is the acclaimed author of *Among the Missing*, which was a finalist for the National Book Award; *You Remind Me of Me*, which was named one of the best books of the year by *The Washington Post*, *San Francisco Chronicle*, and *Entertainment Weekly*, among other publications; and *Await Your Reply*, which was a *New York Times* Notable Book and appeared on more than a dozen "Best of the Year" lists. Chaon's fiction has appeared in many journals and anthologies, including *The Best American Short Stories, Pushcart Prize*, and *The O. Henry Prize Stories*. He has been a finalist for the National Magazine Award in Fiction, and he was the recipient of the 2006 Academy Award in Literature from the American Academy of Arts and Letters. Chaon lives in Cleveland, Ohio, and teaches at Oberlin College, where he is the Pauline M. Delaney Professor of Creative Writing.

MORE GREAT FICTION FROM **DAN CHAON**

AWAIT YOUR REPLY

"A riveting thriller chock full of plot twists, and a sober meditation on the erosion of identity in the age of technology."
—*Los Angeles Times*

YOU REMIND ME OF ME

"Remarkable . . . weaves the threads into a whole that is not only satisfying but devastating."
—*Entertainment Weekly*

AMONG THE MISSING

"Unforgettable . . . hums with life and wry humor."
—*The New York Times Book Review*

FITTING ENDS

"Each story pulls you into a subtle emotional vortex, largely because of Chaon's knack for simple but poignant detail."
—New York *Newsday*

BALLANTINE BOOKS